PLAYING IN THE SAND

The least safe place will be Australia: as lots of things will land there by mistake.

Peter Ustinov

PLAYING IN THE SAND

Christopher Hudson

MACMILLAN
LONDON

First published 1989 by
MACMILLAN LONDON LIMITED
4 Little Essex Street London WC2R 3LF
and Basingstoke

Associated companies in Auckland, Delhi, Dublin, Gaborone,
Hamburg, Harare, Hong Kong, Johannesburg, Kuala Lumpur,
Lagos, Manzini, Melbourne, Mexico City, Nairobi, New York,
Singapore and Tokyo

A CIP catalogue record for this book is available from the British Library.

ISBN 0–333–45198–8

Typeset by Matrix, 21 Russell Street, London WC2

Printed by WBC Bristol and bound by WBC Maesteg, Mid Glamorgan

For Cecilia

Acknowledgements

'All Alone Am I' (Min Ton Rotas Ourano). Composer: M. Hadjidakis. Original author: Jean Ioannidis. English author: Arthur Atman. © 1959, 1962 Sope Athens, Greece. Reproduced by permission MCA Music Limited. All rights reserved.

'Please Please me' by John Lennon and Paul McCartney. © Northern Songs, under licence to SBK Songs Ltd, 3–5 Rathbone Place, London W1P 1DA.

'After Apple Picking' from *The Poetry of Robert Frost*, edited by Edward Connery Latham and published by Jonathan Cape Limited. Acknowledgement is made to the Estate of Robert Frost.

On Adultery

The phenomenon of nuclear fission is caused by a neutron invading a nucleus. The nucleus is made up of particles which interact intimately with each other. The neutron intruding among them generates so much extra heat that the nucleus in a very short time is split into two parts, the parts separating with enormous energy.

Playing in the Sand

Normandy, 6 June 1944

This is no time to sleep. He can hear the crump and whine of the enemy attack. But he's afloat. They must be attacking by sea. In the blackness Corporal Douglas Manifold turns away from the bulkhead in case a torpedo smashes through. Then Nick Kemp is shaking him awake.

'Come on, Duggle. Breakfast's in five minutes. Assembly on deck at oh-five-thirty.'

And it's real, he wasn't dreaming it, the long pummel of the German guns. So much official secrecy, and still the Panzers were ready for them! Cold fingers grapple for boots and battledress top, for kitbag, ammunition-pouches, water-bottle, bayonet. Trust Lieutenant Nick Kemp to be up on his feet – Nick who pushes and jokes and yells Aussie curses and keeps them moving, Nick who turns all their fear into something like excitement. . . .

No hope, in this heavy swell, of keeping down eggs, sausages, coffee. Escape up on deck, and into the racket of the guns. The dawn mist is thinning out over the knifing seas. Douglas can make out the dim shapes of transport ships on either side, and ahead the Normandy beach, the cliffs, the farmhouse roof – all the landmarks they've been shown in the training photographs. The German gunners must be dug into those cliffs, pinning down the first assault-wave . . . and as the pale sun rises he can see the bodies clearly now, littered among the burned-out tanks and trucks, the bodies in the sand.

Nick has come to stand beside him. Douglas points, but smoke has swirled across the shoreline. Nick blows a raspberry.

'Bloody poets! You're always seeing things!'

'Bloody Australian! What do you know about it?'

'I know we're going to find out soon enough.'

And soon enough, too soon, the last Assembly, the last orders, the last issue of sea-sickness pills, and condoms to put over the muzzles of their rifles to keep the water out as they wade ashore.

3

Then down the netting into the pitching landing-craft, wedged together in a stink of fuel oil and vomit, heads down, nothing for it now as they putter slowly into the bombardment except to pray to God and check their ammunition.

The LCA noses in through a floating litter of hawsers, ammo-boxes, bits of timber. The ramp goes down. Nick leads the platoon. Douglas, as junior NCO, brings up the rear. The water's deep here; they're in up to their necks, holding their guns above their heads as they fight to keep their balance. As he jumps, Douglas slips on a puddle of oil; he falls awkwardly into the water, his pack a dead weight on his back. He surfaces, gasping, but his foot's caught, it's a rope underneath the LCA, it's trapping him, it's dragging him down. He screams out, but it's lost in the bedlam of fire and smoke.

He battles to free himself: this is no way to die, in five feet of water; but his ankle must be broken, every time he pulls he almost blacks out with the pain. Then Nick is at his shoulder, yelling something in his ear. Nick's got a knife. He dives down.

Five seconds. Ten. Then Douglas Manifold feels his foot come free. Half-fainting he drifts backwards. Nick holds him up.

'Not much further now, Duggle,' he says.

'I can't go any further. Look after the others.'

'They're under cover. Lean on me.'

Together they struggle up the shore of France. Then, behind them, a shell explodes the world, hurling them across the sand. Their D-Day is over.

ONE

They were eating lunch on the back veranda. Multicoloured birds sang angrily. Georgina Manifold had made a whitish potato salad to accompany the greyish lamb. Helen came up in a silk robe from the swimming-pool, towelling her hair.

'George, would you be an angel and trawl the net over the pool after lunch? It's full of dead things again. Urgh! They just fall out of the air.'

Georgina, her mouth full, nodded. She passed her stepmother the jug of iced lemonade. Helen scanned the surface for dead things and poured it carefully into her glass. 'At least you can keep your body in shape out here,' she remarked. 'It's like California. Your mind goes to pieces but your body looks sensational. And since looking good is all that matters when you don't have a brain, everybody's happy.'

'It doesn't sound to me as if you've entirely lost your mind,' said Douglas Manifold.

'Give me another month, darling. I'll be the beautiful zombie you always wanted me to be. Did you get that message, by the way? The one I left on the table?'

'What message on what table?'

'I'll bring it on a salver next time. A gentleman of the press intends to come to interview you this afternoon around five. A man called Vellacott, I think he said. *South Australian Gazette*. Doing a profile of you, he said. Sounds wiser than full-face. I wonder why none of the hacks has been round before to write you up?'

'Because I don't want any bloody journalists around, that's why. I thought we agreed to avoid publicity! So that we wouldn't be hauled off to endless bloody boring dinner-parties.'

'Did I? That must have been before I knew the true meaning of boredom. Its name is Australia.'

Georgina sighed and looked away. Helen should have stayed in London instead of playing the tragic actress out here to her husband and her stepdaughter in the front stalls. Georgina had been present at one of the rows in Holland Park when Helen had accused Douglas right out of destroying her career. Only two weeks earlier she'd gone to Chichester to be interviewed by Larry (sic) for a job with the new National Theatre. To listen to Helen, it was as if Zeus had descended in a shower of gold and here was Douglas blocking her from picking up the pieces.

Larry had been in his dressing-room after *Uncle Vanya*, taking the wrinkled loneliness of Astrov off his face with cotton-wool. Helen sat behind him; he prompted her out of the mirror while she reminded him of the rôles he should remember her for – first in repertory, then at the Shakespeare Memorial Theatre, lately at the Old Vic ('Helen Callender's spitfire Emilia passionate enough to make the dark Moor pale', *Daily Express*).

Before she could finish, Olivier had lifted his hand. He was ready, according to Helen, to offer her the moon (even though at this preliminary stage all he was actually allowed to contract for were attendant ladies to start a progress, swell a scene or two). 'But come back in the spring, darling, when we've got some productions lined up, and it will be a different story. Promise me.'

Helen had promised. But what could Douglas do? He had already accepted Michael Balcon's commission to compose the screenplay of a film about Gallipoli. It was to be a film about the courage of fighting men, and the bond, sealed in their blood, between Britain and Australia. It was to be an epic of heroism in the jaws of defeat – and who better than Douglas to write the first draft? The University of Adelaide, seeing its chance to bask in the reflected glory of a famous war poet, had offered him a generous stipend for the time it took him to complete the script. It was winter. Douglas yearned to get out of Britain for a few months in the sun. Besides, he could use the money.

He had thought for a while that Helen would refuse to go. Had she not always insisted that her vocation came first? But she was, regrettably for her, between jobs. In London she could survive without work or without Douglas, but not without both at the same time. So out they came – Helen genuinely appalled at the prospect of living in a country which, as she said to Douglas, had not so far as she knew produced anything of utility or artistry on a par with Switzerland's cuckoo clock, with the arguable exception of Peach Melba.

'But of course,' interjected Douglas. 'Dame Nellie Melba.'

'Isn't the ice-cream more famous?'

With such sarcasms did Helen attempt to express her resentment for having been brought to a continent from which she felt she would be lucky to escape with her life, let alone with her health and her translucently ivory complexion. Flying in from London, Australia had looked to her like a fatal accident. The hideous pinkish red of scalded flesh ... mile after mile of raw desert and wrinkled riverbeds to the far horizon. It was like a titanic burned *body* dragged senseless out of the furnace of creation, grey-brown blisters of rock erupting in long weals across its belly. Nothing moved. Nothing. It had lain there for millions of years, exposing its weals to the burning sun; nothing had happened in all that time. Only at the extremities could one see minute creatures at work, feeding off what still had life in it, hurry-scurry over the flaking skin.

Now the Manifolds were a part of it: Douglas, Helen and seventeen-year-old (almost seventeen-year-old) Georgina. Husband, wife, her stepdaughter. Or, looked at another way, father, stepmother, his daughter. Either way, they weren't exactly kith and kin. Whichever way, the corners of the triangle didn't quite meet.

It was like that before, of course. The fashionable painter, Douglas's friend from Oxford, must have picked up some of it when he came to do the family portrait in the drawing-room in London. He's got Douglas Manifold sitting with tensed shoulders at his desk, glasses on the blotting-pad, his hand splayed across the writing-paper as if to conceal, what you can't help noticing if you look closely, that he hasn't put anything down. The lamp on the desk-top throws half his face into relief, highlighting the profile, flatteringly aquiline, and the small red wrinkle above his left temple where the shell-splinter went in, and the flakes of silver in his carefully unkempt black hair.

Georgina Manifold on one of her infrequent visits (it must have been half-term at Malvern) is standing right over the other side, by the window. The painter hasn't been so kind to her. She's wearing yellow slacks, a shapeless green sweater and silly bows on her auburn plaits. Whatever it is she has seen outside in the street, her lips are pressed together. You'd have to know Georgina to realise that the prissy expression comes from keeping her mouth shut over the metal band she used to wear round her teeth.

And here, impossible to overlook, is Helen Manifold, a.k.a. Helen Callender the actress, reclining on the brown button-back sofa in the middle of the picture. You can tell she's an actress by the way her hooded eyes totally disregard the painter, having first established that she's centre-stage commanding his attention. One slim long-fingered hand rests along the back of the sofa; the other droops over the arm. Her scarab-green cotton sheath dress is excessively modern: in conjunction with her small head, oval face and dark hair cut boyishly short it gives her an almost Japanese look. Fine nylon stockings the colour of an expensive tan, and high-heeled shoes kicked off on to the Persian carpet complete the effect. All that's missing is a small fluffy dog to gaze up at her adoringly.

It would be satisfying to be able to pinpoint material symbols of the sitters' unease such as the Victorians liked to put in their conversation pieces. A crumpled handkerchief dropped on the rug? A singing bird on the floor of its cage dead with its feet sticking up in the air? But frankly it's not necessary. Nobody is looking at anybody else. The space between the three of them is impenetrable; even their shadows hold back.

The artist has allowed himself one *plaisanterie*. Above the primitivist pink-and-gold Mexican candlestand on the mantelpiece he's worked in another, miniature painting of the drawing-room. The same scene exactly, it's very clever. Same perspective. Same furnishings. But the room is deserted.

At the lunch-table now, Helen drained her glass of lemonade.

'George, did you ask the man in the shop about ordering yoghurt?'

'Yes.'

'And?'

'He'd never heard of it. He thought I said "dog food".'

Helen groaned and sank back in her chair, clutching her robe as if it harboured a poisonous asp. 'I'll have to ask Edward,' she murmured. 'He'll know where to get yoghurt. Darling, do you know what he told me yesterday, the story about Anthony Eden? That, directly after Suez, he actually tried to assassinate Colonel Nasser with an exploding safety razor?'

'Oh, yes?' Douglas grinned.

'Not in person, of course. He gave orders to the Security Service to arrange it, just before he flew off to stay with Ian Fleming in Jamaica. The Head of British Intelligence refused to pass the instruction on to his secret agents in Cairo. Apparently they all decided that Eden was suffering from delusions brought on by reading too much James Bond. He wanted Nasser to be blown up while he was staying at Goldeneye, so he could have a good laugh with Fleming. But all that happened was that Nasser arrested all our agents in Cairo, and then released them again to show he didn't care!'

'Who spun you that yarn, poppet?'

'Edward Catchpole.'

'Catchpole?'

'Darling, I told you. The man who's organising the Royal Visit in February. He was stationed in Cyprus at the start of Suez. Something about running communications between Whitehall and the RAF. He's totally open about it. He actually came under fire, he said, from the Canal Company offices in Port Said, when hostilities were supposed to have ceased and he was being rowed across with the Chiefs of Staff to receive the Egyptian surrender. They were all cursing Eden like mad. Especially when it turned out the Egyptians weren't surrendering at all.'

Douglas grunted. 'Why was he telling you all this?'

'Why? Because, darling, unlike you he makes conversation. He actually listens to what I'm saying. I know I seem totally empty-headed to you, which is why you don't bother any more, but there are people who give every impression of enjoying my company.' Helen jabbed at a sliver of potato. 'Georgina, please would you pass the mayonnaise?'

Georgina, her mouth full, passed the mayonnaise.

'So tell me, is that why he was boasting about Suez? Because he was enjoying your company so much he couldn't stop himself?'

'There's no need to look so grim, darling. You know I don't mean to snap, so please don't take it out on me. I know how much this Gallipoli script means to you and—'

'Money. Just money.'

'And what a lot it's taking out of you. Out of all of us. I'd just like you to have some consideration for how *I* feel, for a change. Do you ever stop to think if I have any life of my own out here, while you're at your desk? Four and a half more months I've got of this. I cross off the days on my calendar, it's the highlight of my morning. Nineteen ghastly weeks of the same ghastly unforgiving sun, day after day, shining uselessly on the same ghastly bungalows, and everywhere the same bungalow mentality, people raking their gravel and checking the racing tips like Mr Whatsit Robbins next door—'

She flung up her arms in a cadence of copper bracelets. The glass jug toppled and smashed on the patio tiles in a pool of prickling, popping lemonade bubbles. Douglas went down on his hands and knees with paper napkins and picked up the shards of glass. Helen pressed the palms of her hands to her temples.

'It's in my head, my head! Douglas, what am I doing out here? Why did you bring me? I know it's my fault. You will tell me if I'm making you hate me? You promise you'll tell me the truth?'

Her eyes glimmered. Douglas, wiping his fingers on a clean napkin, came round the table, and put his arm round her, stroking her hair. Georgina studied her plate. After a minute, Helen's hands withdrew from her forehead, hovered and came to rest on her husband's protective arm.

'My head is beating,' she murmured. 'I'm going to go and lie down.'

'Shall I take you inside, poppet?'

'No. Leave me. All of you.' Pulling the lapels of her silk robe tightly around her, she rose to her feet and went inside the house, and closed the french doors at her back.

It wasn't a bungalow actually, this Wellington Square house. It was a villa, even though Helen persisted in ignoring the fact. Some would have said that *villa* was too inflated a description for this neo-Georgian single-storey bluestone dwelling, kin to hundreds of other neo-Georgian bluestones, sandstones and brownstones dotting the North Adelaide suburbs. But Adelaiders evidently held to the dictionary definition of *villa* – 'a detached superior middle-class dwelling-house of some size' – which so encapsulated the ethos of this Australian city that no other word would serve.

This detached et cetera, with its green tiled roof and verandas round three sides, was situated upon a fenced plot with enough tall flowering bushes in front to provide an illusion of privacy. Nevertheless, when the bamboo blinds were raised, a passer-by with curiosity and a ladder would be able to discover that the sitting-room of the Manifolds' rented home was furnished in impeccable Adelaide taste. Saucer chairs were disposed around a fake fireplace. A vinyl-topped coffee-table squatted between them, underneath a styrene crystal-style basket chandelier. On the floor, fake Aboriginal scatter rugs and Numdah rugs quarrelled with the solid Axminster carpet. Above the ferns on the mantelpiece, either side of the starfish-shaped gilt wall-clock, stood two turquoise Italian glass vases.

A similar crystal-style chandelier hung in the dining-room, which doubled as the sun-room with voile-draped glass sliding doors out on to the tiled patio. The centrepiece here, undoubtedly, was the maple dining suite. It was Early American Colonial in design, set off by matching place-mats and coasters decorated with scenes of Old Adelaide. In the Early Colonial buffet was displayed a thirty-six-piece luncheon service with an Autumn Leaves motif.

In every room (as the rental agent remarked) the sights and smells of Nature abounded, with flower arrangements in glass bubbles and indoor plants in picturesque bamboo cages – even in the master bathroom with its tiles featuring black French poodle motifs on a pale pink background. Helen sometimes lay in the master bath and looked up at these, and wondered if they, too, would melt when, as she daily promised herself, she poured petrol over the Early American maple, the scatter rugs, the washable voile drapes, the chenille bedspreads – and burned the house and all its contents to the ground.

On the tiled patio meanwhile father and daughter went

on with their lunch without saying much. Georgina peeled the skin off a grape.

'I'm not bored,' she said. 'I like it out here.'

'Do you?'

'Yes.'

'Even school?'

'It's okay.'

'You could have stayed on at Malvern. You only had two more terms.'

'Is that what you wanted me to do?'

Douglas was silent. Eventually he said: 'It's your exams I'm thinking of. It's a different system over here, isn't it?'

'Yes, but it still counts. I mean for university, if I'm going to go. If I do really okay in the Certificate I can still get a place at Cambridge.'

'Oxford?'

'Cambridge is much better for biologists. And for medicine, if I change.'

'Oh.'

She looked him in the face. 'It's what you'd have preferred, isn't it. That I didn't come out here? That I stayed on at Malvern?'

'Only because you're finishing at school,' he said uneasily. 'It is a big uprooting.'

Georgina looked away, past the swimming-pool and the neatly clipped hedges to the blue haze of the Adelaide hills. 'You told me we were going to meet Captain Kemp again,' she declared.

'Meet Nick? Did I say that?'

'Yes, you did. In London. You said he was out here. It's one reason I came.'

'Just because he's in Australia doesn't mean he'll necessarily want to see us.'

'Oh, Daddy, of course he will! Don't you want to see *him* again? After all that he did?'

Douglas pushed his plate aside. 'Why must young people bloody well romanticise everything they read?' he exclaimed. 'Poetry isn't autobiography. Don't you realise? When I write poems I don't have to be truthful to anybody or anything except my own self. It's not history, it's me. Mine. My name on

14

it. I'm not responsible for other people I might include, Nick or anybody else!'

Georgina stared at him, her mouth open. She seemed on the point of tears. 'Are you telling me it didn't happen like that at all?' she cried. 'Nick said— '

'No, I'm not. I'm not saying it didn't happen like that. But in *DogDay*, if that's what you mean, I fulfilled an obligation. I didn't immortalise it so that posterity could hang it like an albatross around my bloody neck. If Nick gets in touch, Georgina, you'll be the first to know about it. Meanwhile I'm here to escape from entertaining people.'

Georgina scowled at the tablecloth, as if she wanted to carry the conversation further. Instead she stood up abruptly and began gathering the lunch things on to the tray. 'I'd better clear up,' she said. 'I've got a whole lot of revising to do this evening. I'll bring you coffee in your study, is that all right?'

Georgina Manifold's scowl didn't last long – and no more it should have because it buttoned up a face which with its broad brow, wide mouth and short straight nose was attractively open and tranquil. After making the coffee, she took a biology handbook out into the garden and sat by the swimming-pool. Out of her father's window, where he was supposed to be writing, she could hear the flat syllables of the Test Match commentator in Sydney.

How she first came to hear the D-Day story she could not remember. Probably she had been told it by Bella, her mother, long before she was able to read the poem for herself. She must have known it by heart by the time it passed down to Aunt Dorothy, after Mummy died, because she could recall so easily the shrinking dread with which she would wait for her mother's only sister to turn it into a bitter illustration of how God moved in unfathomable ways – rescuing Douglas Manifold, the wicked adulterer, and later not lifting a finger to stop the bus which careered up on to the pavement and killed Bella, the poor wife he abandoned for an *actress*. Each time Aunt Dorothy, speaking coldly enough to freeze a judgement on stone, would

15

make herself plain. It was Georgina's father, Douglas, who should have been struck down by the hand of fate. Brave young Nicholas Kemp should never have gone back into the water for him.

At any event, the story impressed itself like a brand upon her young mind. Stories endlessly repeated to young children always carry the intensity of myth, but this one more so to Georgina, because it was hers alone. In every practical sense fatherless from the age of four, she was presented with her very own morality play in which two fathers appeared to be contending to save her unborn life. Superhuman was Captain Kemp, selflessly risking his own life to save another's, struggling to release his friend's trapped foot as he pitted his strength and courage against the forces of destiny. All too mortal was Douglas Manifold, yielding to his fate, rescued from a watery grave at his last breath in order that he might marry Bella and begin working out the long cycle of sin, guilt and repentance.

If this sounds fanciful, remember the solitude in which this young girl's imaginings had room to flower. How many times did Georgina replay that scene on the Normandy beaches, dressing up her dolls in uniforms stained with mud and red ink for verisimilitude? She would make up dialogue for the two men in which a simple 'Help me!' and 'Here I am!' expanded over the years into dramatic pledges by them both to be faithful husbands and fathers if ever they came through alive (all the while drumming her heels on the bare floorboards to produce the background thunder of guns and shells).

Inevitably the promises made by the Douglas Manifold puppet grew more personal, more relevant to the sparse little alimony-sustained flat in which Georgina lived with her mother. And her sense of betrayal grew more acute. The daring rescue sometimes, Aunt-Dorothy-like, didn't work out. The dolls would be battered in a helpless rage against the floor until their uniforms came away and their faces were as swollen and puffy as drowned men's faces.

It cannot have seemed odd to Georgina then, playing with her puppet fathers (or, later, writing the story down and drawing a picture of it in her school exercise-book) that the two men should be interfused, one incomplete without the other. If she paused to think about it, she accepted that Douglas Manifold must be her real father, the one who went out of her life when she was four except for the name she carried. Nevertheless it was Captain Kemp who made the greater claim on her imagination. He was a hero in the mould of Sir Philip Sidney and Beau Geste. To her classmates at Malvern she was the daughter of a writer who must be famous because his poems kept turning up in their examination papers. But whereas most of *them* subconsciously looked to their fathers for the qualities they wanted to find in the boys they fancied, Georgina looked to her image of Nicholas Kemp, and read into this one act of D-Day valour a set of ideals no boy she met had ever lived up to.

Once, early on, he had come out to Malvern to see her. It was a summer Saturday. She'd watched from the top of the stairs as parents arrived to take their daughters away for the weekend. Then, in a loud scattering of gravel, an old army jeep had driven up to the entrance hall. People stopped talking; even the senior girls turned round . . . and in came a man in a bush-hat, leather boots and a safari-suit. He stood in the doorway and flipped a coin which sparkled in the sunlight, and said: 'A Yankee dollar for the first girl to bring me out Georgina Manifold!'

She'd recognised him at once, of course. And she knew, as she walked solemnly down the stairs with the sixth-formers watching, that it was the greatest moment of her life. Nick had taken her out to lunch and she'd drunk cider – probably more than she should have done: anyway, enough to ask him, a little tremulously: 'You know my father's poem. The famous one. *DogDay*. Can I ask you – did it really happen like that?'

Nick Kemp looked at her. She thought there was something mocking about his smile. 'What does your dad say?' he asked.

'I don't know. I don't think he wants. . . . I haven't asked him.'

Her look must have been pleading, because Nick relented. He took her fork and laid it prongs-upwards, and introduced a knife between the prongs.

'The knife is the landing-craft,' he said. 'The tips of the fork are the waves on the beach, because it was a choppy sea. The haft of the fork is the Normandy cliffs where the German gunners are dug in, and the valley between is the beach. The landing-craft comes in *so*, under heavy bombardment. You never want to hear such a racket. I lead the men ashore, but your father slips and falls sideways. He gets his head up above water all right, but his foot's trapped. I've got a knife and I dive down, and luckily it's a rope round his ankle, I can cut him free. Trouble is, the Huns must have seen us by now, because just as I surface this damn great shell lands behind me. I'm holed in six places, but poor old Duggle's knocked out by a shell-splinter, you know, the scar above his eye. So I haul him on to the beach and the next thing I remember is this very ugly nurse in a dressing station tying me up in bandages. Strewth! I was more frightened by that woman than I was in the water!'

She'd never forgotten that lunch. It meant more to her than she was ever able to explain. It was why she had to see him; why she was sitting here by a swimming-pool in Australia instead of looking out of a school-room window at the grey snow.

She sneezed.

'Bless you!'

Turning, she saw their next-door neighbour, Mr Robbins, leaning across the privet hedge. A broad, stubby man with a brown face under a khaki bush-hat, he was holding a can of beer with which he saluted her grandiosely.

'According to my daughter, you sneezed at the speed of one hundred and seventy miles an hour!' he shouted. 'And she should know, she's a statistician in the Premier's office, the Premier of South Australia. What do you think of that?'

'Oh! Well— '

'What are you going to do when you're older, girl?'

'I don't know.'

'Well, then, take my advice. Don't end up any place where you can't see the stars at night when you walk out through your front door.'

'Oh?'

'My word. I've been to London. By the time my late-departed wife and I had finished seeing the sights, I'd have swapped you twenty Harrods department stores for one clear view of the horizon. Know what I mean? Well, then, I won't keep you from your books.'

Mr Robbins turned away, whistling for his dog. Georgina

looked up at the raw blue sky. It occurred to her that she knew almost nothing about Australia, no more really than when she first arrived. The heat and the brightness, of course. And the accents. But that kind of unfamiliarity quickly wore off; and, as for the rest of Adelaide, it didn't seem so different from those dreaded school holidays in Woking with her Aunt Dorothy and Uncle Frank.

She was out here with the father she scarcely knew, and still felt resentful towards. She was at a new school. Naturally she felt the need to look more for similarities than for differences; and, God knows, there were enough similarities. It was as if Woking had flown bodily through the air and transplanted itself upon Adelaide, its inhabitants waking up one morning, blinking *en masse* at the tropical scene that greeted their eyes, and immediately deciding that life must go on in this oven exactly as before – shaving the lawn to a defenceless stubble, cooking hot roasts, washing the car, following the cricket scores, spying upon their neighbours and sitting under a beach umbrella with a handkerchief knotted on their pates.

Adelaide. At least she'd looked it up in *Britannica*, which was more than the others had troubled to do. Adelaide had been dreamed up by a gaolbird in Newgate Prison, which (her father said) must account for all the bars. Colonel Light, who founded it, planned to call it after his great hero Wellington; but by 1840 the place had been settled by nonconformists (Methodists mostly) and Wellington had just outraged them by helping Peel emancipate the Catholics. So Adelaide it became, a model city of squares and intersections laid out from Acre One, the nucleus and birth-site of Adelaide upon which there shortly rose a boozer, proudly catering to the carriage trade.

And for people fresh out from England it must indeed have seemed like Home. The cows grazed on the banks of the Torrens, leaving and entering the parkland through gates marked 'Cows Only'. Silver-haired legislators who had come up through Elders GM lunched off cold saddle of mutton at the Adelaide Club and discussed declining standards, Asian immigration and the scandalously relaxed licensing laws. Teenagers sat swinging their legs in a milk-bar in Rundle Street, while Richard Chamberlain puffed out his chest and crooned 'Love Me Tender' on the corner jukebox. The *Advertiser* serialised

19

Lord Avon's memoirs, down beside its etiquette column. In the Botanic Gardens elderly ladies in long skirts glanced guiltily over their shoulders before stooping to trowel up a Banksia. . . .

This was all as it should be: but something somewhere was not quite right. It might have had to do with the stillness of the air in the early morning of a north-wind day, before the wind came blowing hot and gritty from the desert heart of Australia, prickling the eyes, clogging the throat, putting down a dust-haze in the street. But on this particular afternoon there was no wind, no haze – and still Georgina felt a restless unease, as if she was waiting for something which she couldn't define, but which was somehow too important to miss.

D ouglas had put his work aside and was writing a letter
to his publisher, Richard de la Mare at Faber.

My dear Richard

I am writing this at my desk by the window. Outside,
the Wellington Square gardener is watering a luxurious
quilt of purple and white Cinerarias. It is basking weather.
I can almost hear the offended buzzing of the honey-bees as
they abandon their pollen under the hail of sun-drenched
water-drops. For days, weeks, it has been like this.

I'm not setting out to gloat over you. I know what it's
like at home. The Adelaide papers have been running stories
about the worst snowstorms since 1881, and Londoners
skating on Hampstead Ponds. I can see you now in your
office: the rime on the glass, the heat clanking through the
ancient Russell Square pipes, your dreadnought and muffler
hanging on the coat-stand beside the draughty door. What
I want you to try to imagine in return is coming away from
a country where the windows are all shut tight to a land
where the windows everywhere are open.

The British winter has not reached as far as Australia
yet, to sclerose its tissues, freeze its warm blood, turn it
in upon itself and huddle it towards the stove and its old
memories. There may be all kinds of misgivings out here,
to do with personal and cultural identity. But to me they
come across as the trials of youth to be overcome, not the
tribulations of middle age to be endured. Frankly, Richard,
Australia makes me feel alive again. I am a greybeard who
has been carried out into the sun, a wintry old bard whose
blood begins to quicken and whose gnarled fingers begin to
uncurl and flex enough to be able to hold a quill. Because
that, as I hear you reminding me, is what I came out for,
is it not? To refresh the Muse, to unfreeze the Pierian
springs . . . to test myself as a writer once more, in a young

21

land which still believes that to strive and to aspire are a worthy ambition even at the cost of failure, not something to be sneered at by the metropolitan critics and all your weevil literary set.

You know what I think about the drudgery of poetry readings, to people too lazy to read for themselves . . . those dreary occasions where one attempts to reanimate dead tissue which has lost its feeling, its coloration, its music, its karma, before politely attentive audiences who can't tell the living from the dead – you know they are what I am gladdest to leave behind. But meanwhile the Gallipoli script will keep me ticking over. And while the Australian sun warms this piece of sullen clay . . .

Douglas broke off. He had caught sight of something, on his desk, under the ink-stand. A piece of stitched hide, the shape of a shoe-heel. He got up and went into the kitchen, banging drawers, and came back with a box of matches. Picking up the shoe-heel, he held it at arm's length as if it were contaminated. On it was inked an address in a free flowing hand: *Nick Kemp, Bellerophon, Mannum Bend, R. Murray. Its walking distance!*

The shoe-heel had arrived in an envelope, addressed to Douglas Manifold, c/o Adelaide University, shortly after he'd arrived. He had thrown it away days ago. The cleaner must have retrieved it and put it back on his desk. Why? Nick, anyway, had probably moved on by now, further up the Murray. Not since the war, when they were in camp together training in landing-craft before the Normandy invasion, had Nick ever stayed for long in the same place. Messages would come through the letter-box in Holland Park; scribbled postcards from the Yukon, from Hong Kong, the Witwatersrand, Rio de Janeiro, Rangoon, latterly from Nick's native land, Australia, which he had quitted as a young man. Their pictures of goldfields, Burmese dancers, ivory-poachers and Himalayan skylines taunted him with their images of adventurousness. *You and I took risks once*, they seemed to be admonishing him. *We walked the trail together; we shared our food, our women, our confidences. We overcame dangers. We set the town alight. . . .*

Douglas put the matches down. He placed the shoe-heel

in an ashtray on the desk. Immediately in front of the window the unnaturally bright sun blazed down on dark green bushes and spiky unfamiliar flowers. He thought of dank back rooms in Liverpool, Brighton, Norwich, Cardiff, London: the stink of beer, the beer-stained tables, the committee in the front row, the denim and donkey-jackets strung out behind them ('Let's have you forward, you at the back there! There's plenty of seats up front!'). Introduced by the chairman with always the same unctuous phrases – 'the celebrated war poet', 'author of *DogDay* about the D-Day landings, the finest narrative poem of the last war'; once, by some patronising twerp, 'the best Second World War poet who survived . . . '. Most of them wouldn't have given a fig if he hadn't survived and gone on writing. Probably they'd have preferred it that way. How satisfying for the academic pall-bearers if they had been able to brush a little chiaroscuro into their blackening of his posthumous reputation . . . *killed at the height of his promise . . . who knows what he might not have gone on to achieve?*

Too bad. He had gone on. But not in the way any of them expected. He had published, since the war, three volumes of formal poetry. Love poems for the most part, they were sculptured, elegant, chiselled verses, armoured against critical barbs. He'd raised two fingers at the pack of them, with their demands for poetry reflecting the new age of concentration-camps and mass extermination, poetry written on the naked edge of experience by poets ready and willing to bite down to the quick of their souls. None of these critics, flailing from their ivory towers like muezzins calling the barbarians to Mecca, had been through the crucible of his war. How many of them had been pinned down by sniper fire, or seen men trapped in a blazing tank? How many of them had watched the enemy shells straddle their position and been humiliated by terror so paralysing that their limbs refused the commands of their brain? In the war he had written the poetry of war from the experience of war. In peacetime to have simulated the same violence, by reaching in and putting his bleeding entrails on public display, would have been a travesty, and a defamation of what he and Nick had been through.

'*So with no further ado, ladies and gentlemen, let me give you Douglas Manifold to read from some of those poems. I'm sure we all hope that "DogDay" will be amongst them'* – as if the poems of these past twenty years were to be passed over in an embarrassed silence. Well, they got more love poems than war poems and sod their looks of disappointment. Even Eliot, the first to accept his poems for publication, had pronounced himself disappointed that the blood had sweetened to honey after 1945. When Eliot's private verdict on the first volume of love poems – 'Graves without the White Goddess' – had reached Douglas's ears, he had demanded another editor at Faber. And got one.

Book reviews, wireless broadcasts, film scripts, readings, lectures: all the hack employments of the man of letters were what brought the money in, not the poetry which was his profession. The critics had seen to that. They'd done their best to destroy his reputation with the metropolitan audience (though his poems sold well enough to the ordinary readers, the kind of people who were not ashamed to acknowledge that they still kept a volume of Yeats or Tennyson on the bedroom table). Meanwhile the froth rose to the top: the Celtic babble of Dylan Thomas, and the sub-Lawrentian sensationalists kindling their *ignis fatuus* over a sunflower or a parrot in a zoo. When everyday trivia aroused such *Angst*, what hope was left for the great heroic subjects, the struggle between good and evil, between light and darkness, in which, less than a generation ago, his own friends had fought and died? No hope, for sure, in the victory-corrupted England of never-had-it-so-good and I'm-all-right-Jack. Nick Kemp had seen it coming. . . .

He heard the patio doors open, then the sound of Georgina at the piano. He lit a match and held Nick's address over the flame. The hide singed and wrinkled. When the words were no longer legible he dropped the shoe-heel in the ashtray, where it went on kicking up, as if it had places to get to.

He looked at his watch: 4.30. That journalist of Helen's would be arriving to interview him. Best to get a drink in first. He strode into the sitting-room, where Georgina was practising her scales, and poured himself a large whisky and water.

'Is there anything to eat?' he demanded.

Georgina stopped playing. 'Sultana cake,' she offered.

'No, no.'

'Crackers? Mrs G always leaves crackers when she comes and cleans. Shall I make some crackers with Vegemite? Or cheese?'

'What the hell is Vegemite?'

'It's a kind of yeast extract. Everybody eats it out here. Mrs G brings it with crackers.'

'Cheese. I'll have cheese, thank you. Where's Helen?'

'She's playing tennis.'

'So long as you're here. I hate it when the house is empty. I've spent too much of my life in empty houses, silent houses, knocking my thoughts against the walls.' Douglas tossed back the whisky and poured himself another, jabbing with the tongs in the ice-bucket. Georgina wondered what her father used to do when he was on his own. Did he iron his own clothes? Did he feed himself? She could have looked after him so much better than Helen.

By the time she got back with the cheese and biscuits, the journalist from the *South Australian Gazette* had arrived. She was conscious of a ruddy face framed by greying curls, and a pair of watery blue eyes appraising her.

'G'day,' said the man, levering himself out of the armchair. 'This, I presume, is the good-looking Miss Manifold, am I right?'

'Georgina,' said Georgina. She held the plate to her chest and shook his hand.

'Winn Vellacott, *South Australian Gazette*. First name as in Godfrey Winn, with whom I have not yet been compared but there's a first time for everything. That was a kind thought, my dear,' he added, taking the plate of biscuits-and-cheese and returning to his chair beside which a large Campari stood in a moist ring on the vinyl table. He crammed a biscuit into his mouth, scattering crumbs on his bow-tie. Then, swallowing a mouthful of Campari, he picked up his notebook. 'Now, if I might recapitulate, Sir Douglas— '

'No. I'm not a knight of the realm, for heaven's sake.'

'Whoops. I'm up a gum-tree there for starters.' Vellacott scored out a scribble heavily with his pencil. 'Always wise to check these things, eh? I presume it would not be libellous to describe you, Mr Manifold, as one of Great Britain's most respected poets. Author of *DogDay*— '

'Among many better poems— '

'Author of *DogDay* among other poems. Winner of numerous literary awards and distinctions. Lecturer, broadcaster— '

'Et cetera.'

'Et cetera. Thank you. So, Mr Manifold. . . . It's not Adelaide Festival time. What brings you to our provincial backwater, eh? Big fish or little ones?'

'I'm here, attached to the University, while I write the script for a film about the Dardanelles Expedition.'

'A Brit movie?'

'Yes.'

'About Australians?'

'Anzac and British. It's about the Gallipoli campaign as a whole. I don't want to go into details.'

Winn Vellacott scribbled fiercely. His large red fingers held the pencil near the tip and pressed down until it seemed the lead would break. 'Are you talking to veterans of Gallipoli during your stay with us, Mr Manifold? To get the Australian point of view of the cock-up by the Brit high command?'

'I expect to. Let's get this straight. This isn't a documentary about military strategy. It's a film about people in war; people fighting and dying; people spilling their guts trying to rescue their mates out of no man's land. That's something I know about.'

Vellacott went on scribbling. 'Blood and guts. Heroism under fire. What you might call your standard war movie, I presume, in that case. In its essentials, I mean?'

'Crudely simplified for your readers, that is what you might call it.'

Georgina, sitting on the piano-stool, watched her father drumming his glasses on the arm of his chair. She knew that sign. The man from the *South Australian Gazette*, on the other hand, appeared to be settling in. He took another gulp of Campari and sat back comfortably in the chair, his long legs in twill trousers stretched out in front of him, his notebook on his lap. Georgina got up to refill his glass. He waved her back.

'No, thanks, sweetheart. I have to manufacture immortal prose tonight. Not as immortal as your pa's; I make no bones about that. *Ephemeral* might be the word; here today and gone tomorrow. But even the poor glow-worm is permitted to think it's going to shine forever, if you'll excuse my poetry, Mr Manifold. . . .'

'Was there anything else?'

'Ah.' Winn Vellacott flipped the pages of his notebook.

'If that's all—'

'Not quite. I want to ask you, is there any other purpose to your visit?'

'Purpose?'

'Any other reason you're here in Adelaide at this time, apart from solely and entirely to write your script?'

'And give a talk or two at the University – no.'

'Nothing else?'

The scar on Douglas Manifold's forehead began to redden. He stood up. Winn Vellacott waved a pacifying paw.

'Not to worry. Maybe I'm up another gum-tree. But the coincidence, you must admit—'

'What coincidence?'

'Are you familiar with Major Freddie Collins?'

'Freddie? I used to know him. What about him?'

'Collins is now head of British defence liaison staff at the British high commission in Canberra. Used to work for British Army Intelligence, yes? Helped organise the bombing of Dresden during the war. He last surfaced in Cyprus, during the little trouble you had over Suez. He's in Adelaide right now – for the cricket, I expect. Is cricket his game?' Vellacott went on flipping the pages of his notebook. 'Do you know Edward Catchpole?'

Douglas glanced at Georgina on the piano-stool. 'I've heard the name.'

'He's down here organising security for next month's Royal Visit. An odd posting, wouldn't you say, Mr Manifold, for a senior civil servant in your Ministry of Supply, especially so far in advance? No? Perhaps not. You know Whitehall better than I do, I think I'm right in saying. When you knew Major Collins – wasn't that in Army Intelligence at the end of the war?'

'None of your damned business. Let me get this straight. You came here to write a profile of me for your newspaper, right?'

'Right.'

'And now you want to include me in your personal theories of some sort of conspiracy by the British government, no doubt to overthrow the Premier and declare South Australia an integral part of the United Kingdom. Is that what they call "creative journalism" out here?'

Winn Vellacott turned on a wide smile which gave his face a look of baby blandness. 'There's nothing like a sense of humour,' he said, putting his notebook away and getting to his feet. 'Always remember, Georgie, never trust a man without a sense of humour.' He sketched a shambling bow to Douglas. 'Thanks for sparing me an audience, Mr Manifold. Pity about the knighthood; p'raps it's on its way. Let me leave you with something to chew on. This is election year for Bob Menzies, our anointed Prime Minister. He's got a two-seat majority: he needs some international kudos to stand a chance of getting back in. The Yanks are already negotiating with him for a naval satellite communications base at North West Cape. My hunch is the Brits are negotiating for something even bigger down here. I intend the *Gazette* to be the first to know about it.'

Digging in his pocket, Vellacott pulled out a grubby white card and held it out to Douglas between the tips of his fingers. 'If you want to talk about it, that's my number on the paper. Thanks for the rosiner. Don't worry to get up, Georgie. I'm used to finding my own way out.'

Georgina brooded on this meeting. The more she thought about what Vellacott had said, the more it appeared to her to be serious and even sinister in its implications. Was her father really involved with Catchpole, and this man Freddie Collins? When she asked him, he just shook his head and dismissed it with a laugh. She had come out to get to know him; but the more time she spent out here the less she understood.

It was Saturday before a solution came to her. Mid-afternoon was the dead time of the day: too hot to stay out by the pool, too stuffy to enjoy staying inside, too much trouble to go visiting, too enervating to work, too boring to sit and read. Dully she was practising scales and arpeggios. Douglas, recovering from painful sunburn, was making notes on a typescript with a towel round his shoulders and zinc cream on the back of his neck. Helen, in a purple leotard, was doing the gymnastic exercises she learned at RADA. Every now and then she would stop to concentrate on breathing from her diaphragm, standing in the middle of the room, her hair tied back, her eyes shut, her fingers pressed against her stomach. Ottoman, the Persian kitten Helen had bought for companionship, crackled against Georgina's bare ankles. She kicked it away and slammed down the piano lid.

They couldn't go on like this. They were falling off the edge of the world. She must find Nick. He had rescued her father once before. He would do it again, rescue all of them, bring them back to their senses. However long it took, she, Georgina, would track him down. Nick would come; he had to come. . . .

'He *will* come,' she said aloud.

'Who will come, George?' Helen had finished her exercises, and gone to rest on the Regency-style chaise-longue against the wall, under the print of a naked ochre-striped Aborigine holding a shield across his middle in one hand and a fishing-spear in the other.

'Who, George?'

29

'Nobody important.'

'Oh, one of your school-friends. I'm so thrilled you're making some friends at last.' Helen tucked her legs up. Ottoman sat beside her and preened obscenely. 'Douglas, on the other hand, has chosen to play the Hermit of Wellington Square,' she continued in a plaintive tone.

'That is absolute twaddle!' Douglas looked up from the typescript he was correcting. 'We've been to the theatre here. Such as it is.'

'By ourselves, darling. At least I make the effort to go out and socialise. I refuse to be like the ancient Stoics, or one of those women who commits suttee on the pyre of her husband's career. In fact you may like to know that I've agreed to do Isabella for a University Drama Guild production of *Measure for Measure* next month. It will be a charade, no doubt, but at least it's preferable to cloistering myself in this kitsch mausoleum, listening to the death-rattle of your typewriter keys.'

Douglas made a wry face. 'I think it's a very good idea that you're getting out of the house. When do rehearsals start?'

'Next week.' Helen stood up and stretched, the purple leotard tight against her small breasts, flat stomach, slim hips. Not for the first time Georgina considered what an enviable figure she might have inherited if she'd been Helen's daughter. Except that she might have inherited Helen's character as well. She glanced at her father. Douglas, bent over his typescript, did not look up.

Georgina thought finding Nick would be easy, a simple matter of a few phone calls. She had the time. As a final-year entrant she had been excused most of the school's extra-curricular activities – ball games, mostly, in which astonishingly large, vigorous, athletic, pink-thighed Australian girls jumped and bounced and screamed. She had sung in the choir a couple of times when it had run short of contraltos; she had joined the Camera Club so she could use the school darkroom. Otherwise she kept herself apart, concentrating on her classroom and laboratory work for the Leaving Honours certificate. The continuity of her schoolwork had so far carried her over the uprooting Douglas had worried about. The human anatomy, she had been relieved to discover, looked exactly the same in South Australia as it did in Worcestershire. Evolution appeared to proceed, here as there, from amoeba through earthworm, dogfish, frogs and rabbits. Apart from the sun's unusual habit of shining warmly, she'd had little cause to ponder the ninety-degree change in her angle on the universe.

She remembered her father saying that Nick had been prospecting for oil. Very well, she would contact the oil companies. She telephoned the Hunt Oil Company, the Woodside Oil Company and Exoil. She spoke to Shell Development (Aust.) Pty, Continental Oil Company of Australia Ltd, and Associated Australian Oilfields NL. She was put through to an endless succession of departments, secretaries and company spokesmen. None of them had any staff record of Nicholas Kemp.

She tried the University. Someone in the registrar's office put her on to the School of Mining. The School of Mining recommended she contact the Geology people, so she biked out across the Parklands. A lab technician in a white coat took pity on her. 'Try the Arcadia,' he advised. 'It's a pub, up by the railway station. That's where the prospectors hang out.'

Georgina made her way back to the railway station. It was late afternoon. This was a quarter of Adelaide she barely knew. Next to the railway station in an open shed, a wizened man with a squint was standing on a tea-chest, conducting a yard sale. He was wearing brown shoes, a brown suit and a brown hat, and kept flicking the brim of the hat with his fingers as he recited bids in a fast monotonous voice. Georgina watched from the back of the shed, conscious that her school uniform set her apart from the shabby little knots of people who stopped among the goods being auctioned – umbrellas, prams, chairs, hockey sticks, battered typewriters and cardboard boxes full of old clothes. It was impossible to tell which piece of junk the auctioneer's patter referred to, but from time to time an anonymous figure would emerge from the throng carrying a cardboard box, and step out of the roped enclosure.

The Arcadia was across the road from the railway tracks. Dingy orange paint flaked off its walls and caught

31

in the netting over the windows that gave on to the street, but its name glowed in red neon above the doorway and there was much coming and going of drinking men. As Georgina approached, two of them stood in the doorway, puce with beer and brawling. One squared up with his fists. The other closed on him and pinioned his arms like a boxer. Both drunks swayed, then slowly toppled over in each other's arms and rolled down the stone steps to the pavement, whereupon they got on all fours, pulled each other up and staggered down the street arm-in-arm.

Georgina stood still, summoning up her courage. Then, hugging her school-bag to her chest, she walked up the steps and in through the doors. She was engulfed at once in a roar of men talking. Dressed mostly in grey suits with white open-necked shirts, they sat and bellowed at each other, or walked backwards and forwards between the steaming tables carrying two-pint schooners of beer.

The stale smells of beer and sweat made her mouth dry. She crossed the slippery brown linoleum to the bar and was brought up dead by a wall of backs, shoulder to shoulder on bar-stools, wedged so tightly that each beer-drinker was only able to address the one beside him by bending his head forward and turning his neck like a tortoise to left or right. Georgina was about to retreat, defeated by the noise, the smells, the sour and strenuous atmosphere of this place, when one back dislodged sufficiently from the wall for the head on it to swivel right round and regard her with a look of astonishment and growing consternation.

'Hey, Bill,' it said. 'There's a young sheila in here, straight out of nursery school!'

Georgina could feel a deep blush starting at her throat and blossoming over her cheeks. It didn't occur to her that her bizarrely incongruous school outfit of white blouse, black shoes and tartan skirt with blanket-pin was actually the best thing she could have worn, because instead of raucous jokes aimed at driving out this under-age intruder Bill (or Joe or Mick) said kindly: 'Lost your dad, have you, love? What's his name, eh?'

'Nicholas Kemp,' said Georgina. 'Nicholas Kemp, I'm looking for Nicholas Kemp.'

The backs had all turned round now, presenting fronts

which were equally forbidding to Georgina's eye – tougher-looking than the farmers at Worcester County Fair, fatter-necked and more weather-beaten. To judge from their bulging muscular frames there were as many drovers and sheep-shearers among them as prospectors (whatever a prospector was supposed to look like). One of them roared above the din, 'Anyone here know Nicholas Kemp?' and some of his mates took up the refrain: 'Kemp! Kemp! We want Kemp!'

Georgina stood rooted to the spot. Bill summoned a barmaid and bellowed a question in her ear. She nodded, and looked at Georgina with frank astonishment. Bill turned to her.

'Is it Captain Kemp you want, love?'

'Yes. Yes.'

Eagerly she gazed at Bill. He regarded her, grinning, and shook his head.

'*He's* a dark horse, the Captain, then,' he declared.

At that instant a whistle blew. As one man, drinkers at the tables stampeded to the bar. Georgina was squeezed and pummelled, cannoned between pressing, straining, sweating bodies. She could hear the rattle of glasses being lined up two-deep the length of the bar and the pissing of beer as it was hosed into them all the way up and down the lines. Falling, she believed it was the last sound she would ever hear – but the next moment a strong pair of arms lifted her out of the ruck and half-carried, half-propelled her through the door and down the steps into the sweet air. She turned round, and saw Winn Vellacott.

'You!' She shrank back.

'You're lucky to be alive, sweetie. Haven't you heard about the six o'clock swill?'

'The what?'

'Bars shut at six. One of Adelaide's more picturesque customs, if you don't get trampled in the rush. Come on, I'll buy you a cup of tea. They don't arrest you, yet, for drinking tea.'

Georgina clutched her school-bag. The strap had broken. 'I have to find someone,' she said, still in a daze.

'I heard. Nicholas Kemp.'

'You know him, then?'

33

'I know everybody, sweet Miss Manifold. Come with me.'

Vellacott took her into the railway station. Her black lace-up shoes rang in the long-windowed stone vault of the station hall. In the buffet he ordered a pot of tea and an egg sandwich. His watery blue eyes studied her with distinct amusement across the table.

'Are you okay, sweetie?'

'Yes, I am, thank you.'

'Your daddy never told you women don't go into pubs like the Arcadia? Let alone schoolgirls?'

'How do you know Captain Kemp?'

'I'll ask the questions, if you please. What's he to you?'

'He's . . . a friend of my father's.'

'If he's a friend of your father's, why doesn't your father go looking for him?'

Georgina was silent.

'Have they been friends for long?'

'Yes. Since the war.' She said impatiently, as if explaining to an idiot; 'He is the Australian soldier in *DogDay*.'

'Nick?' Winn Vellacott whistled. 'The bastard. He never told me. I've known Nick for years; we went to school together.'

'In England?'

'Ah, no. I'm the local boy. Nick was always the tall poppy. Captain of cricket, football star, scholarships all round; he went on to Oxford. We lost contact. But I knew he was back, and there's no way old Nick would miss the Adelaide Test, not with Cowdrey and Dexter playing. No, I had the same idea as you, Georgie. I thought I'd find him in the Arcadia. I've heard that Nick's been prospecting up in the Nullarbor Desert, and I had a few things to ask him about that.'

'Mr Vellacott. . . .' Georgina hesitated. 'I really need to find Captain Kemp. I don't know where else to look for him. If you find him, can you tell him how important it is?'

Vellacott sipped his tea and spat it back into the cup. 'Piss on that.' Glancing quickly round, he poured the cup back into the teapot and refilled it with the contents of a flask he palmed out of his inside jacket pocket. Georgina watched him drain it down.

'That's got the taste out of my mouth,' he said, breathing

34

whisky at her. 'It can rot your brain, that tea. They come for you in the green cart. Now, Georgie, I'll help you if you help me. What's your dad's connection with Edward Catchpole?'

Georgina started. 'I don't think there is a connection.'

'That's not what I call help.'

'Only . . . I mean only what my father told you.'

'Really? I thought your mother was seeing— '

'No.'

'What?'

'She's not my mother. Helen's not my mother. She's my stepmother.'

'Sorry. Okay. Your stepmother is seeing quite a bit of Mr Catchpole, isn't she?'

'Is she? I don't think so.' Georgina paused, remembering Helen's tennis game. 'I mean, I don't know. Is she? Are you sure? Have you been following her?' This was rather intriguing. Pondering the possible scenarios, she poured herself a second cup out of the teapot before recalling that Vellacott had spat into it.

'I'm not accusing Helen of anything, sweetie. I just want you to keep your eyes and ears open. If I find Kemp for you, I want you to promise me you'll do that. Ask your stepmother . . . anything. Then ring me on this number at the *Gazette*.'

He scribbled a telephone number on a paper napkin and passed it over the table. 'Just between ourselves, Georgie. We'll keep it a secret. Okay?'

Georgina looked at the napkin and put it in her school-bag. 'Okay, if you find Captain Kemp,' she said.

He had come to the immortal landing of 25 April 1915. The young man William Anderson, into whom he breathed life and friendship and sympathies, whom he had fostered in a chalk valley in the South Downs, trained as an officer near Grimsby, filled with courageous hope and sent out, all innocent of love and battle, in a troopship across the Mediterranean, was now with his men in a towed lighter silently approaching the glimmering cliffs of Cape Helles, which bounded the deeper darkness of the Dardanelles.

Lieutenant Anderson's throat was dry. There was dirt in the corners of his eyes and stubble on his chin and in his nostrils the hot sour smell of herded human bodies. They were still thirty yards from the beach when the Turks opened fire with everything they'd got, ten thousand shots a minute singing into unprotected bone and flesh and stirring the bay into white foam, while the troops screamed and groaned and drowned as they jumped overboard and tried to swim. . . .

And it all flooded back to Douglas, as it was bound to. Not Gallipoli, where his young lieutenant was about to step on to the soft sand and be slaughtered by the Turkish machine-guns dug in under the ruins of Sedd-el-Bahr, but the Normandy beaches, in the grey dawn light of another war, with a cold wind off the sea. The German gunners were still enfilading the beach. He could feel his heart pounding, his clammy fingers slipping as he steadied his rifle and stood up amid the hail of bullets to run ashore. He has checked his ammunition. He knows what he has to do. Stay a distance of six feet from the man in front and keep running –

> Run towards him, he has seen you, he
> Is Death, he flings out his arms

The pen slipped in his fingers. It lay on the paper in a gout of ink. His breath came shallowly; his heart pumped in his chest. In his dreams he had not relived those moments so vividly for years. He was tormenting himself as an act of penance, because it was himself he saw on those beaches, and this time there was going to be no reprieve, no second chance to learn how to be a coward.

He could take the easy way through the Gallipoli script and castigate the British high command – Churchill and Kitchener, Hamilton and Wemyss, who between them bore much of the responsibility for the Dardanelles Expedition. But that would be to submit to the fashionable sanctimoniousness about the Great War, the insidious white lie that civilians behind the lines in every war were eager to repeat because they could not face the knowledge that they had sent the flower of their young manhood to die in vain.

Warring nations were like families in this respect. Domestic violence and bereavement were glossed over with self-deluding pieties which quickly took hold as truth. Sometimes these pieties lauded the valour and glory of battle: *dulce et decorum est pro patria mori*. Travestied as a classical heroic drama by John Masefield and Ernest Raymond, Gallipoli had suffered enough from such hypocrisies. More often nowadays the popular cant was that governments made war; soldiers were the helpless victims of the pride and avarice of statesmen who sent them out to fight. By such means did the liberal humbugs, the Tartuffes and Pecksniffs and Joseph Surfaces, whitewash the instincts of human nature and lay all the blame on the perverted impulses of men at the top.

Neither was true. Orwell had been right when he argued that aggression was a fundamental part of human nature. Aggression welled up in the young, after interludes of peace, and spilled out almost of its own accord into riot and battle. In this film-script Douglas would have nothing to do with either of the fashionable hypocrisies. He would show the heat, the flies, the mud and litter of the communication trenches terracing Achi Baba, the frothing blood, the gangrenous wounds – and he would leave cinema audiences to draw their own conclusions about the morality of it all.

But the images of his own war would not go away . . . the hospital ship with its cargo of weeping and shouting men, the fractured images of fear and pain as he lay on cool sheets recovering . . . and then rejoining his regiment as it fought through

37

towards Paris, the blackened villages and charcoaled corpses, the trail of bright arterial blood on the spring grass which they followed into a copse of flowering hawthorns to confront a young German soldier too weak to throw the grenade which exploded in his hand.

Douglas pushed back his chair and opened the window. Outside, heavy crimson cannas gushed uncontrollably over the fence. *Dulce et decorum* . . . he couldn't work any more now. He needed air; he must have air. Helen was out somewhere. Georgina was at school. On an impulse, he took the Morris and headed westwards towards the beaches.

Driving through the suburbs it occurred to him how rarely any longer he acted upon impulse. Helen had been an impulse. Perhaps that was why he no longer entirely trusted them, even while depending on them for inspiration. His imaginative energy was as strong as ever but he invested it in his writing, his poetry – and in some strange way it neutralised him. It was a contrariness in his nature. His love poems were the product of strong emotions, of imagination charged with erotic longings, anger, lust, jealousy, bitterness, sexual triumph. But in distilling the raw spirit of himself into the vessel of formal verse, what he achieved was permanence at the expense of realism, sculptured beauty at the cost of the rough edges and loose ends which reflected the common experience of life.

Helen sometimes charged him with shutting her out of what he wrote. It was a weapon she used against him, and yet it had a kind of truth in it. She was there, but unrecognisable, like a painter's flesh-and-blood mistress transmuted on the canvas into an icon of womanhood.

Blue sea appeared at the end of a decorous suburban street, which at once lost its decorum and opened up into a sprawl of ice-cream stands, candy stalls, carparks and beach huts the length of the marina. Douglas drove into a parking-space beside a coin-in-the-slot telescope, and walked down on to the sand.

A salt breeze roused a thin white topple of breakers north towards Port Adelaide, south towards Glenelg. Although it was mid-morning, on a weekday, the beach was disagreeably cluttered with people, most of them old and in deck-chairs, though a flurry of truant schoolboys showed off on surfboards in the water. Bending down, Douglas took his sandals and socks off and kicked his feet into the warm sand.

It was not for this – this *banality* – that he had come away from England. Elsewhere, north towards the centre, west across the Gulf, he was conscious that there existed another Australia which had not been wrenched into a simulacrum of the British way of life. There the sun ruled over a vast boiling emptiness. No walls or roofs could keep it out. Four nights ago he had dreamed that a giant fist had put him down in the middle of this emptiness and like a vacuum it had sucked him clean. Words fled from him; in a trance he had moved and breathed through his imagination, soaring and dipping over the sand-hills at whim, and then up and up and up towards the sun itself. He had awoken with a cry of triumph, to find the morning light transfixing him through a gap in the curtains, and Helen in the bed beside him looking at him with frightened eyes.

Gingerly in his bare feet Douglas trod up hot concrete steps to a stall on the marina where he bought a Coke. Sitting on a bench beside his socks and sandals he sipped the Coke slowly as he now did all drinks. Not that he'd felt the need out here to use drink for oblivion, the way he had in London. That was something he'd left behind, along with the writing block. Along with the memories, too.

After the war, in his bemedalled uniform, he had taken time off from his writing and his intelligence work with Freddie Collins to lecture the students at RADA on verse drama and poetry. He had gloried as much in the dashing figure he had cut as in his blossoming reputation. In full flow he would find his hand lifting (he blushed to think of it) to touch the war-wound on his brow. At some such moment the young RADA student Helen Callender had, he supposed, fallen in love. Already, even then, an unforgettably fine actress, she had seen in this handsome soldier-poet (what he had seen in her) a combination of beauty and talent to set off her own.

That was when he had learned that the soldier-poet was a coward at heart. Like most acts of cowardice it had seemed to be easiest for everyone at the time, so much the natural solution. He left his wife and moved into Nick's flat in Marylebone (Nick was already on his travels most of the year by then, working for a shipping company). To Bella whom he had loved all through the war years, Bella who had given her life to him, he explained simply that he wanted space to breathe, to rediscover himself. Bella wept, protested, eventually had no choice but to give in. Her energies were all directed towards their daughter Georgina, then two years old. She must have thought that a combination of patient steadfastness and the adorable child they had made together would draw Douglas back.

She was wrong. Douglas drowned his guilts and slaked his ego at Helen's inexhaustible beauty and high spirits. Bella took a job at a bookbinder's, engraving the dies of patterns provided by a man who had come bottom of her art course. At the end of that year, by which time his relationship with Helen was common knowledge, Douglas went back to the flat to discuss the divorce settlement. Georgina toddled across the frayed carpet and clutched his knee. He picked her up and put her beside him on the sofa. While Bella was alive, he never saw either of them again.

Cowardice was an unmentionable disease, so it always seemed to Douglas. Kept secret, it preyed upon the will. Moral cowardice became physical cowardice and vice versa. As happy with Helen as any proud seducer, Douglas found a succession of good reasons for not visiting Bella and Georgina, until it was too late. By then his shame was so great that he could not bring himself to meet anybody connected with that episode – Nick included. Surreptitiously the disease infected his life, his surroundings, his relationship with Helen. When he suspected her of taking other lovers, it was less through any circumstantial evidence than out of a perverse desire to see justice done to him. An eye for an eye; a heart for a heart. This was the fifteenth year of their marriage. Helen was still a superb actress, still beautiful. And he? What had he become?

He was still holding the Coke-bottle. He threw it into a litter-bin. As the sun climbed, he brushed the sand off his feet. He put on his socks and sandals and walked back along the marina.

Channel 5AD was relaying the throaty wistfulness of 'Stranger on the Shore'. Georgina stood on a chair, stringing up a bulbous white Chinese paper lantern she'd bought in John Martin's. Above her bed a black-and-white poster of the pianist Van Cliburn exchanged intense looks with Russ Conway and Cliff Richard on the opposite wall. A bookcase, a large balding teddy-bear and a desk littered with schoolwork were disposed at ankle-level around the room.

The phone rang. It went on ringing. Georgina stepped down. Mrs G came to the door holding a can of furniture-spray.

'For you, Georgina darling.'

It was Ursula Miller, inviting her over to listen to an Elvis Presley LP.

'No. Thank you,' said Georgina.

'Why?'

'I'm working.'

'So stop working. Exams are weeks away.'

Reluctantly Georgina wheeled out her bike for the ten-minute journey to Walkerville. She rang her bell in greeting to Mr Robbins, who was polishing his already spotless Vauxhall Victor in the next-door driveway. Sprinklers in the Wellington Square gardens made local rainbows in the afternoon. A black huddled object on the roadside, which she could have sworn wasn't there when she'd looked a moment ago, had been caught in the spray. As she bicycled past she recognised (with the slight shiver that still came every time) the beetling brows, thick lips and flattened nose of an Aboriginal, refreshing himself in the white man's rain.

Where was it she had seen that look before, that blank-shadowed deep-set gaze which once or twice before had looked up at her out of a squatting bundle of clothes on the pavement, or from a bench in the park? Of course – last summer, when she had travelled out with a school party from

41

Malvern to Florence. There, in the Brancacci Chapel of Santa Maria del Carmine, she had been mesmerised by Masaccio's ancient fresco of the Expulsion from Paradise. It was not so much the setting of the naked couple, hand in hand, stumbling in flight from the fearsome angel, as the despairing *faces* of Adam and Eve which had transfixed her – their mouths and eyes blank round holes of loss. . . .

She concentrated on her hand signals. A breeze out of the hot stillness lifted the brown curls on her forehead. Ursula was okay, but far from being a close friend. It was the stories she told about her father, Professor Miller, which fascinated Georgina: how he got out of Vienna at the time of the *Anschluss* and went to England, thinking it would be safe; and how, when the war started, the British put him and several hundred other Jewish communist émigrés on a boat to Australia, like the old convict ships; and how the only job he could get when he arrived in Adelaide was working as a security guard in the museum in North Terrace.

She wanted very much to meet Professor Miller. That was the chief reason she'd agreed to come to tea. Meanwhile Ursula, she supposed, was jolly enough ('Call me Sally. Ursula's some gruesome Catholic saint who was martyred with an arrow up her you-know') even if she was insisting on introducing Georgina to her elder brother Dirk who would be amazed at her knowing a war poet's daughter. . . .

She wheeled her bike through the gate in the thatched fence and up to the Millers' greyish-white brick villa with its green corrugated-iron roof. Sally and two small brown-and-white puppies erupted at the door. With her tight black skirt and puffed blonde hair Sally looked like Gaye Gambol in the strip cartoon.

'Aloha!' she cried.

'I'm sorry?'

'Aloha, birdbrain. Do you mean you haven't seen the new Elvis yet? Oh, c'mon, Georgie. *Blue Hawaii*!' Sally lifted her arms above her head as she took Georgina through the house, wriggling her hips as much as the skirt would allow and crooning in a breathy, drawly voice: 'Aloha-oe! Aloha-aiee!'

A tall bronzed boy with a long face and a prominent

jaw sat in the living-room, flicking through the pages of a motor magazine.

'Sis?'

'Oh, excuse *me*. This is Derek. Who likes to be called Dirk because he thinks it's sexier. This is my *amigo* Georgie Manifold, whose dad's famous, and she expects *gentlemen* to stand up when a lady enters the room.'

'No, no,' protested Georgina. And immediately wished she hadn't, since Derek, or Dirk, showed not the least inclination to get up but merely waved his hand in her direction. That he was good-looking even she had to admit, the sullen jaw giving him a James Dean look which he accentuated by brushing back his fair hair in a casual quiff.

'Any friend of yours, sis,' he said, taking one look at Georgina and dropping his eyes back to the magazine. 'Who's your dad? Anyone I know?'

'He was a war hero,' said Georgina quickly. 'So I don't suppose you'd know about him. A famous war poet, who was adviser on *The Longest Day*.'

This last detail (not strictly true, although one of the co-directors had taken Douglas out to dinner once to talk about the film while it was in production) never failed to impress the kind of people who didn't read poetry. It impressed Dirk Miller, who lowered his magazine for a moment before saying in a casual tone: 'Speaking for myself, I'm a pacifist. An international-socialist pacifist. I don't believe in war. It's the rich who wage war and the poor who die.'

'Gosh,' said Georgina. 'Did you make that up?'

'I don't know. I expect so.'

'It sounds as if you made it up. For the reason that it's totally not true, as my father would tell you. The working classes were as much against Hitler as anyone.'

Dirk lowered the magazine again. 'Sis, isn't your friend waiting for her tea? Don't worry about Sally,' he went on in a friendlier tone when his sister had strutted off to the kitchen playing an imaginary guitar. 'She has no brain at all. But she can do simple things quite well, like boil a kettle of water and pour it over a tea-bag in a cup. You girls do go in for this tea-drinking, don't you? I wonder if it damages your nervous system? Please sit down. There's a lot of caffeine in tea, you know. Twice as much as in coffee. It's an alkaloid, related to uric acid, and it stimulates the adrenal glands. Are you at her school?'

'Yes. For my last term. Doing biology.' Georgina sat down in a dog-hairy armchair, examined her shoes and tucked them under her. 'Sally says you're at the University. Daddy's giving a lecture at the University this term, so you might hear him.'

'Not unless he's lecturing in my chemistry laboratory. Do you always talk about your dad? You know, you would be pretty if you had your hair longer.'

'Thanks. Thanks very much. Do all chemists talk to other people as if they're talking to a . . . a test-tube?'

'Test-tube? Oh. No. Test-tubes you have to concentrate on.'

Georgina was aware of Dirk gazing at her. Having suddenly nothing to say, she looked at her watch.

'Are you in a hurry?' he asked.

'No. Except I have an essay on Browning to write some time.'

'Is it complicated? I thought you just put things under the grill.'

'Very funny. Browning the poet.'

'God, I'd forgotten about girls' schools. They won't let you do science, will they, until you can hold your own in polite society? What a joke.'

'What do you do in polite society? Apart from con-centrating on test-tubes.'

'I like cars. I'm good with cars. And surfing. Studying as hard as you do, I don't suppose you've ever seen a surfboard. Have you?'

'Aren't they those things carried around by small boys in swimsuits?'

She was pleased with that. Dirk sighed deeply and looked at his watch.

'Jeez, is that the time? We're picking up Vince on the way. You coming?'

Georgina began to get up, and sat down again. 'Where?'

'Swimming, of course. Didn't Sally tell you? I thought you were all fixed up. We're going down to the beach.'

44

Georgina shook her head, just as Sally appeared in the doorway.

'Never mind. Sis will find you a costume.'

'Don't bother,' said Georgina quickly, as Sally went running upstairs. 'Listen, you and Sally go. Really. I don't feel like going swimming today. Thanks all the same.'

In the awkward pause Sally could be heard bounding down the stairs. 'Ta-raa!' She held up a one-piece bathing-costume in a luminescent apple-green. 'It'll stretch,' she added.

Georgina blushed a deep and furious crimson. 'No, thanks,' she repeated. 'You two go and have fun. I must be off anyway. Thanks.'

She stood up.

'Okay.' Dirk pointed an imaginary pistol at his sister's blonde locks and winked at Georgina. 'Any enemy of Sally's is a friend of mine,' he declared. 'Now. Can I give you a lift?'

'I've got my bike outside.'

Georgina watched them depart, in a shabby sprayed-silver Beetle which was probably Dirk's pride and joy. Then, ignoring the pleading yelps from the puppies on the veranda, she wheeled her bike out of the gate.

Do you always talk about your dad? Dirk's question returned to her as she pedalled home through the late afternoon. It was unfair: it had stopped her asking him about his own father, who had obviously lived a much more fascinating life as a refugee. And now here he was in Australia, a settler among all the other white settlers, living in close proximity to the Aborigines whom they had made settlers and refugees in turn. Did they ever think about what they had done? Was it a source of unconscious guilt? Or did most of them secretly think that Aborigines were subhuman so it didn't matter? She resolved to ask one of the teachers at school about it. Better still, she would bring the subject up with Captain Kemp when Winn Vellacott traced him and put her in touch with him.

At the thought of Winn Vellacott all Georgina's old anxieties returned. Dismounting at the front gate in Wellington Square, she was quite relieved to observe that Helen and her father must have gone out on some social occasion because the house, crouched down in the dusk shadows behind its tall bushes, gave forth not a glimmer of light.

The Union Jack broke from a freshly painted flagpole and began snapping in the vicious breeze. The plane, an RAAF Convair Metropolitan, taxied to a halt and a gangway was attached, its metal steps striped in consecutive daubs of red, white and blue. Helen and Georgina emerged and stood at the top of the steps, clutching at their hats. Helen was wearing a belted wattle-yellow outfit which seemed designed to avoid flattering her slender figure. Her arms were covered by long white gloves; a cumbersome white leather handbag dangled from the crook of her elbow. The hat consisted of an arrangement of yellow silk petals stiffened with gauze. Georgina was dressed Pollyanna-fashion in a bonnet with ribbons and bows, and a flounced pastel-blue dress which she was trying to stop blowing up in the wind.

As they began to descend the gangway a sixteen-cannon salute boomed out across the tarmac, startling a galah into the cloudless sky. Tea-cosy helmets bobbing, the Central Command band launched into a fast-tempo 'God Save the Queen'. An Army Guard of Honour in green combat-dress clicked to attention and gave the Royal Salute. Across the tarmac glided a brood of Humber Super Snipes, led by a black swan of a Rolls-Royce limousine. Little knots of airport workers cheered and applauded. As the two women reached the bottom of the steps, the Governor of South Australia's private secretary detached himself from the rack of important dark suits on the runway. Trouser-legs flapping in the wind, he came forward, described a bow and shook a long white glove.

'Welcome to the City of Adelaide, Your Majesty.'

'Thank you. It's so nice to be back with you all,' declared Helen, and swatted at the pestering flies.

'Might not be a bad idea if we get the others right up beside you, Symes,' said a voice behind them. 'Then we can move the Queen sharply along the line-up and into the Roller before the flies start getting on her wick.'

46

'No trouble,' replied the Governor's private secretary.

The voice which issued that instruction fairly typified the man who now joined Helen and Georgina at the foot of the gangway. It was quick, soft, light, with the affected hesitancy of someone who never needed to hector to impose his point of view. And the man himself, Edward Catchpole, was perfectly cast for the rôle of mandarin. Tall, and relaxed in his morning-coat, his black hair was sleeked down over an impressive pink cranium. Sun-glasses accentuated the strong-boned handsomeness of his face. Nodding to Symes and the others, he now took the two women by the elbow and encouraged them in the direction of the Guard of Honour.

'Do give the mob one of your waves, ma'am,' he murmured. 'They are doing their best. Actually we imported forty-three Aboriginal girls from one of the Adelaide girls' homes to keep up the decibel rating.'

'How very charming.'

Helen Manifold gave a queenly wave (arm stiff, fingers polishing a very small pane of glass) to the black girls in their Sunday hats clustered in front of the Arrivals door, singing the British national anthem in well-schooled tuneless voices. Standing in for Her Majesty, who was shortly due to undergo her second Royal Visit to Adelaide in the space of nine years, was not a rôle which naturally appealed to Helen's histrionic talents. All the queens she had played on stage were Royals who in their tragic dignity embodied the history of their nation. Their every gesture – of bereavement, of felicity, of prostrate suffering, of sovereign grace – was instinct with drama and significance. But times had changed. Now Helen found herself having to impersonate a queen whose diminished rôle no longer entitled her to sweeping gestures: a queen whose walk, whose clothes, whose voice, whose mannerisms all spoke of a more prosaic destiny.

But she was getting the hang of it, Helen; she was nothing if not professional. As the last shrill Aboriginal pleas to save the Queen were blown heavenwards, she tripped past the Guard of Honour holding her handbag in front of her and smiling the famous purse-lipped smile, while the bush-flies danced in her yellow crown of gauze and silk. If she wasn't careful, she'd catch one of these beefcake recruits making eyes at her. Hurriedly she turned to glance at the bemedalled tunic of the top brass clanking along beside her.

'Gallipoli?'

'Hardly, ma'am. The fall of Singapore.'

'Gracious me.' She hastened her step. In front of the last Guard in the line, a pimply youth with an insistent Adam's apple, she assumed familiar regal pose, leaning back slightly so that she didn't have to raise her chin.

'And what is your name?'

'George Jenkins, Your Majesty.'

'How very nice.'

Having exchanged the required amount of conversation, she wheeled left and walked across the tarmac to the waiting Rolls. A cluster of baby Union Jacks unfurled along the gloved ranks of the Aboriginal girls. The clanking person halted and saluted. Helen shook the hands held out to her and ducked into the back of the limousine.

Georgina Manifold and Edward Catchpole followed her in. Catchpole unhooked a transceiver from under his coat and spoke into it.

'Cars on their way now. I make it twenty-six minutes and twenty seconds.'

'Roger,' replied a tinny voice.

'Those Godawful flies,' said Helen. 'Didn't you think, George, or didn't they go for you? And my feet! What that poor bloody woman must have to go through. I hope I didn't disgrace you, Edward.'

'You were sensational. Absolutely queenly. I never expected you to *act* the part, but you were bang on. I'm most obliged to you. We all are.'

Edward Catchpole gazed at Helen warmly. Of course he had expected her to act the part. He had set up the idea of Helen standing in for the Queen precisely so that he could be impressed with her professionalism and openly display his admiration as he was doing now. Catchpole was the kind of man who never lacked the means or contacts to do anything he set his mind to.

'It is what we need to know, you see,' he explained. 'The timing. Very important. And details, such as the flies. Her lady-in-waiting always keeps a larger size of shoes in her bag in case the Queen's feet swell in the heat. But we'll suggest she puts in a can of fly-repellent as well, this being Australia. Really, I can't thank you enough.'

Helen let out a long breath and rested her head back against the seat, just far enough to expose a curve of white throat above the wattle-yellow.

'Getting the walk right,' she murmured, 'that's always the hardest part. Larry, Olivier you know, says that once you've got the walk right everything else about the character falls into place. George, darling, as my lady-in-waiting, I know it's a problem, with that thing on your teeth, but you really will have to try to smile a little more confidently.'

'I don't see why,' said Georgina. 'I'm not an actress like you. I don't pretend all the time. It wasn't my idea to come on this rehearsal.'

Helen snapped her bag shut.

'It's plain sailing from now on,' Catchpole soothed. 'Just the timing, actually. It is now ... what, nine thirty-five by my watch. That gives us bags of time to get to Port Adelaide. If everything goes according to plan, we'll have you home for Sunday lunch. And Georgina back with her chums.'

Georgina winced. Sitting opposite them in the folding seat, she pulled at the gloves she'd been made to wear. They were too small; they made her fingers look like stumps. Her brown hair scraped back under the ridiculous hat with ribbons, the papery petticoats and hateful suspenders – it was not as if she'd ever enjoyed making a public exhibition of herself. The whole theatrical costumier's outfit might have been expressly designed to transform her into a Helen-figure, when her firmest resolve in life was to be as removed from Helen as possible.

Catchpole had taken out a town map of Adelaide and smoothed it across Helen's wattle-yellow lap, the better to illustrate the route. His fingernails were burnished with a rich pink sheen and prominent moons. Helen had run into him when she went up to Canberra for a theatre inauguration – 'Someone near the top of the High Commission,' was how he'd been introduced. 'Lucky I don't suffer from vertigo!' she'd brightly replied, and they'd made small-talk about phobias. Now that Catchpole was down in Adelaide, it was the most natural thing in the world that he should prolong their little joke by asking

Helen to impersonate the Highest of the High at the rehearsal. *It might amuse you*, was what he'd actually said.

So here she was. Acting – always acting in Georgina's eyes, as she was the very first moment she met Douglas, and seduced him away from Georgina's mother, and broke up the family, and destroyed their lives. . . .

'Georgina darling.'

'Yes?'

'Wave to our loyal subjects. Wave. That's right.'

The cavalcade had reached Commercial Road. The sun was already high, jewelling off the Port River. On the far side, workmen with buckets of white paint swarmed over rusty galvanised-iron grain-warehouses. More paint was being plastered on the concrete of the wharf, right down to the green waterline. Everywhere the cosmeticians could be seen working overtime, scraping off grime, clipping trees, splashing whitewash, stringing bunting, fixing flags in brightly painted oil-drums, so that the Royal eyes, wherever they roved, would not be confronted by any evidence of Nature's disloyalty.

At precisely 1005 hours the motor-cycle escort took up position either side of the Rolls. Catchpole contacted Operations HQ, murmured *Roger and out* and tapped on the driver's window. They set off at a steady 16 miles per hour, a hundred yards behind the pilot car packed with tour officials clicking stop-watches. As they rounded the end of the wharf shed, the rest of the Humber Super Snipes fell in behind them.

'We can't take any chances on the day,' commented Catchpole, waving at a group of catcalling workers. 'You wouldn't believe what precautions have to be organised for the Royal Progress. Crowd barriers. Special passes. Armed security officers will be scattered through the crowds at strategic points. Troops if need be. Anyone in the front with an unscheduled bouquet of roses is a security risk; you don't know what the flowers might be concealing.'

'And you are in charge of all this, Edward?' asked Helen, widening her eyes.

Catchpole gazed at her. 'It was worth it, to have you as my Queen for a day,' he said.

Georgina tossed her head, and let her gaze wander over the limousine. Certainly the accessories were impressive.

A foot-rest. A back-seat adjuster. A push-button radio with an electric aerial-control. Intercom switches (in case you wanted to tell the driver to let you out for a pee, she supposed). Behind her a cocktail-cabinet, not yet stocked. Beside her arm a button – which she pressed. The sun-roof slid forward, bathing them in light and air.

'George darling, we don't want that open.'

'Why?'

'You know how I hate direct sunlight on my face.' Helen darted a smile at Catchpole. 'We may be in Australia; that doesn't mean we have to behave like Australians.'

'It won't give you wrinkles, you know.'

'Please, George. I don't want to argue about it.'

'Anyway, none of us is going to live that long. We'll all be blown up before then. I'm sure Mr Catchpole agrees. Did you think we were all going to be blown up last year, Mr Catchpole? In the Missile Crisis?'

'The window, George.'

Edward Catchpole leaned forward and pressed the button. The sun-roof expunged the sun. 'We're all going to live to a great old age,' he said cheerfully. 'That's why we have the Bomb, Georgina. To protect us.'

Children's voices outside the car. Something flew in the window and rolled on the floor. Helen gasped. Catchpole bent down and picked up – an apple. Georgina looked out to see an urchin running across a used-car lot, pursued by one of the police motor-cycle escort. She laughed aloud. Onwards they rode. At every intersection with their route – at Cheltenham Parade, Woodville Road, Government Road, as far as the Hindmarsh Bridge – roadside stands were being hammered together. When the auspicious day of the Royal Progress arrived they would be decorated with councillors, Girl Guides, church elders, pensioners, war veterans, Sisters of the Resurrection, people from the senior citizens' clubs and spastics' homes, all waving their toy flags more or less freely, hurrahing, clapping, keeling over in the heat and being borne away by the St John Ambulance Brigade.

Even now as they passed the Queen Elizabeth Hospital (where a large 'E2R' had been picked out in begonias, cinerarias and marigolds on a raised bed) they could distinctly

51

hear the strains of 'Rule, Britannia' from an upper balcony where a blind crippled veteran, egged on by two smirking nurses, was sawing away patriotically at a violin.

'I suppose we'll live longer in Australia,' Georgina continued reflectively. 'Like in *On the Beach*. The fallout could take years to come this far.'

'How are we for time, Edward?' asked Helen. 'I need a cigarette. Please don't be like Douglas and tell me it's bad for my tennis.'

'We're dead on schedule.'

'And once we're at the Town Hall?' Helen dipped her fingers at a group of bare-chested construction workers banging beer-cans as they passed.

'That's all we have permission for today. Three or four more routes have to be tested, but they aren't complex. We shan't need such distinguished understudies for them. Unless of course— '

'I bet you,' said Georgina, 'the Aboriginals in the Nullarbor Desert will be the last people on earth left alive. The first men and the last men. Isn't that a thought?'

'Not much of a thought,' said Helen, smiling. 'A very uninteresting thought in my opinion, since you ask. I didn't come out here to escape some sort of holocaust. I came out to be with your father.'

'And me,' said Georgina.

'Yes, when we knew you were coming. I didn't suppose Douglas would be very good at looking after sixteen-year-olds.'

'He's never had to be.'

'That's because you've been at boarding-school.'

'That's what I mean. He's never had to bother.'

'This is where the Lancers should be waiting for us,' interrupted Catchpole, peering out of the window. 'Ah! Here they are.'

As they reached North Terrace, where the city proper started, the motor-cycle escort peeled away. A mounted detachment of South Australian Police Lancers took over, their Police Greys keeping pace with the cavalcade which had slowed to seven miles per hour. Catchpole checked his watch and spoke into the transceiver. Helen poked a white glove out of the window.

Policemen holding back the Sunday traffic grinned and whistled. A scuffle of small children darted among the horses with shouts of glee, and then went back to splashing water at each other from the pool behind the South Australian War Memorial. As they turned down King William Street, the brave flagpoles already in position along the median strip, Georgina saw workmen on painter's hoists attaching giant turquoise pasteboard letters to the façade of the Bank of New South Wales –

WELCOME TO OUR ROYAL VISI

– and as the three mock royals pictured the stark grey business buildings of the city centre afire with bunting and bright window-boxes, and the shuttered shops and near-deserted arcades crammed with flag-waving Adelaiders in shorts and sandals, they could hardly be blamed for supposing it to be the homage of loyal colonials, rather than the neutral curiosity which brought as many locals out each year to applaud the John Martin department store's Christmas pageant.

In their upholstered Rolls-Royce they cruised through the echo of next month's euphoria, and came to a stop, on schedule, at Adelaide Town Hall. The rehearsal over, Edward Catchpole bowed profoundly over Helen's hand and hailed a taxi to take the two women home to a light salad lunch in Wellington Square.

'You mentioned tennis,' he said, hailing a taxi. 'I have the court at Government House for an hour at five-thirty this afternoon. Might you be free for a game, Helen?'

'I should be delighted,' said Helen graciously, and waved her gloved fingers at him through the window, as the cab bore the two women home.

Interlude: tennis match. Helen is serving. She cuts a boyish figure in her white tunic and white shorts; but there is nothing boyish about her game. Helen likes to win, and for most of her life she has known that the way to win is to compete on her terms. Tennis isn't so different from sex in this respect. Playing against a man, unless he's a complete boor, you generally win the psychological points by drawing him gently into a trap. Making it plain that you are only pretending to take the game

53

seriously, you confront him with a dilemma. He can choose to appear ludicrously aggressive by playing his usual competitive match. Or he can run the risk of looking idiotic or patronising by lowering his game to parry yours. Both ways, poor fool, he's a loser.

So it is that Helen's serve is a model of good coaching – ball thrown well up and slightly forward, racket arm stretched back, up on the balls of her feet – except that instead of following through with a hard first serve she goes for style. She hits the tennis ball with a graceful tap which lands it harmlessly in front of her male opponent, Edward Catchpole.

Not to be outdone, Catchpole treats her service with every bit of the respect he might show Laver or Rosewall. First he runs on the spot. Then he crouches, back behind the baseline, staring intently and twirling his racket. At the last moment he pads in fast to meet the ball as it sits up and waits for him. His shot across court makes Helen scamper. Her return sails straight to where he stands, dominating the net; but somehow it appears to give him problems, he fails to put the ball away. Helen has time to return this one on her forehand. Although Catchpole makes a half-hearted lunge, the ball floats past his racket into the open court.

'Good shot!' cries Edward Catchpole.

'Jolly lucky!' laughs Helen.

'Not a bit of it! Your game, I believe.'

They play four more games like this. Then without warning Helen sinks down, a dying swan on the perfect grass. Edward Catchpole runs, faster than he has moved all morning, and goes down handsomely on one knee by her side. She brushes him away, smiling, her face prettily flushed.

'Gosh! Isn't it hot!' she exclaims.

'Helen. My dear. Are you all right?'

'I'm all right. Just puffed. You've run me ragged, Edward.'

Waving away his ministrations, she nevertheless with one hand clasps his arm and permits him to pull her to her feet. On cue, a waiter in a slim-cut white jacket, a discreet gold chain round his bronzed neck, patters down the terrace steps with two glasses of iced lemon barley water on a tray.

'Can I get you anything restorative, madam?' he asks, a smile lifting the thin moustache on his upper lip.

Helen declines. She sits in a bamboo garden-chair in the shade of the red, white and blue umbrella and sips the lemon barley water. In her line of vision the white-pillared and rounded façade of Government House billows gently in the heat, shielded by tall oaks from *hoi polloi* on North Terrace. Catchpole drops into the other chair. He takes off his glasses and wipes his face with a silk handkerchief.

Helen enquires, without turning her head: 'Is it Regency?'

'Almost. Classical Revival, actually. That bit we're looking at is eighteen thirty-nine. Difficult to believe, but it's the earliest surviving building in South Australia.'

'How sweet! That's exactly the date of our London house. Do you know, for the first time since I've been here I feel at home?'

'Do you? How nice.'

He offers her a cigarette, and lights it for her. She leans back, stretching her legs, and lets the smoke curl out between her parted lips.

'Surroundings matter so much, don't you think?' she says after a pensive silence. 'Vulgarity depresses one so. In England, in London, you can keep it at bay. Out here you can't do that. It's pervasive; it sticks to you like smells from a chair you've sat in. England I associate – awfully boring, I know – with honeysuckle. South Australia with boiled cabbage. For you it's different, Edward. You have a job to do out here.'

Catchpole smiles and serves up a lob. 'Couldn't you have stayed behind? You must be missed dreadfully back in London.'

'You say all the right things. You should work for the Diplomatic Service.'

Fifteen–love.

'I do. When I have to.'

Fifteen all.

'Do you? Do you really? I suppose the Royal Visit must be a test of diplomacy.' She laid long fingers on his sleeve. 'Are you in charge of all the Royal guest-lists? I do hope so, Edward. Then you could smuggle me in to a dinner on board *Britannia.* . . . '

'I wanted to talk to you about the Visit. There's another rehearsal, you know. Even grander this time, in a Royal Barge rowed down the Torrens to Elder Park for a Music Festival. I can promise you everything except the burnished throne— '

'Oars of silver? A poop of beaten gold?'

'Ha ha. Not on Adelaide's budget. But allow me to say that gold and silver would be superfluous, Helen, with you as our Cleopatra. What do you say? Are you game?'

Helen uncrossed her legs. 'When do you want me?'

'If you can spare me one more hour of your time, I can give you all the details.' He stubbed out his cigarette. 'Are you free to join me for a light supper?'

'What, now?' Putting out her hands, she weighed the invisible decision. 'I suppose I am. Do they bring it to your rooms?'

'No, I've moved out of Government House. It became . . . inconvenient. They've given me a hospitality flat, just across North Terrace. Shall we go?'

What street this flat was in Helen had no way of telling, since Edward Catchpole took her by a circuitous back route which involved a series of stairs and passages and somewhere a small courtyard which he hurried her across.

'A standard precaution,' he explained, as they arrived in what could easily have been a hotel corridor, with numbered doors on either side. 'I have an aversion to the kind of journalists they nurture out here. Always hanging around in the front lobby, asking questions. They're like leeches: you have to pour petrol over them and set fire to them before they'll drop off.'

'I know. One of them came round to see Douglas the other day. A man from the *South Australian Gazette* . . . Winn something. But I don't understand why they should pester you. Surely there can't be a big story in the security side of the Queen's visit?'

Catchpole stopped outside a door identical to the others and carefully studied his key-ring. 'Do you mean Winn Vellacott?' he asked.

'He's the one.'

A telephone began to ring. Catchpole threw open the door. 'Here we are. Sorry about the mess. There was a cleaning woman for all the crockery, but she started poking her nose into things. Would you excuse me for a minute?'

There was no mess. The apartment was large, clean and expensive-looking, with leather sofas either side of a polished glass coffee-table. Opened double doors allowed Helen a glimpse (before she looked away) of an equally spacious connecting room where invisible venetian blinds cast slatted shadows on the white coverlet of a double bed. The 'crockery' was all around her: on the window-sills, the coffee-table, the top of a bookcase and in two beautiful small satinwood display-cabinets – tiny porcelain bowls and dishes, bottles and cups, with oriental designs of flowers, birds and mythical creatures painted in garish colours on the white glaze.

She heard Catchpole's voice on the telephone. *I can't discuss that now, Freddie. . . . No, I've talked to the Premier, there are no suspicions. . . . A journalist, I can deal with him. . . . On schedule, yes. Very smoothly, no snags at all.* She put down her bag and tennis racket and sat on the sofa, as still and upright as a porcelain doll. Had it not been for the papers and books on the writing-table, the room itself would have felt like a display-cabinet. The windows were closed against the traffic many floors below. Only the hum of the air-conditioner disturbed the silent antiseptic chill. Helen put her arms round herself, and smiled brightly as Catchpole reappeared.

'Are these yours? I've never seen such a collection. I thought you were only here for a week or two. Did you bring them all the way from Canberra?'

Catchpole hesitated. 'I'm caretaking them for the chap who lives here,' he said. 'He travels a lot. But aren't they splendid? Hard and delicate as bone. Did you know that there were clay pots actually fired in the atomic blast at Nagasaki? I should give a lot for one of those.'

He opened one of the display-cabinets. Gone was the clumsiness he'd displayed on the tennis-court. His movements were deft and precise as he lifted a plate off its stand and brought it over for her to examine.

'It's Japanese,' he explained. 'All Japanese. An early eighteenth-century Kakiemon-ware saucer dish. Look at the brilliance of that enamel. All hand-painted before the dish was glazed, you can see the hairline cracks overlaying it. Tokugawa period. It was the great age of Japanese porcelain.'

He stopped abruptly, as if he'd been giving himself away, and put the dish in Helen's hands. It was surprisingly light; cold to the touch. Round the centre swirled a turquoise-and-red dragon trying to bite its feathered tail. A convoluted pattern of flowers, leaves and fans embellished the rim. She had never admired or coveted oriental artistry. It was too remote, unaccommodating.

'It's very pretty,' she said with distaste.

He took it away from her and went into the kitchen, his shoes soundless on the thick carpet. He returned with two glasses of wine. In his tennis whites he towered over her, his face still pink and glistening from his exertions.

'To my Cleopatra!' he toasted her.

They both laughed. The air-conditioner hummed. Edward Catchpole looked down at his glass.

'It's Australian, a nineteen-sixty Quelltaler,' he said. 'They call it a hock but it's almost more of a Gewürtztraminer, *I* think. Rich but dryish, if you see.'

She sipped. 'It's one thing we English have learned to do well out here, the wines.'

'The Germans actually. But yes.' She caught him gazing at her. The pinkness swelled on her throat and cheeks. He turned, abruptly, and went into the kitchen. 'Will a ham salad be enough?' he called.

'Yes, of course!' She drank all the Quelltaler in her glass and went and stood in the doorway. By comparison with the two main rooms, the kitchen was cramped, but everything again was ordered and spotless, lined up on the shelves or hanging on the wall. When Catchpole opened the fridge door to take out a lettuce, she saw a fresh T-bone steak moistening on a white plate. She watched him clean the lettuce under the tap. His fingers brushed the leaves, then tore them off with a jerk.

'Can I please do something?' she asked.

'How about an egg for the salad? There's a saucepan on the ring. Eggs in the rack on the wall.'

She put the egg on to boil. 'Would you mind if I used your bathroom?'

'Round the corner. On the right.'

Helen collected her bag and went in. The mirror was on the bathroom cabinet. With a few quick strokes of pencil and powder puff she restored the near-immaculate canvas of her face, toning down the flush that lingered on her cheeks from the tennis. Her complexion hadn't yet succumbed to the Australian sun: with her hooded grey eyes, high cheekbones and downward-pouting mouth, she looked as if she had stepped off the cover of *Vanity Fair*. With a satisfied look, she quietly eased open the cabinet door. Sun lotion . . . the usual shaving stuff . . . an aftershave from Trumpers of Curzon Street . . . aspirin . . . sticking plaster . . . a bottle of pills which appeared to be laxatives . . . and another large bottle of some dark liquid. She unscrewed the top, sniffed it, tipped a drop on her finger. Hair dye! Smiling, she slid back the bottle and shut the cabinet door.

Fifteen–thirty.

Edward Catchpole had arranged supper on the glass coffee-table, facing one of the sofas. He came out with the bowl of green salad. 'I hope you approve of my dressing,' he declared. 'Some people find it sharp but, if you ask me, a pinch of sugar is all you need.'

'Sugar?'

'Yes.'

'That's a good idea. What a good idea.'

'It tastes the way it should?'

'Delicious.'

'I believe in perfectibility in all things.' He gazed at her again, and blinked. 'I'm sorry. What an idiot I am. I should have brought napkins.'

'Oh, no. No, please. Tennis things won't hurt.'

'Are you sure? They look so spotless on you. It would be a pity to spoil that perfect white.'

'Quite sure.' Helen gazed round the room again, as if conscious that Catchpole had eyes for one thing only. Her glance fell upon a grey folder on the table. It was stamped, in black letters, 'AEC'. 'Is that one of the anarchist groups you're having to watch out for during the Royal Progress?' she asked, leaning forward.

Catchpole was there before her. He picked up the file and dropped it on the carpet, near his feet. 'Atomic Energy Commission,' he told her. 'Just another of the hats I have to wear.'

'What exactly is it you do in Canberra?'

'Ah.' Catchpole was chewing.

'You aren't going to tell me it's hush-hush, are you?'

He grinned. 'Between ourselves?'

'Between ourselves.'

'If you want the title I go under, it is Permanent Secretary at the Ministry of Supply. On secondment to the British defence liaison staff in Canberra.'

59

'That doesn't tell me very much.'

'It's not supposed to. My job, I suppose you could say, is to be a nightwatchman. I look out for fires on the horizon. I raise the alarm. I help develop fire-fighting equipment. You could call me a security guard outside Great Britain Incorporated. Protecting the Queen is one of my tasks.'

She nodded. 'And are there fires on the horizon?'

'I don't know about fires. There is plenty of smoke.' He frowned. 'These are perilous days for the civilised world, Helen. The Chinese are massing on their border with India. The Russians are on the offensive: don't think we've seen the last of it with Hungary and Cuba. The Americans, right now, are fighting an undeclared war against Russian-backed troops in Indo-China. The point is, we can't rely upon the Americans to defend us in a nuclear attack. We in Britain have to maintain our own independent power of retaliation. Power to hit back is the only kind of deterrent our enemies understand.'

'I can see that. But why Australia? Where does Canberra fit in?'

There was a pause. She looked at him. Catchpole had begun to clear the plates away.

'The next war will be a global conflict,' he said finally. 'We have to be prepared here in Australia, too. We have to be vigilant. That's what I admire about Bob Menzies. He's prepared to take a tough line.'

'You know the Prime Minister?'

Thirty all.

Catchpole nodded. 'I had to brief him recently in Canberra. He doesn't go around whining about disarmament, like some Australians, like your pacifist acquaintance Winn Vellacott. Menzies knows that the only way to negotiate is from strength. That's why he gave the go-ahead for the US Navy to build a telecommunications base out on North West Cape. He told me so. He's got a majority of two in the House of Representatives, and the Labour opposition is talking about nuclear-free zones, but Menzies isn't the kind of man to listen to defeatists. He believes in the balance of power, and we're backing him all the way. Coffee?'

'No, thanks. Do you mind if I smoke? I shouldn't of course.'

He sat beside her and produced a lighter. She leaned towards him without lifting her eyes from the flame, then sat back, crossing her legs. Catchpole couldn't take his eyes off her. There was no question where the balance of power on the sofa lay.

'It's one of the curses of my profession that one has to keep in condition,' Helen remarked, dragging on the cigarette. 'It's like you, Edward, one has to be prepared. I remember last autumn – no, the one before – we had a glorious Indian summer. I'd just finished a gruelling season at the Aldwych, Ibsen and Shakespeare, and I just sat in the sun and got fat. Suddenly, my agent rang to say that the Lyric was desperate to get me for Peter Pan in their Christmas pantomime.' She laughed. 'All that athleticism, swinging on wires! I thought I'd die!'

Catchpole didn't take his eyes off her. 'I remember. I saw you in that Aldwych season. You were the best Viola I've ever seen. Do you come from a theatrical family? It must be in your blood.'

'Mama and Papa? Good heavens, no. Papa would have had a fit. He'd have disinherited me if he'd still been alive. Not that there was much to inherit, you know, because all his estates were in Poland, but he'd have had a damn good try.'

'I can see it now,' said Catchpole. He lit a cigarette himself. 'I can see it, the Polish side in you. Something devil-may-care, a wildness. And in the cheekbones! You shouldn't be here, Helen. You should be on a stage. Any stage.'

Forty–thirty.

She patted him on the knee, playfully. 'But you're putting me on a stage! I'm your Queen, remember? On a Royal barge, going up the Torrens! And in return I expect to be invited— '

'No, no – a proper stage! Hasn't anybody tried to get you?'

'Oh, but they have, Edward. Believe it or not, I've agreed to play Isabella at the University Theatre here. *Measure for Measure* is a set book this year. We start rehearsals tomorrow.'

She shook her head. 'I don't know why I'm doing it. Acting with amateurs is almost as bad as acting with children or animals.'

'But you must do it! The whole of Adelaide will come and see you. A parochial audience, I admit, but it's all about what you said, about keeping in condition. You treat it as an exercise, an energiser, a toning of the muscles. And Shakespeare is Shakespeare, even in Adelaide.'

Animated, Edward Catchpole got up and strode into the bedroom. He came out with a copy of the Collected Works.

'Let me remind you,' he said, laying the book open on her lap. 'Isabella pleading with Angelo that he save her brother's life – isn't it an engrossing scene? Some of the cleverest dialogue in Shakespeare.'

'Some of the most anti-feminine, surely?' returned Helen.

Deuce.

She picked up the book and read aloud in a low voice. ' "Women! Help heaven! Men their creation mar In profiting by them. Nay, call us ten times frail, For we are soft as our complexions are, And credulous to false prints." '

Catchpole read Angelo over her shoulder. The hesitant note in his voice was replaced by a roughness she could not have heard before, because her hands quivered and she set the book down on her lap. ' "Let me be bold; I do arrest your words. Be that you are, That is, a woman; if you be more, you're none; If you be one, as you are well expressed By all external warrants, show it now, By putting on the destined livery." '

' "I have no tongue but one; Gentle my lord, Let me entreat you speak the former language." '

' "Plainly conceive, I love you." '

' "My brother did love Juliet, And you tell me that he shall die for't." '

' "He shall not, Isabel, if you give me love." '

Catchpole's arm rested along the top of the sofa. His head was very close to Helen's. She went on, uncertainly: ' "I know your virtue hath a licence in't, Which seems a little fouler than it is, To pluck on others." '

' "Believe me, on mine honour, My words express my purpose." '

'And so they go on.' With a bang Helen shut the book on Angelo's reckless passion. 'She's a prune, that Isabella. Even by the standard of Shakespeare's women. *More than our brother is our chastity.* You have to play her as a suppressed hysteric.'

She looked straight ahead as she spoke these words. Her shoulders were trembling. Neither of them moved for a moment. Then Edward Catchpole rose above her.

'I've always thought Angelo deserved better,' he commented.

'What about Cleopatra?' Without waiting for his reply, Helen stood up. 'Look at the time. Edward, I'll have to fly. Douglas will be wanting the car.'

Advantage, Helen.

'Of course. I'll see you back to it.' Picking up a bunch of keys, Catchpole went to the door and began turning locks and sliding bolts. 'We can talk about the rehearsals on the way. If you still are sure you want to stand in for the Highest of the High.'

'Oh, yes,' cried Helen, brushing past him with a swing of her tennis racket. 'The show must go on. Shouldn't it?'

Game and set.

In England the snow rose towards the ground-floor windows. Down under, the heat was building up like a kiln-fire. For three successive days Adelaide had sweltered in 100-degree temperatures and no wind. Helen Manifold lay naked on the bed-sheet, gazing up at the beating fan, which sent light fingers of air to explore her body. Outside, garden sprinklers dripped soundless water on the burning leaves.

Douglas could not write. The pen slipped in his fingers. The pages of script stuck to his sweaty hands. He was drinking too much again and sleeping badly, waking exhausted from vivid dreams which pursued him night after night. In them always he was a child again, a boy stumbling on a mystery he had not known he was seeking. Sometimes he was climbing a hill towards long-deserted mine-workings on a hill in Westmorland. Other times he relived the spiritual outpourings of his confirmation – the South Coast retreat, the soft drizzle of prayer, the long walks in the gorse at sunset resolving the purpose of man on earth, until that moment prostrate on the cliff's edge far from any other human presence, when the molten sky, the vast darkening sea and the tussocks of grass beside his cheek all spoke to him with one voice of the glory of God.

And last night in the small hours, when a thin breeze through the open window nudged the heat off his skin, he had dreamed he was back with Bella at Callanish, the ring of stones. He had gone on ahead, impatient as he always was with her, and found himself in that prehistoric spot alone with the wind off the sea and the Lewis hills and the grey menhirs blindly circling him like ancient courtiers welcoming a king back to the birthplace he set out from before time began. He always woke from the dream before Bella came up beside him. But every evening, as he drew down the blinds and moved sluggishly from room to room in the humid darkness, he feared he would sleep on until, one night, she spoke and the stones retreated, and left him defenceless.

It wasn't only Bella. Daytime ghosts pursued him. Nick was on his mind. Then there was Freddie Collins – what the devil was he doing in Adelaide? That bloody reporter had hinted at secrets, conspiracies – the usual journalistic twaddle. On the other hand, you didn't find a man like Freddie taking time off to fly across the world to shoot the breeze with a few old chums. Straws in the wind . . . but in this heat every wind carried a smell of burning.

In the late afternoon it was possible to go out and swim, or sit by the pool, and pretend it was an English summer's day. Douglas swam up and down the length of the pool, thrusting himself onward with a furious panting and splashing which helped to compensate for the sedentary intellectual exercise he took at the writing-desk. Helen lay in a deck-chair, ostensibly exposed to the sun but fighting it off with every weapon in her armoury: sun-hat, dark glasses, and a thick protective coating of oils and creams which demanded constant checking and renewing and made relaxation impossible.

Georgina sat beside her. She wore a cotton shift over her bathing-costume. An orange Penguin paperback copy of *Nineteen Eighty-Four* lay in her lap, but her eye hardly fell upon it. Minutes had passed since she last turned the page. She had arranged for something momentous to happen that evening, and she was contemplating how she should impart the news to the others.

Her father swam to the edge of the pool. He rested his elbows on the cement and picked up his glasses. As always when it was wet, the red worm of his war wound stood out on his forehead like a birthmark.

'What are you reading, Georgina?'

'Oh.' She looked down. 'It's *Nineteen Eighty-Four*.'

'Very good.' Douglas heaved himself out of the water, breathing heavily. 'I knew him slightly, Orwell. He was no fool, though he sometimes acted like one. He wrote something once which I've never forgotten. *The energy that actually shapes the world*, Orwell said, *springs from emotions – racial pride, leader-worship, religious belief, love of war – which liberal intellectuals mechanically write off as anachronisms, and which they have usually destroyed so completely in themselves as to have lost all power of action.* I can't remember which essay it comes in. It may have been in one of his war broadcasts. But it is one of the most unfashionable truths ever uttered by a man of the Left. I would like to see it implanted in the brains of the London intelligentsia – the kind of people who stamp on success and cut every hero down to their own littleness. You'll find out, Georgina! It's because of them the British have lost touch with their instincts. I remember Freddie Collins telling me that. We've lost confidence. I won't be surprised if we end up like Winston Smith in the end. Or like the farm animals being ordered around by Napoleon and Snowball.'

'I don't see why—' Georgina began, but was interrupted by Helen who had lowered her sun-glasses.

'Darling, there's nothing new in any of that. Shakespeare says exactly the same thing in *Hamlet*. And it's the whole point of *Measure for Measure*, it's the struggle between reason and instinct. I wish it weren't. I'd be much happier if Isabella was the instinctive one instead of the ghastly repressed creature she is, freezing everything with cold reason and her brother, too. How am I supposed to make her feminine? Making her sympathetic on stage is like trying to melt an iceberg with a match. . . . Christ! These insects!'

'When will it open?' Douglas asked.

'Oh, I don't know.' Helen yawned and got up, as if to signal that this topic of conversation no longer interested her. Wandering up the garden, she held on to her sun-hat and gazed at the tattered victims of heat exhaustion in the flowerbeds. When she came back she was swatting the air.

'Bloody flies everywhere! It's that man's dog shitting all over the garden. And look at the pool! Georgina, did you trawl it this morning?'

'It's your sun lotion,' Georgina explained. 'It attracts the flies.'

'Don't be silly, George. It repels insects. It says so on the bottle. Anyway, there are flies on the water.'

'That's because your sun-cream comes off in oil-slicks on the pool. It attracts them down.'

'I'm not going to argue with you. It's too hot to argue.'

'G'day!'

Helen slid into the pool. Mr Robbins, in a red vest, was standing by the low hedge that separated them from the garden next door. He was holding up by the legs a bright green frog.

'How you going?' he bellowed.

Helen back-stroked. Georgina smiled. Douglas raised his arm.

'Very well, thank you, Mr Robbins,' he said.

'I've got something for you, Georgie. A tree-frog. Isn't he a beaut? There's no better pet, that's a fact. Very friendly. Lives on flies, so there's no need to feed him. Just make sure that he's not around when you're barbie-ing, ha-ha!'

Georgina went and collected the tree-frog. She had dissected one identical to it that morning. 'Thanks, Mr Robbins.'

'You're welcome.' Mr Robbins showed no inclination to retire. 'How's the writing, Mr Manifold?' he called out cheerily. 'Bit hot, eh? My word. It's enough to make an Abo frizzle.'

'It's very hot,' Douglas agreed.

'Makes people go troppo, you know? Did you see that double suicide in the papers? A brilliant nuclear scientist, they say. Him and that young nurse after a New Year's party. They think they tried a new kind of drug together and it killed them. But they don't know, they're just guessing. My wife, now departed, used to say that Australia isn't a country for eggheads. It turns 'em.'

'A girl I know's father is Sir Martin Amory. He's a nuclear scientist. He's supposed to be brilliant.' Georgina put the tree-frog down carefully by the side of the swimming-pool, close to her stepmother who swam away. 'According to Robyn, he thinks everything's contaminated from the radioactivity in the air, which is why he lives in the hills.'

'Too right, Miss Manifold. It's a polluted society we're living in. Pollutants scorching the grass. Pollutants in the grain, bringing the horses down with colic. Pollutants in the sea; and of course pollution of people, and I don't just mean Abos, blimey. Look at our beaches south of Glenelg – cars right down by the water, churning up the beach, it's a bleeding disgrace. Excuse my euphemism, Mrs Manifold.'

Helen wrapped herself in a towel. 'Your dog's no better, Mr Robbins,' she said. 'It's been coming through the fence and making messes on the lawn. There's one over there.'

Mr Robbins shook his head. With a tolerant chuckle he waved his arm as if to encompass the land-mass of Australia. 'To a dog, this is a free country,' he replied. 'It's us humans who ought to know better. According to my daughter Terrine, who as you know is a statistician in the office of the Prime Minister of South Australia, the world's human population excretes over fifty thousand million gallons of waste on to the land and in the water every twelve months. She also mentioned, Mrs Manifold, that she has seen your face several times in *Woman's Weekly*, and I know she'd like to make your acquaintance. . . . '

'Mr Robbins, I can see steam coming out of your window,' Douglas interrupted.

'Strewth. My kettle. What a pest. Nice to talk to you people. Any time you want a hand, just ask me, no worries.' With that, Mr Robbins vanished from above the hedge as abruptly as he had appeared.

There was a moment's silence.

'Bloody 'ell,' said Georgina, and giggled.

'Did we know his daughter was a statistician?' asked Helen. 'I don't know anything about the man at all, except that he appears to take us for granted. Do you know anything, darling? Our neighbours in Holland Park were bad enough but at least they didn't stand and talk at us over the fence – I suppose because the fences were too high at home, thank goodness. George, what are you going to do with that frog?'

'Barbie it?' Georgina giggled again.

'I talked to him when we first arrived,' said Douglas. 'It's a bit of a sad story really. He obviously married up a grade. Then his wife died, and left him her old man's house. They had a son called Terry who apparently didn't live beyond two, and then this daughter they called Terrine. *Terrine*. God knows what he does. Probably a bookie at Adelaide racecourse to judge from his conversation— '

'I think he's a manager at the Chrysler works in South Adelaide,' said Georgina.

'Something like that, but what fascinates me about these people is their unaffected racism. You heard him say

68

"enough to make an Abo frizzle" and you find the same thing with all these Australian working-men – *ockers*, they call them. They have all the prejudices of the uncultivated and uncouth. They won't tolerate anything new or foreign or different. They have no spiritual qualities at all. But there's a not unattractive quality about a man like Robbins, don't you think? He reminds me a little bit of Nick Kemp— '

'Oh, darling!'

'No, I mean the straightforwardness. Cheerful. No-nonsense. Obviously resourceful.'

'Yes, but Nick was different.' Helen glanced at Georgina who was sitting right forward in her chair, her book fallen on the grass. 'I mean Nick was . . . *exciting* isn't the word I want. He was unboring, he kept one interested and entertained. He wasn't *Australian* at all.'

'Nick is thoroughly Australian.' Douglas grinned. 'He's always boasted that New South Wales has a Prick named after him. It's a pinnacle of stone, Kemp's Pinnacle, in the Falls Country. It's named after Major William Kemp who fought at Waterloo and came out to Australia in eighteen thirty-seven. He's Nick's great-grandfather. And one of his uncles, or great-uncles, was a governor of South Australia and built a baronial mansion up in the Adelaide Hills. Nick's a native all right.'

Georgina took her courage in both hands. 'He's coming round tonight,' she said.

Douglas laughed. 'Great-grandfather Kemp? Heaven help us.'

'No– '

'Who, George?' Helen said sharply.

'Captain Kemp. I invited him round.'

Douglas began to redden. 'What are you talking about? Nick's miles away.'

'No. No, he's in Adelaide. He phoned up while you were in the pool. I'd left a message, you see. He's coming round for a drink before dinner, Daddy. I know how much you want to see him again. So I asked him for tonight.'

'You little fool!' Douglas stood up. 'Why didn't you tell me? Why did you have to go behind my back?'

'What do you mean?' Georgina's lips trembled. 'He's your friend!'

69

'How did you find him?' Helen wanted to know.

'I asked that reporter. Winn Vellacott.'

'That skunk!' cried Helen, remembering what Edward Catchpole had said.

'Oh, what does it matter?' Douglas flung off his robe and tossed his glasses after it. 'She's done it now. That's it.'

So saying, he dived into the pool and swam underwater, away from them.

Later they sat in the saucer chairs, facing towards the turquoise vases on the false chimneypiece. Helen Manifold was wearing a cotton sheath dress of pale heliotrope. Douglas for some reason had changed into the unfamiliar costume of slacks, a sports-shirt and canvas shoes. He was flicking through a book on the Atomic Age. Georgina, in her usual jeans and blouse, put her Coke down on the coffee-table.

'It's six-thirty,' she said.

Helen sipped her white wine and brushed one of Ottoman's hairs off her lap. Douglas drummed his fingers on the side of his whisky-glass.

'Listen to this,' he said. 'From Bohr and Wheeler, the perfect definition of adultery and divorce. "The phenomenon of nuclear fission is caused by a neutron invading a nucleus. The nucleus is made up of particles which interact intimately with each other. The neutron intruding among them generates so much extra heat that the nucleus in a very short time is split into two parts, the parts separating with enormous energy." How about that?'

No response came back. In the evening beyond the mantelpiece, the crickets had begun racketing.

'Surprisingly comfortable, these shoes,' Douglas went on. 'If I must talk to myself. After all, there's no pressing reason why one should keep on with suits and ties and heavy shoes out here. One should travel light; one should dispense with the past. Don't you agree, poppet?'

'It's too late to dispense with the past,' replied Helen. She tapped a cigarette-packet and drew one out between her lips. 'I would be happy to dispense with that hideous

70

clock, though,' she added, nodding at the starfish above the mantelpiece. 'How can one believe the time told by anything so vulgar?'

'I think I can hear a car,' said Georgina.

In the silence, they listened. The sound went past, and faded away.

Helen said: 'I wish you could do something about our car, darling. Can't you change it? Nobody drives a Morris Major Elite, least of all the élite. Even on our apology for an income, surely we could afford a Rover.'

'It's no smaller than the car we've got at home.'

'Maybe, but we're not in England now. And when we went to the States for that year, even on your lecturer's salary we had something with a bit more style. . . . '

'Shush!' Georgina put her finger to her lips. They listened again. This time they heard the crunch of gravel. Georgina jumped up and ran out. The front door opened, and shut. Georgina came back into the room, her face dark with embarrassment, followed by a man who was exclaiming: ' . . . never knew I'd got so handsome that you wouldn't recognise me after five years!'

Douglas got to his feet and stood holding the back of Helen's chair. The man sauntered up to them and produced from behind his back a bunch of flowers. Vivid scarlet petals knifed out from a black heart.

'Desert blooms,' Nicholas Kemp said to Helen with a cheerful bow. 'Tomorrow they'll die but tonight they'll put on a show for you. *Ave, morituri te salutant*. Douglas, you old buzzard, how've you been?' he went on, shaking Douglas by the hand, clapping him on the back and hugging him all at once. 'I feel like a pilgrim who's arrived at the hermit's cell. And where have you been hiding Georgina? She's grown into a fine sprig of a woman and you never told me! Then she had the face to tell me that I've changed!'

But he had changed. Surely he had changed. At Malvern that time he was still the hero of *DogDay* in the eyes of the small girl who had come down the stairs – tall and handsome like any of the chivalrous knights in her *Child's History of England*. But, instead of Sir Philip Sidney, Georgina saw before her an all-too-human being of average height, with a fair complexion, wavy copper-coloured hair and a friendly grin. Only his wide shoulders and muscular frame conformed to her preconception. The rest of him – blue eyes, broken nose and all – belonged more to a prizefighter than to the Achilles she had worshipped in her imagination. Dominate the room as he might, he was not the real Captain Kemp. Childishly she resented him for it.

She brought him a glass and a can of lager (he'd asked for a stubby; she wasn't about to ask him what a stubby might be). After that she went quietly out of the room and sat alone at the dining-table, nursing her resentment. Faintly she could hear the clink of glasses on the coffee-table and the murmur of voices, sounding exactly as they had on all the drearily genteel social occasions of her childhood.

She went to the french windows, and pressed her nose against the glass. The bright stars had flung up over the darkened garden. As she watched, one star seemed to detach itself from the canopy of the night sky and fall diagonally across it, like a living thing travelling so fast that it was consumed by its own fire. It fell and fell and went on falling, and the earth under her feet turned to observe its progress. When at last she could see it no longer, she turned her face away and rested her back against the corner of the door. Slowly she let her feet slide under her until she was sitting on the floor, where she stayed, without moving, for a long time.

On the basket chairs in the sitting-room Helen and Douglas sat with drinks in their hands. Nick Kemp was sprawled on the floor, his head resting against the armchair. With one hand, expertly, he opened a can of lager, and carried it towards his mouth before remembering to pour it into the glass beside him.

'There's no mystery,' he said. 'I had a three-month furlough; Adelaide had the Fourth Test. Watching the bludgers in the English side, I'm starting to wonder which of us is taking time off. Truman's getting no lift with the ball. The one watchable batsman in the team – Sheppard, you know, the Youth for Christ preacher – he's gone sick with pharyngitis.'

'So much for muscular Christianity,' interjected Douglas.

'As you say. Not that the Aussies are cutting the mustard, either. Benaud took two and a half hours to make forty-eight runs today, and got slow-hand-clapped by the Oval crowd or what was left of them. Playing a straight bat . . . I used to think it was an English vice.'

He laughed and drank, talked cricket and laughed again. Helen got up, tapping out a cigarette.

'Would you like something to eat?' she enquired. 'We've eaten, but I could make you a ham omelette. I'm afraid it's all we've got in the house.'

Nick gazed at her as if seeing her for the first time. 'What could be more delectable!' he said admiringly. 'You don't need any help, do you?'

'No,' said Helen. And went out.

Left to themselves the two men were silent for a time. It was not the comfortable silence of old friends who know each other well enough to avoid the tiresome necessity of producing interesting things to say; far from it. There was too much to say, too much to discover; and the first bridge across that gulf of ignorance had to be thrown warily if it was to hold.

'I'd decided that you didn't want to see old Nick,' said the visitor. 'Then I heard Georgina was trying to get in touch. It's gone down in legend, you know, Georgina turning up in her schoolgirl kit at the toughest pub in Adelaide. Winn Vellacott told me how he saved her from an early grave. I thought if she wanted to see me that bad there must be something up.'

'Georgina's a free agent. She does pretty much as she wants to. She gets these quixotic ideas sometimes. She thinks she understands me better than I understand myself.'

'Perhaps she does.'

Douglas forced a laugh. He walked over to the record-player and began to sort through records in the cabinet. 'I had a Benny Goodman somewhere,' he said. 'You used to like Benny Goodman.'

'I still do.'

Douglas couldn't find it. He put on Johnny Hodges instead, playing a rich blue saxophone. At once it became a clumsy embarrassing attempt to evoke the past that they had in common, when it was the past Douglas was trying to evade.

'The record's cracked,' he lied, and switched it off. 'I can't believe you're still with that Melbourne oil company,' he went on. 'I'd have thought you'd be back on your travels by now. You know, Yokohama, the Yukon. . . . ' He stopped, as if for the moment unable to think of any more exotic place-names beginning with Y.

'I'm an old man,' Nick replied. 'Money is all I'm interested in now. Money and a good time.' He rapped his stomach. 'This is the belly of a businessman, soft and white and full of Foster's. Soon I'll only be able to keep my girlfriends by proposing marriage to them. Then I'll know it's time to hang up my boots. Do you remember that little girl in Evreux in forty-four when you had to dress up as an army chaplain for me?'

'Of course I bloody well do. If I hadn't arrived at top speed by motor-bike to join you together in holy matrimony, her family would never have let you out of the house. You were damn lucky I kept them talking so you could make your escape!'

Nick Kemp raised his can in salutation. 'To the smoothest tongue in the West!' he proclaimed, and downed the lager.

'You could be pretty damn smooth!' Douglas protested. Neither of them noticed Helen make an entrance with the food on a tray. 'What about that time in Berlin after the war? When we drove past the Russian sentries to go and look at the Führerbunker, or what was left of it? I brought out an armful of soup-bowls with the Chancellery stamp on, and you talked us back past the guards by telling them we were having a party in the British sector and inviting Marshal Zhukov to attend!'

Nick threw back his head and roared with laughter. Helen advanced and placed the tray on the floor beside his recumbent figure.

'It's late,' she declared with a charming smile. 'I've got rehearsals in the morning, so if you'll forgive me I'll leave you two old soldiers to your memories. Good night, Nick. Come and see us again.'

Nothing was said, as she left the room, though Nick smiled grimly into his drink. Douglas broke the silence, joining Nick on the floor, his back to the wall.

'I'm worse than you,' he said.

'Worse how?'

'Backing away. I backed away from things. Still do. You saw yourself in relation to the whole damn world; you plunged into it. I saw myself in relation to my family and my work; that was it. I stayed in London. I wrote commentaries on life. You lived it. That was the difference between us.'

'Horse shit! Do you think I gained some sort of wisdom, bumming around the world? Not half so much as you. You had time to reflect on what you were doing. I never had time to reflect. I was always working like a blue-arsed fly to pay for steamer tickets, abortions, gambling debts . . . excuse me. . . . ' Nick was eating the omelette. 'I'm older, and I'd be sadder if I was any the wiser.'

Douglas poured out more whisky. 'Anyway,' he said, 'it's all in the past.'

'Old soldiers.'

'That's what the lady said.'

Nick crumpled an empty beer-can in his hand, and placed it carefully on the floor. He said: 'It's not us, you know, Duggle. It's not because we're older. It's that the world's a smaller place. It's too small for heroes. It's too small for adventurers even, unless you're darn lucky. That's why I'm out here prospecting, if I'm honest with myself. It's the last frontier' – he rapped the carpet – 'what lies under our feet. Especially in the outback. You've got thousands of square miles of sand and scrub out there and it could be hiding anything, it could be hiding oil or water, opals, gold, uranium. . . . It's the last chance at Eldorado.'

'Isn't that what your old man used to say?'

'He didn't know what he was saying, half the time. Too drunk by the end. It was my grandfather who went out during the gold-rush in eighteen seventy-two and made his fortune, up around Leigh Creek. Lost most of it again on gambling and whisky of course. That's been the story of the Kemps in Australia. Flying high until the sun got to them and burned their wings. That's why I stayed away.'

'Until now.'

'Until now.' Nick was silent. Suddenly he said: 'I'll tell you something queer. I've been doing some prospecting off my own bat up in the north-west of the State. I came across a blackfella I'd met before, name of Nelson, in a dump on the

75

Transcontinental Railway. Do you know the story of Ooldea? There's a tribe of Abos called the Pitjantjatjara who lived around there for generations. It was the only unfailing source of water for hundreds of miles around, at least until the railway tapped the wells. Their ancestors way back had come there for initiation ceremonies. Then, for some reason, they were all picked up and transported south, to a reservation at Yalata. Tribespeople who tried to get back home were rounded up and driven back.'

'Why?'

'I should ask Nelson. He's a Pitjantjatjara from Ooldea. He abominates Yalata. He says that his Pitjantjatjara tribe are red-earth, spinifex people, and Yalata is a grey-earth place. Living there ages them and makes their hair go grey. Anyway, he'd managed to get away from the reservation and wandered back north. He took me aside and started telling me about this fairy-tale place in the desert. A place of green stones, he said, somewhere in the far outback, near the edge of the Nullarbor. I knew he wasn't bullshitting me because he'd taken me out near the site of the old Mission, where the Soak used to be . . . there are a lot of ancestral spirits hanging round there, it's like swearing on the family bible. So then, what he does, he fishes a stone out of his pocket and gives it to me.'

Douglas leaned forward. 'And?'

'It was green. Bits of it were green, no mistake. I thought it was copper at first, but then it seemed volcanic, possibly a rhyolite. To be honest, I didn't know what I was looking at. One-eyed Nelson wanted money to guide me to where he found the stone, but I said I'd need to check it out. They're running tests in the lab on it now.'

'I'm amazed he let you take it from him.'

'Nelson's sitting pretty. He must know that there's no one else who could lead me there. If it turns out to be worth following up, why don't you come along?'

'Me?'

'Yes.'

Douglas sprang up off the floor. He paced over to the window. Outside, the moon had turned the leaves of the cannas into gunmetal, fragments of steel. He felt absurdly excited, like a little boy again, and at once derided himself.

'Just Aramis and D'Artagnan?' he asked mockingly.

'And Nelson.'

'Very well. Let's see what it's made of first.'

In the dining-room, Georgina stirred and opened her eyes. Her bottom ached and her back was stiff from the hours spent slumped against the french windows. Groggily she got to her feet and stumbled out into the hall. She could hear voices coming from the sitting-room. What time was it? Putting her ear to the door, she heard a great happy belly-laugh, a boozy beer-swiller's laugh such as had echoed around her in the Arcadia. She ran upstairs, and lay awake and unhappy on her bed, until the sky paled and the birds began to sing, when she fell asleep.

Nicholas Kemp left in the early hours of the morning. But for Georgina his visitation marked a turning-point. The time of her dreaming was over. In the days which followed, before they heard from Nick again, she castigated herself repeatedly, recognising in her reaction to Nick the immaturity of her hopes and imaginings.

It wasn't Nick Kemp's fault, she decided. It was hers. But the sense of betrayal lingered, and perhaps it was this as much as any new-found independence of spirit that impelled Georgina to spend less time at home. She took her science books to revise in the school library, often getting back to Wellington Square later than Helen (whose *Measure for Measure* rehearsals for some mysterious reason occupied her into the early evening several times a week). She put herself out to be friendly to other girls at school, and since she was no threat they accepted her. Bookish, reserved, but friendly, Georgina fitted into a category they could comprehend.

But she needed to be by herself as much as she ever had. She walked in the Botanic Gardens, and took shelter from the heat of the sun in the cool alcoves formed by the arching roots of the giant Moreton Bay fig trees. In the Eastern Parklands she sat by the shallow pool and watched while a white-haired old gentleman launched a beautifully constructed model of *Queen Elizabeth*. On the opposite bank, a boy with a shock of yellow hair wound up an American-style speedboat and sent it roaring past the fragile liner, near-capsizing it.

Probably most boys were like this. She thought about Dirk Miller, who had rung her up out of the blue three days ago and asked her, abruptly, to come with him to see James Whale's *Frankenstein* with Lon Chaney as the Monster at the University Film Club that night. To her astonishment she'd said yes – and then found herself in a party of eight, with Dirk and his friends loudly discussing a surfing competition at Victor Harbour while she ate scorched almonds out of a paper bag and refused to pretend the smallest interest in their silly one-upmanship. What made it so hard for men to grow up?

At the Zoo she strolled past reconstructions of extinct Australian birds and mammals, several of them killed off in modern times by the foxes, rats and rabbits introduced off the ships from Europe. The pouched mammals, apart from the kangaroos and wallabies, were too freakish to hold her interest. What drew her back, time and time again, was the White Earless Dragon. The White Earless Dragon lived in the middle of the vast dry salt lakes of the interior, miles from any species of plant or animal life save only its prey, a tiny harvest ant, which existed on seeds blown out across the surface of the lake from the shoreline, below the pale horizon.

Such an extreme of detachment from the support systems of the universe filled Georgina with wonderment and humility. She gazed and gazed at the immobile salt-white scrap in its glass cage until she seemed to see it quiver with the effort of sustaining its remoteness of being.

If anybody wondered why Georgina took off on these solitary rambles, she would point to the camera round her neck. Photography was becoming a passion as engrossing as the piano had been (before her piano teacher had managed to extinguish her interest by refusing to let her graduate from arpeggios and 'Chopsticks' to any kind of serious music). At the end of term a new Leica was being offered as first prize in the Picturesnapper competition open to members of the Photography Society. With the ancient Nikon that had belonged to her father, Georgina was gradually putting together a portfolio of nineteenth-century Adelaide ruins: the demolished remains of the Theatre Royal in Hindley Street where Sarah Bernhardt and

Sir Laurence Olivier had played; a disused prison building in Enfield; a Victorian workman's cottage built of slab; the relics of an old smelting works in Glen Osmond; and, best of all, the blackened ruins of Marble Hill.

A great high-towered Gothic mansion near Mount Lofty, Marble Hill was the vice-regal residence built in the 1890s by Nick Kemp's great-uncle. In 1955 it had been gutted in a devastating bushfire which came close to incinerating the Governor too as he sheltered with his house-guests in a gully, wet blankets over their heads. It kept drawing Georgina back, this grand desolate building, although it was a long ride into the Adelaide Hills. Occasionally at weekends she would come across local Adelaiders who had ignored the 'No Trespassing' signs in order to picnic in the grounds or wander in the roofless shell. More usually she had the ruin to herself, and would make her way up the steps in the collapsed tower until she could look out, as the governors had, over all of Adelaide and the plains beyond, to the sea.

On the road back through Glen Osmond lived Robyn Amory. In her class at school, Robyn was as different from Ursula Miller as Georgina could have wished. For one thing she didn't have a brother. For another, she was Georgina's intellectual equal, the free-thinker she had not expected to find. Tall, impetuous, rangily good-looking, Robyn Amory affected an Olympian detachment from school affairs. She reminded Georgina of Wendy Veevors at Malvern – a bit reserved and shy at first but, when you got to know her, incredibly sensitive and funny, in a wicked sort of way. Perhaps because they were both outsiders, Robyn had taken her up as an ally and a confidante.

They had in common the burden of a famous father. Sir Martin Amory was the most distinguished nuclear scientist in Australia. Georgina already knew something of his background. He had been a student of Enrico Fermi, and worked under Oppenheimer on the wartime project to develop the first atomic bomb. But Oppenheimer's morality had rubbed off on him. Repelled by the devastation of Hiroshima, he had spoken out against atomic weapons research after the war, and returned to Australia where he set up committees and research programmes to explore the peaceful uses of atomic energy. Along with Niels Bohr and Oppenheimer himself, Amory was known (according to Georgina's physics master at Malvern) as one of the dissenting trinity – a man who had renounced his lifetime's study rather than watch his research adapted for the purposes of death and destruction.

He and his daughter lived in Mountfoot, a rambling ivy-clad stone house on the lower slopes of Mount Osmond. Robyn never talked about her mother. Georgina had no way of knowing for sure if Lady Amory was alive or dead, although once she saw a pale, lined face at an upper-storey window, which withdrew as soon as Georgina noticed it. A housekeeper attended to Sir Martin's needs when he was at home. When he wasn't, Robyn seemed to have the run of the place.

Not until her second visit did Georgina get to meet the physicist. She had gone to pick up some biology notes which Robyn had borrowed. They were sitting on the white wooden veranda at the front of the house. The ground in front of them fell away steeply in a wide crescent of lawn, cleared of trees to help protect Mountfoot from bushfire. It was the kind of day when that felt like a necessary precaution. A hot wind blew southwards from the Flinders Ranges, carrying a grit which burned their cheeks whenever they stirred out of the shade. As they sat over bottles of Coke – actually Georgina was in a hammock, one leg dangling to the floor – their conversation had shifted from schoolwork to arguing the relative merits of the Jets and the Sharks in *West Side Story*. Then Georgina described last Sunday's trial run for the Queen's visit – coming down in the aeroplane, and being escorted by mounted police through the streets of Adelaide in the Royal limousine.

'It made me see what it must be like to be in a play with Helen,' she finished. 'Someone who has to be centre-stage all the time, taking the curtain calls. The man in charge, Mr Catchpole, came round for a drink the other day. You should have seen her! All her ever-so-funny rehearsal stories about *Measure for Measure* – poor old Daddy hardly got a look in. He started telling Mr Catchpole about the university lecture he's giving on the play, to coincide with the end of the run, and he was actually quite funny. Especially about the head of the Literature Department who's very trendy and writes outback Westerns with Aborigines as the good guys. But Helen and Mr Catchpole just sat staring at each other, and then Catchpole got up and said he was sorry, he had a dinner engagement. Just like that!'

'Talking of culture, I saw the best film ad ever in the *Gazette* yesterday,' said Robyn. 'It was for the Australasian première of *Sodom and Gomorrah*, can you imagine? *See Lot's wife turned to Salt!* It had it in big letters. *Pagan pleasures – and then the Hour of Reckoning!* Actually I wouldn't mind the hour of reckoning, just so's we had the good time first. Don't you think Adelaide's like a convent, Georgina? I mean— '

She was interrupted by a dog barking. A piebald terrier came bounding up the veranda steps and into Robyn's lap, knocking her Coke-bottle to the ground. A tall man with thick glasses and an untidy thatch of white hair came round the side of the house. Although he was holding a stick, his step was full of vigour. A pair of binoculars swung at his chest.

'What's all this about an hour of reckoning?' he enquired.

'We were saying it's what Adelaide's never going to get, Dad.'

'Don't be too sure. Who's your friend?'

Robyn introduced Georgina. Martin Amory blinked at her.

'So your father is D. J. Manifold?'

'Yes, sir.'

'These days in poetry there's too much straining for effect. Your father, never.'

He excused himself and went inside. When he returned, it was in carpet slippers, carrying a can of beer.

'I've been up the mountain looking for smoke,' he said, stretching back in the hammock which Georgina had vacated. 'It's one of the Red Alert days. I thought I could smell burning on the air.'

'Did you see anything, sir?' asked Georgina.

'No. But the woods are like tinder just now. All it takes is one spark. With this wind our fire-break wouldn't save Mountfoot. And that' – he chuckled – 'would save people the trouble of making any arson attempts.'

Georgina looked at Robyn, puzzled. Robyn explained.

'Dad's writing his memoirs, and people want to stop him. They're full of nuclear secrets, and stories about all the conspiracies that went on. That's why they won't ever be published, under the thousand-year rule.'

'Hundred-year rule,' Amory corrected.

'I know all about you, sir,' Georgina said shyly. 'Mr Willis our physics master used to talk about you, along with Professor Oppenheimer and Professor Bohr.'

This was greeted with another chuckle. 'That's very flattering, but I'm afraid I'm small fry.' Amory took a swig of the beer. 'I'd never have had the nerve to try to argue Churchill and Roosevelt round, like Bohr did. You know he warned them that the Russians should be let in on the Manhattan Project to avoid a terrifying arms race when the war was over. A month later, Roosevelt signed the Hyde Park Agreement with Churchill which kept the Bomb an Anglo-American secret. And he ordered round-the-clock surveillance of Bohr to make sure he didn't leak any information to the Russians.'

'That's so hypocritical!' cried Georgina. 'Why, they could have stopped everything, straight after the war, there and then! They could have stopped nuclear research, nuclear weapons . . . don't you think?'

'I wish I did.' Amory half-turned in the hammock and sniffed the air. He went on: 'I wish knowledge could be turned back like the hands of a clock, but it can't. And nuclear energy is knowledge so elemental and destructive it's like Promethean Fire. You steal it from the Gods, and sooner or later Zeus will take his revenge. Except that next time Zeus sends Pandora down to be the ruin of man there might not be Hope left at the bottom of her box.'

'Dad, you're so gloomy.' Robyn had her sandalled feet up on the seat of her rattan chair and was examining her toes. 'Men have been around for millions of years and never created anything they can't control.'

'They have now. It's called Plutonium. It can only be created artificially, by neutron bombardment of uranium. An element which doesn't exist in Nature because it's too dangerous, that's Plutonium. It's about the most lethal carcinogen known to man. Imagine Frankenstein creating a monster which is invisible and goes on existing and killing people for at least twenty-four thousand years. That's what one gram of Plutonium can do. And twenty-four thousand years is just its half-life. Created out of nothing, indestructible, it will go on living and pulsing for hundreds of thousands of years.' He stopped. 'Now, what the dickens . . . ?'

The dog had started to growl. Putting his boots back on, Amory seized his stick and set off up the steep hillside behind the house. Robyn and Georgina followed him, hurrying through the scrub heath and past the molars of grey rock and clumps of hard-leaved stringybark and yellow gum trees. The burning smell was getting stronger. Amory set a fast pace. Suddenly he halted. He gestured at them to be still. Faintly they could hear a crackling sound. It was coming from their left, and as Georgina strained her eyes she saw a disturbance in the air from heat rising behind a thick clump of eucalyptus.

They ran towards it, and stopped dead. An Aborigine was squatting over a fire of hot coals. The fire was sheltered from the breeze by a leaning boulder which was blackened and cracked on the underside as if it had been used as a primitive fire-shelter for generations. The Aborigine was naked except for cotton khaki trousers cut off just above the knees so they looked to Georgina absurdly like Bermuda shorts. On the fire was an aluminium saucepan in which he was cooking a meal. Georgina saw, with a sense of utter inappropriateness, that it was full of tinned baked beans, in the moment before Sir Martin Amory rushed forward, scattering the coals with his stick and kicking over the saucepan.

Amory beat at the fire as though it was the Aborigine he wanted to thrash with his stick. Embers and ash rose in the air and settled on the leaves of the eucalyptus. The Aborigine stayed squatting. He watched Amory scatter the coals. He watched the saucepan with his meal tip over on the scorched ground. Still he did not move.

'No fires!' shouted Amory. 'You know there's a law, no open fires! You could go to prison. Prison, understand?'

The Aborigine nodded. The ash drifted on to his rounded shoulders and whitened his grey curls. Still without looking up at Amory, he reached out his hand and picked up his dented saucepan, apparently his one possession. It had a few baked beans adhering to it; he scooped them out with his finger and put them in his mouth. Then he stood up and walked away, vanishing in the shadow of the eucalyptus almost before

Georgina realised he had gone. Amory jabbed his stick at the scorched grass.

'Blast them!' he exclaimed. 'Confounded people! That fool could have set the mountain alight. Us with it.'

'Wouldn't he have known that?' asked Robyn.

Her father finished dispersing the fire. He leaned on his stick taking deep breaths.

'Of course he did. He didn't give a damn. It's a kind of revenge, I sometimes think. An Aboriginal revenge on white people. They've lost their land and now they don't care if they destroy it, or what happens to us if they do. Nothing means anything to them any longer. I sometimes think they've declared a kind of silent war.'

Robyn took his arm. Georgina went down with them, back towards Mountfoot. The idea of unforgiving Aborigines conspiring to take revenge on the whites seemed to her ridiculous, as ludicrous as if . . . as if stones flying up and hitting the car window were taking revenge for being run over! But *fire*. She remembered what Amory had explained about knowledge as the Promethean Fire. If so, it wasn't the Gods who should be angry at the theft of it; surely it was the Aborigines, who had been robbed of the knowledge of their dreaming. And if ever they determined to fight back – here in South Australia, here of all places, *fire* was the weapon.

As she walked up the lawn to the cool veranda the dry grass crackled under her feet like bones.

The barge she sat in would have burned in the water if clouds had not obscured the sun. The poop, though not beaten gold, was draped in yellow crêpe de chine. Instead of silver oars a prosaic eight-cylinder engine puttered beneath her buckled shoes. But Helen on her red-canopied throne was content. At her feet – or more precisely by her right knee – stood Edward Catchpole consulting his stop-watch.

It would be late evening, on the Day itself, although the floodlit stands on either bank would make it as bright as noon. A procession of fifty boats decorated with lanterns and bunting would be preceding them up the Torrens River. On her left at this moment Australia's oldest male-voice choir, the Taninda Liedertafel, would be in full throat on the steps of the Rotunda, with Mr Fritz Homburg conducting. In a few minutes their lowing would fade on the ear, to be replaced, on her right, by the warbling note of the ABC Adelaide Singers. Precariously embarked in a riverboat, they would be positioned one down from the Police Band whose trumpets and tubas would reach new heights of discord as the wash from the Royal Barge rocked their shallow craft at its moorings.

This, too, would pass. Sweeping up the Torrens a curious new outcry, something between a bellow and a screech, would command the Royal ear. As the barge chugged on towards the Morphett Street bridge it would resolve itself into 'The Song of Australia', sung by a massed high-school choir of two thousand voices joined in patriotic refrain:

> 'There is a land where, floating free,
> From mountain top to girdling sea,
> A proud flag waves exultingly,
> And Freedom's sons the banner bear;
> No shackled slave can breathe the air,
> Fairest of Britain's daughters fair –
>   Australia!'

Frankly, Her Majesty was welcome to it. Helen, once again in her wattle-yellow, basked more in the admiration of one man than would the Queen in the admiration of twenty thousand. The dark waters of the Torrens chuckled past under the keel, revelling in their conspiracy. Sporadic clapping reached her ears from the riverbank. It gave her a continual thrill of sexual excitement that anything so illicit and intimate could be conducted in such public view; almost as if they were on stage, she and Edward, making real love in front of an audience who thought they were faking it. She squeezed her stockinged thighs together under the yellow skirt and pressed the bulky handbag down on her lap, rubbing it against herself in time to the throb of the engines.

Less than two hours ago Edward Catchpole had supervised her dressing. She had come to him in his flat, in the bedroom with the venetian blinds, and he had made her draw on the long white gloves and pin in place the yellow hat with its crown of silk petals. He had made her stand in front of his

mirror and powder her face and paint her lips with Royal Red
lipstick—

And then he had taken her apart.

Standing over her, his big hands working smoothly at first
and then more hurriedly, clumsily, he had lifted the crown off
her and unpinned her hair; he had taken off her ear-rings and
unclipped her pearls and unbelted her yellow dress and pulled
it over her head. Dropping on his knees, he had unbuckled her
shoes and pulled them off her stockinged feet. Her petticoat,
lifted off her shoulders, fell on the carpet, and then he could
unhook her stockings from the girdle (her appearance becoming
less queenly by the second) and peel them down her legs.

Finally, when she stood naked before him except for a pair of
pink bikini briefs, all majesty stripped away, he had picked her up
and thrown her on the bed, and begun ripping at his own clothes,
tearing them off as if they were catching fire from him, while she
lay, her heart beating, and looked up in supplication.

'This is the first time,' she said.

'What?'

'I haven't done this before.'

Catchpole, tugging at his collar, paused. His eyes flickered
at her.

'I mean, except with Douglas. I've never been unfaithful
to him in our marriage. There's never been anyone else.'

The collar went flying across the room. 'Is this the time
you want to talk about Douglas?'

'No. I'm sorry. I just wanted you to know what you mean to
me.' She pulled a sheet over her nakedness. Inside she started
to whimper like a little girl lost, *Help me! I'm scared!* But Edward
Catchpole left her no time to be scared. Laying his rimless glasses
down, he kneeled on the bed and stopped her whimpering mouth
with his tongue.

She had expected him to treat her . . . differently. That is,
with the gentleness, the discretion, with which he caressed his
Japanese porcelain bowls and plates. But her he handled as if she
were the potter's clay, pummelling and kneading her, squeezing
her breasts, spreading her legs and roughly exploring her. If this
was tenderness, it was a ferocious tenderness, an animal tenderness, and to her satisfaction she found herself rising to it like
the professional she called herself. With exclamations of joy she

86

fought him; she bit and scratched and arched her slender body; she acted the part of the wild mare tamed by the bit and the crop, not the *ingénue* whom Douglas liked to initiate into lovemaking.

When they separated, she and the stranger who was now her lover, it was more out of exhaustion than satiation. Streaks of blood dashed the white pillow. She had thought it was the Royal Red, but Edward was dabbing at a scratch on his cheek.

'Fee, fi, fo, fum, I smell the blood of a panjandrum,' she murmured with a little laugh at her own wit. But the panjandrum, although smiling, was displeased.

'Take a lesson from me, Cleopatra,' he said. 'Do the damage but don't leave marks.'

He lifted his legs out of bed, still dabbing his cheek with a tissue. Helen held on to his arm. She raised his hand to her lips and kissed it.

'That was good,' she said. 'That was the best.'

'Was it?'

'The best.'

Edward Catchpole put on his glasses. He gazed at her, frowning slightly, as if attempting to reconcile the figure sprawled in his bed with the Royal facsimile he had denuded a few minutes previously. Picking up one of the long white gloves, he held it by the sleeve and ran it softly over her face and breasts, and down her belly.

'You are a wonderful actress,' was what he'd said.

And she was. She knew it. She had Edward Catchpole where she wanted him: the most powerful man she had known was in her power. She looked down at him triumphantly now as the barge neared the Morphett Street bridge; she wanted to put her hand out and stroke the plaster on his cheek. He was signalling to men on the bridge, security men by the look of them. As he did so, the engines revved and the barge began to turn in the current to go back to the landing. Catchpole clicked his stop-watch.

'Eighteen minutes and forty-one seconds,' he announced. 'That's a minute and a half behind schedule.' Turning to Helen, he added in a softer voice: 'I think we can do better next time, don't you, Mrs Manifold?'

'And the next time and the time after that,' she murmured, and waved a white-gloved hand at the scaffolders erecting the stalls from which the choirs would sing their alleluias.

It brought out the insects, this long spell of hot weather. Helen slept with a spray-gun beside her bed. Having thoroughly drenched the bedroom before switching out the light, she would keep the gun under her pillow to kill any late arrivals who had survived the poison in the air. Only regular visitors to Wellington Square, of whom there were few, could accustom themselves to the curious mixture of odours – sweet, bitter, musty, sharp – which surrounded them as they moved through the house in a mist of repellents, attractants, air-fresheners and insecticides. True, the DDT powder Helen put down in small saucers by the wainscot to poison cockroaches was odourless – but, then, as Mrs G constantly remarked, it never killed cockroaches. Ottoman always got there first.

Helen's self-protectiveness seemed to gather strength as she approached the end of rehearsals for *Measure for Measure* at the Union Hall. She stopped smoking, as she usually did before a show. Under her stage name of Helen Callender she was featured on posters all across Adelaide (to say nothing of Gawler, Elizabeth, Port Victor, west as far as Renmark and north up to Port Augusta) and at home she was already clothing herself in the aloof and tragic airs of the pious Isabella. When Douglas suggested arranging a Sunday dinner at Wellington Square for a senior British Lion executive coming over from England later in the month, Helen raised no objection. Her mind was on the play.

Nine days before the dinner, Nick Kemp got back in touch.

'Duggle? Why haven't you come out to see me, you bastard?'

'Where are you?'

'On the houseboat. Mannum Bend. An hour and a half in that limo of yours, straight across the hills.'

'OK. Let's make it next week.'

'Bugger next week. Tomorrow, Saturday. Bring Georgina, she ought to have a dekko at Australia's most famous waterway. I've got some news that can't wait.'

'About the place of green stones?'

'Yes. But not over the telephone. Come for lunch. I'll catch some Murray cod and we'll have 'em grilled, with yabbies.'

They took a box of cigars with them, father and daughter. It was Georgina's idea, perhaps a kind of penance. Even though secretly dreading this second encounter, she squirmed to think of her childish behaviour that first time when she had run and hidden herself away in the dining-room. Really it was all too silly. What did it matter?

That shock of Nick's appearance had propelled her into an indiscriminate cynicism about men. They wrote and talked about themselves as heroes, but not one of them lived up to his self-advertisement. Even the ones who died young – she thought of Chesterton, Rupert Brooke, James Dean – were probably insufferable to live with, always looking in the mirror and popping their acne and telling dirty stories about girls. As she considered the great men of past centuries they stepped out of their grand portraits and stood before her, short and thickset with coppery hair, guffawing at an ancient joke. The whole of history seemed to her a conspiracy to present its leading men in a false light of nobility and idealism, in order for women to conclude that with their smaller-scale virtues they could not compete.

They had passed the Amorys' house (*there* was a man she could admire) and driven up into the rolling wooded hills. Her father had kept to wearing light casual clothes since Nick's visit. His manner, too, had altered, become lighter, younger . . . she didn't know whether it was the clothes or whether he cast off a heaviness whenever he left the Wellington Square house behind him. Increasingly, Georgina appreciated her differences from him. It wasn't the physical difference so much – her eyes blue, her hair less dark. She felt herself to be altogether more sensible, more practical, more down-to-earth – and in these qualities she sensed the inheritance of her dead mother supervening like a comforting presence when the rest of the family seemed remote and estranged.

She asked suddenly: 'Do you think that anything exists of us after we're dead?'

'Really, what a question!'

'If not, you see, then every death is the end of the world, in a way. Like a nuclear apocalypse. That's what Robyn Amory says. No man is an island because every man is the world – or woman. I don't believe that, do you? I think that if you're a Christian you have to believe that everything goes on after you, with a little bit of you in it. Otherwise there'd be no point in trying to make the world a better place to live, would there?'

Douglas drove on. Past Birdwood the hills were flattening out, with tall stands of eucalyptus in the fields. Eventually he said, so quietly she almost missed it: 'Nobody you love dies completely. They go on existing in your memory. They hold conversations with you. Sometimes they wake up beside you in bed. Only people who were never loved go straight into the dark.'

Georgina could not look at him. She stared straight ahead, her heart beating painfully in her chest. They were coming into a country which was new to both of them, a landscape bleak with loss, stony with guilt . . . but somewhere, surely, a water-table of shared memories where they could slake the unspoken sadness. All it needed, to break through, was to speak aloud her mother's name, to say *Tell me about Bella, you must have loved her once!*

'It's so empty out here,' continued her father in a brisker tone. 'I don't think I've seen an animal for miles. Have you, Georgina? I can't understand where they've all gone. Rabbits I know about. That's the myxomatosis. But cows! Sheep I've seen, but where are the cattle?'

Georgina let out a long sigh. Eventually she said: 'There's been an epidemic. According to our biology mistress a lot of cattle are suffering from a mucosal disease. It can be deadly, a sort of murrain. But where it comes from, and whether the cows breathe it in the air or as dust off the ground, no one knows, she says.'

'Is that so? You mean it gets up their noses and it finishes them off?'

'I expect there's something left,' replied Georgina cruelly. 'Even cows, I should think, leave some memory behind, some dumb animal who loved them.'

In the silence that followed this remark they came out on to a plain. Down here it was easy to imagine that the whole country lay under a blight. The ground was hard, the grass burnt the colour of corn-stalks in this height of summer. The midday sun stabbed painfully off the cumbrous metal pipeline which snaked along the road carrying water to Adelaide from the River Murray. Even the clumps of eucalyptus trees looked stunted, although this wasn't the outback or the bush but what passed for good arable country.

'Has Captain Kemp got any children?' Georgina asked.

'None that I know of.'

'Oh.'

'Nick travels light. Ask him, he's got some very amusing stories.'

'Do you believe them?'

Douglas hesitated. 'Nick reminds me of Nostromo,' he said finally. 'He's very tough. Very proud. Very straight. He commands enormous loyalty from his friends, while always somehow keeping his distance. Like Nostromo, whatever he tells you, it's with complete sincerity.'

'Does that mean they're always true?' persisted Georgina.

Her father laughed, and pinched her ear affectionately.

'Read *Nostromo*,' he said.

Two hours out of Adelaide the narrow bitumen road dipped down towards Mannum and the broad slow-moving river. Following Nick's instructions, Douglas turned left through the old riverside town and headed north in the direction of Purnong. In the summer drought the Murray lay on the flat landscape like a flood, brimming its shallow banks with an ample majesty. Black swans floated very upright on the yellow-green water, among half-submerged small islands and scattered trees. On either side, beyond the dark green river-grasses, the land shrugged up dusty brown shoulders as if this vast lake of moving water was a gigantic hallucination, a mirage of light refracted through the parched Australian air.

After a couple of miles they turned off the road on a narrow dirt track which ran past a boat-builder's yard and disappeared behind a clump of stringybarks. The river was all around them. In amongst the trees they came to moorings dug into the riverbank. All were empty except the last, where a pontoon-boat lay in the water, tethered with a looped rope flung over the stump of a tree. Stencilled green letters on the yellow superstructure spelled out the name BELLEROPHON.

Captain Kemp was on deck. He had a skillet in his hand. Georgina got out of the car, clutching the box of cigars. To her relief there was no intense churning of her emotions. Nick, bare-chested, a dirty blue engineer's cap shading his red mariner's face, looked much more at home in this makeshift anchorage than he had in Wellington Square. He waved the skillet at them.

'Come on, you lot! What've you been doing, feeding the ducks?' He held out a hand to help Georgina up the gangway. 'Come aboard, pal. Come and see how the other half lives.'

'We got you these,' she said awkwardly.

'Exploding cigars?'

'No.'

'Real cigars? What a sport.' He threw his arms round her and hugged her to his bare chest, lifting her off her feet. 'Put them on the table, will you? I'll help your old man on board. Can't have him falling in the water.' Winking at her, he reached up and tweaked a klaxon, which gave a startled burp. Georgina laughed aloud. Flushed, pushing her hair back, she marched inside *Bellerophon*.

It resembled a luxury caravan which had been dragged at high speed over bumpy roads. Books, fishing-rods, cushions lay in a jumble on the frayed carpet. The galley at the back looked as if it had been blown up in an explosion and no one had bothered to clear up the mess. Cupboard doors hung open. Saucepans cluttered the sink. Three blackened fish lay in a frying-pan on top of the blackened cooker beside herbs on a chopping-board. Through a half-open door Georgina caught sight of a rumpled double bed, and a dressing-table with what might have been a message scrawled in lipstick on the mirror, although with the curtains drawn against the sun she couldn't make it out. Only the ship's wheel, and the controls built into the front of the cabin, were in spotless condition. She dropped the cigar-box on the table and turned to leave. Captain Kemp stood in the doorway.

'Put some plates on the tray, Georgina,' he said, pointing to the open cupboard, 'and I'll get the chairs and we'll go and sit outside.'

'Knives and forks?'

'In there. Pull hard. That's right, pal. Have you ever been in one of these old bathtubs before?'

'No.'

'On the Murray they're called plank-boats, don't ask me why. Probably because you have to be as thick as two planks to want to sail one. I'll show you round it, but let's have lunch first, before it's cooked to pieces.'

They ate on the shaded front deck. Trees on either side of them bowed grey-green branches into the dappled water. As Georgina might have known, the fish on its bed of Murray crayfish was perfect, done with herbs and lemon and new potatoes, deliciously moist and fresh. Instead of beers, Nick pulled up a couple of bottles of a dryish local wine which had been cooling in the river. They ate and talked, hearing the noisy mynah birds and occasionally seeing pelicans belly-flopping upwards on ponderous black-tipped wings. A feeling of detachment stole over her . . . it was as if the afternoon was already floating into the memory it would become: the wine, the warmth, the water, the trees, the play of sunlight and shadow, and she herself in a blue cotton dress listening to the rise and fall of the men's voices.

With fascination she observed how much more at ease Nick was away from cities and drawing-rooms. Among city people he drank and got drunk in company – it was his way of preserving his isolation in the crowd. Out here he didn't need to drink. He was among the practical solitary people of the river and the open country who tested their understanding against the forces of Nature.

This had to be the Australian-ness in Nick, and the reason why he had come home. He told them about his childhood out in the back of nowhere, and talked about it with such affection that all the stories Georgina had heard from her father about Nick's exploring, hunting, treasure-seeking across half the globe began to sound like an unceasing search for something he had already discovered as a boy, and put aside, and was only now remembering.

He'd just read this newspaper article about the town where he was born. Ducking inside, he brought it out to show them. The accompanying picture showed wide clean streets and sturdy pale rubble-stone houses set in a valley among arid hills. There were no people in the streets, none. When Georgina looked more closely she realised that the houses were all empty. Their neatly rendered windows opened into vacant dark.

'Where is it?' she asked.

'Hammond? Up in the hills, miles from anywhere, on a dirt road that ran from Quorn to Orroroo. It's a ghost town now, but, strewth, those houses were built to last. They wanted them to last, they thought they'd settle there for ever, this wasn't some fly-by-night mining community. My pa had all his furniture brought to the railhead at Port Augusta and he carted it over the hills in a wagon. First thing I remember was being woken by tremendous thunder all over the house, and bawling my head off. It was the workmen putting on a corrugated-iron roof over the thatch, to protect the walls. Hammond was a town to be proud in. I was walloped if I went to Sunday school with dirty fingernails.'

Douglas was silent, reading the newspaper story. Georgina asked: 'What happened?'

'According to my pa, there were three good seasons in a row. The valley was planted out with crops, miles and miles of waving feed for the sheep and cattle, it was like swimming in gold. Then there was a bad season. Pa had two hundred head of cattle and every one survived. Then another good season. Then two more bad ones, very bad. The crops blew away. Pa's cattle ended up eating out the dry-country saltbush and tearing the leaves off the trees. People were leaving. The shops shut. No more Sunday school. There were more starving cattle than people. I never knew cows had so many bones. Every day their eyes got bigger, staring at you as if it was your fault the rains never came. Pa's good furniture started cracking. We all started cracking. But Pa didn't give up easily. He believed experiments had to be carried through. By the time we loaded up the wagon and drove up that main street for the last time, Hammond was looking just like it looks in this picture.'

He took back the newspaper and studied the photograph. Then he chortled with laughter. 'See what the caption says? *Hammond – a town ready for tourism?* What did I tell you: Hammond was built to last!'

'You told me once you hated the place,' said Douglas.

94

'I did. But only because of what it did to Pa. The outback, no, crikey, I loved it. As soon as school-term was finished in Adelaide I'd get out of stiff collars and on to the first train north. I'd go and work as a young jackaroo on one of the outback stations, the kind of place where the water out of the artesian well was so hot it boiled the shit in the lavatory pan. When I was older, it was prawn-fishing up Cairns way. Come on, Duggle, you old buzzard, I must have told you about that!'

'Probably. You used to tell a lot of stories at Oxford. Most of them were as tall as the Empire State.'

'Bloody oath, it's as true as we're sitting here. It's where I learned quick reactions, because if you missed your footing you drowned and no questions asked. The prawn-fishing crews were all as full as a tick with beer and whisky, and youngsters like me had to get tanked up too, or else we'd never have worked up the courage to transfer the catch. It's the same thing now, you know. There are as many unlicensed prawn-fishing boats in Queensland as licensed ones. You can't land your catch from an unlicensed boat; you have to transfer it to a licensed boat out at sea, and it's the most dangerous bloody high-wire act ever invented. Three boys drowned during the times I was up there. All vagrants, so there was no inquiry. I was sucked under myself once . . . so full of rotgut liquor the cook had siphoned down my throat that the chap who hooked me up said I was rolling around underwater with a silly grin on my face.'

The sun suddenly spilled over a bough into Georgina's face. She blinked and moved her chair back. Downstream, boys were swimming off some kind of raft; she could hear splashing and laughter. A goanna scuttled along the white guard-rail, checked, and ran for cover inside a rubber tyre. Nick was talking about the motley prawn-fishing crews he'd sailed with as a boy – something about a giant of a man with six toes on each foot who would pick out the worthless blackbug prawns and eat them still wriggling; and a lawyer with a black belt in karate; and an ex-prospector who spent his free time staring over the side into the slapping sea looking for buried treasure; and an opera-singer who would sing the prawns up with arias from the foredeck . . . all of them people escaping, on the run, from a world whose civilities stuck in their throat.

95

She blinked again. The wine-bottles were empty. The shadows had advanced down the deck of *Bellerophon*. Nick had taken a tissue from his pocket and unrolled it on the table. In the middle lay a stone, about the size of a hen's egg, blackish with streaks of green. 'Nelson's stone,' he announced. 'The reason I brought you here.'

Douglas picked it up, weighed it in his hand.

'It's heavy,' he said.

'Yes.'

'What is it, then?'

'Uranium.'

Douglas dropped the stone on the table.

'Don't worry,' said Nick. 'It's not present in sufficient quantities to do you any harm. But, yes, uranium. What that Aborigine said he picked up off the desert floor. The lab couldn't believe it. They wanted to know where I got it from. They said it had the highest proportion of Uranium-235 they'd ever tested.'

'You'll have to tell me what that means.'

'It means we could be sitting on a gold mine, pal. It means our Abo may have located out there in the desert the biggest deposit of almost-pure uranium minerals the world has ever seen.'

Georgina stared, open-mouthed. Her father picked up the stone with shaking fingers and dropped it again.

'It's purer than the davidite mined at Radium Hill,' continued Nick. He, too, seemed drawn to finger the blackish rock and test it in his hand to make sure it existed. 'Besides, Radium Hill's deposits of primary uranium are exhausted.'

'The green. Is it the green?'

'It's dispersed right through the agglomerate. Copper and uranium minerals you often find in the same piece of rock. The green deposit probably isn't important except as the key to our location. That's its significance, at any rate to Nelson. He said he could only find this place-of-green-stones at a time of full moon. Full moon's two weeks away. It's what we've got to go for.'

'We?'

Nick tipped his cap back on his head. 'You're not backing out now, Duggle?'

Douglas looked across at his daughter. She could see he was considering Helen. He frowned.

'Of course not. Give me ten days, that's all. I've got a university lecture to give.'

With a shout of pleasure, Nick leaped up and clapped him on the shoulder. Running down the gangplank, he untethered *Bellerophon* and jumped back on deck.

'We can discuss that,' he cried. 'You've come all this way, I'm going to take you out on the river!'

With a loud clanking that scared five pelicans into the sky, line abreast, Captain Kemp started up *Bellerophon* and steered her out into midstream. Birds swooped and plunged. Small waves danced away from them and drowned in silver bubbles.

'How far have you come?' shouted Georgina. Pink-skinned in her swimming-costume, she was standing next to him at the wheel.

'From Renmark. I'm taking her down as far as Tailem Bend. A mate of mine will bring her back.'

'It goes incredibly fast. Why isn't there a wake?'

'She floats on pontoons, great big barrels underneath. That's why I have to watch where I'm going. Hit something sharp at speed and it could rip them open like sardine-tins. She'd turn turtle and sink – and the water's thirty-five feet deep out here.'

'Will you take me with you?'

'Where?'

'To find the uranium.'

Nick Kemp grinned. He shook his head. 'It's no place for a woman out there, pal. Not where we're going. It's subsistence living. Hot as Hades, and if you lose your bearings you're done for. I'll tell you what, though. I'm having lunch with a friend of yours at the *South Australian* tomorrow. Winn Vellacott.'

'Him!'

'And I need someone there to remind me not to open my silly great mouth about the uranium. If Winn gets hold of the story, we can forget the whole thing. Will you come along for lunch and hold my hand?'

Georgina blushed. 'I'd love to. Thanks.'

'Good on you, pal. Tell your dad I'll pick you up at twelve-thirty.'

She left him and wandered out through the back. Her father was standing by the guard-rail. She put her arm through his.

'Are you really going into the bush with Nick?'

'It looks like it.'

'Why?'

He squeezed her arm. 'Old times' sake.'

'But it's not like old times. I mean, I wasn't *born* the last time you did something like this!'

'It's something I have to do. I can't explain it.' He grinned at her and flicked her hair. 'You think I'm too old for adventures, you and Helen. You're both jealous of my past because it doesn't include you. Am I not right?'

'No!' She was cross. She wanted to say that he'd misunderstood her and what she meant was that the past surely wasn't like that, it wasn't something you could go back to. But her attention was distracted by something black in the water. She pointed.

'Look. Do you see? Daddy?'

Douglas had vanished round the other side. The thing was coming closer. It was a swan, a black swan; but its head and neck were plunged down under the water. Its feathers stood up untidily along its back. It was turning in a slow circle.

Tears came into Georgina's eyes. She shouted for Nick to stop the engines – but how could he hear her? In a moment they would be up-river; the swan would be past saving. Turning, she saw a boat-hook fastened under *Bellerophon*'s flat roof. She grabbed it and stretched over the side. If she could just lift its neck. . . .

The hook missed. It snagged on something else in the water. In an instant she was overboard in the cool fast-flowing river. She surfaced, still clinging to the boat-hook, struggling to get her breath back to scream for help.

Douglas heard her and saw her and shouted for Nick. *Bellerophon*'s engines spluttered up; it began turning hard in the water. But so slowly, and she was disappearing downstream, she couldn't swim against this current, it was too strong for her.

Long seconds passed. Strangely, she felt no fear. Had

she been alone on board with her father . . . but Nick she trusted. Turning her head, she saw him come out on deck – he was looking for the boat-hook! She screamed and laughed at him. Now he was taking off his shoes and his shirt and tying a rope round his waist.

'Are you okay?' he called out.

'Yes!'

'Hang on to the boat-hook! Don't let go!'

Her father had tied the other end of the rope to *Bellerophon*'s railing. Nick dived into the water. He had to swim against the current to reach her and there was no sign of him, just the tumbling brown water of the Murray dragging her further downstream. Then he surfaced right beside her and grabbed the boat-hook.

'Hold tight,' he said.

Back on the house-boat, a towel wrapped round her shoulders, pink with apology, Georgina explained what she'd tried to do.

'It's been happening a lot,' said Nick, replacing the boat-hook. 'I must have seen a dozen swans, dying or dead, coming down from Renmark. River people thought it might be lead poisoning, but it isn't, it's some strange sickness they've been getting. It weakens them; they can t hold up their heads, and they drown. Now, Georgina, you're steering us back. Come on!'

'What!'

Nick Kemp put his arm round her, led her over to the wheel and shoved his cap on her head. For the next twenty minutes he showed her how to steer and how to vary the speed of the engine, how to tell where the Murray ran fast and how to recognise shoal-water. With his hands over hers on the wheel, she managed to bring *Bellerophon* back to its mooring as docilely as stabling a Shetland pony.

The two men cheered her like boys at a football match.

'There's another bottle of wine somewhere,' said Nick. 'Let's toast the new midshipwoman.'

They drank to Georgina. They drank to adventure. They drank to Australia, the one land still fit for heroes. By the time they left, it was dark enough for Nick to light the storm-lantern and guide them back through the trees to their car.

99

That Saturday night Douglas sat in the armchair, a reading-lamp illuminating the book on his lap. He was listening to Mozart's G Minor Symphony, a work that seemed to overflow with passion and violence, so that it pierced him with heartache each time he played it. Into the room stepped Helen, wearing a yellow robe embroidered with glistening butterflies.

'What is it?' she asked. 'Mozart? It's very pretty. Darling, are you coming to bed?'

Douglas, smiling, got up and turned off the record-player. 'That's what Schumann called it. A work of exquisite charm. Mozart's most tragic, passionate symphony, and all Schumann could find in it was prettiness and grace. . . . '

'Meaning that I'm too insensitive to understand music?'

'No. Not in the least, poppet. It's up to you what you find in music. I'm trivialising Mozart anyway to describe him in terms of the sentiments he arouses. Did you see that Robert Frost has died?'

'It was on the radio.'

'He was the best of all the Americans. There's nobody left like him.' Douglas sat down and picked up the book. 'I was reading his apple poem:

"My long two-pointed ladder's sticking through a tree
Toward heaven still,
And there's a barrel that I didn't fill
Beside it, and there may be two or three
Apples I didn't pick upon some bough.
But I am done with apple-picking now."

That's the hardest thing to get right in the whole of poetry, that kind of casualness. My old man used to quote Frost. His taste ran more to Bridges and Longfellow, but he liked Frost. He'd come back for supper from his rounds, gripping his black bag, dog-tired, and he'd quote that bit, you know: "The woods are lovely, dark and deep, But I have promises to keep— " '

' "And miles to go before I sleep, And miles to go before I sleep." ' Helen bent over Douglas in the chair, her yellow robe open, her breasts unpicked apples under heaven. 'Come on, darling. I can't sleep, either, when you're not there.'

Douglas pulled her towards him and kissed her. She offered no resistance, but when he made to take off her robe she stepped back.

'I'm going to bed,' she declared. 'It's my first dress rehearsal tomorrow.'

'Poppet— '

'Will you switch everything off before you come?'

Frowning, he turned off the light. This was unlike her, even before a performance. The way their game went, she would come to him like a lost thing, an orphan in the storm, and he would put his arms round her comfortingly. She would sit in his lap and he would cuddle her, waiting for her to put her face up to be kissed like a baby, her eyes half-closed, her mouth pouting that the kiss was not already bestowed. Then he would pick her up in his arms and carry her through to the bedroom, muttering little endearments, baby words, and licking her ear. Passive, unblinking, she would let herself be undressed, put to bed and tucked up like a doll – except that she never wanted to leave go of him, she was always holding on to something, his tie, his belt, his arm, even while he was attempting to take his clothes off before getting in with her and showing her, father-like, what to do to bring him all the way.

Tonight, she had started the game and then broken the rules. Or had she? There was another game they used to play in the early days, he remembered now. She would tease him, stroke him, arouse him and then run away. He had chased her, grabbed at her, missed her, run after her again, pretended to get angry, threatened to punish her, to put her across his knee – finally catching her in the bedroom where she stood contrite, chastened, as rapt as he for what was to follow.

Stumbling over a Numdah rug in his hurry, Douglas trotted after his wife. He opened doors and shut them; he blundered round ostentatiously in the dark. But Helen wasn't leading him on at all. When he reached the bedroom she was sitting up in bed with a magazine. She put it down and stared at him.

'What were you making all that noise for?'

Douglas didn't reply. His back turned, he took off his clothes and hung them up.

'Is there something wrong?' he demanded.

'No. Nothing. Why?'

He stared at her. She was looking prettier than he'd ever seen her, her cheeks flushed, her eyes sparkling.

'What is it?' he asked again.

'Nothing.'

'Are you sure?'

'Of course I am.'

'Come to me, then, my pretty poppet, my baby-love. Come and let me hold you tight.'

Obediently Helen came to him. He could feel the tenseness in her, it was like holding a stringed instrument. He stroked her hair. He would have to play her carefully, tune her to the right pitch. He stroked her, and touched her. She lay still.

At last, when he could wait no longer, Douglas lifted himself over her, still murmuring the words they always used into the stillness below him. No response.

'Do you love me?'

Helen took his face between her hands. 'Of course I love you, my darling. I want you and need you and love you. . . . '

But it was no use. She stiffened every time he touched her. He rolled aside and lay looking up at the ceiling. Moonlight cut across it like a dagger pointing at the door.

'You've changed,' he told her.

'You're imagining things.'

Propped up on one shoulder, Douglas gazed down at her impassivity. All at once he felt a terrible jealousy. It came from nowhere, it had no name, but it rose in a bitter taste to the back of his throat until he felt like spitting. All that he loved in Helen – her feline grace, her self-centredness, her beauty, her intelligence – should now be at his mercy, pleading to be cherished and protected, leading him on. That was how it was played. And here she was, refusing her part in it.

With a groan he lay back and closed his eyes. He tried to tell himself that he'd witnessed this transformation before, when Helen was about to open in a play; that this was the chaste Isabella who lay beside him. Then Helen turned and got out of bed. She went to the window and pulled tight the curtains, cutting out the moonlight. He felt her lift up the sheet and crawl in on top of him. Curling up her cool body like a caterpillar on an autumn leaf, she rested her small dark head beneath his chin.

'I think we can do better next time, don't you, Daddykins?' she murmured.

'Oh, Helen. Oh, my baby.'

'Put your arms around me, Daddykins. That's right. Baby's so cold and sleepy . . . so sleepy, that's what it is. But next time Baby will make up for it. Promise, promise.'

'Oh, my baby.'

'Sleep now.'

The milk-bottles that Sunday morning arrived on the Manifolds' doorstep with a crown and the letters 'ER' embossed on the silver bottle-cap. As Nick Kemp drove Georgina to lunch at the South Australian Hotel, the verges were sprouting red, white and blue. Workmen were testing the jets on a brand-new ornamental fountain in Pennington Gardens.

Nick was telling her about Winn Vellacott, a man he'd known from his schooldays.

'Is he very political?' asked Georgina, remembering what he'd said about Edward Catchpole.

'Political? There aren't any political journalists in Adelaide to touch him; you won't find a better one in Australia. Winn lives and breathes politics. He knows where to look for the skeletons. I've heard some people say that he's over the hill, he's gone to seed, but don't believe it, pal. I grant you that he looks that way sometimes, after he's passed out behind the filing-cabinets in the *Gazette* after a hard night picking up gossip in the bars, and his deputy's had to kick him awake and pour black coffee down his throat. But Winn's powers of recovery are phenomenal. He's never more alert than when he looks as if he's about to topple forward into his whisky chaser. He's drunk me under the table a couple of times, and there aren't many can do that.'

For an instant Georgina felt a clutch at her heart again at the gulf between the Captain Kemp of her dreams and the man sitting beside her. She liked him enormously now. But, since Mannum, she had found herself constantly puzzling why two successful men in their middle age should still be planning boys' adventures together, as if searching for some grand design in order to make sense of their lives.

She asked: 'Where does he come from?'

'Winn? An Irish Catholic; you'll learn to tell these things. A solid labour man all his life. Some people say his pieces are prejudiced against the English since his wife . . . well, that's how it is.'

'What about his wife?'

'Mm?'

'His wife. You were saying about his wife.'

'Yes . . . well, this isn't for repeating: she ran off with a Brit a couple of years ago. He owned a chain of vending machines, penny-in-the-slot. There were some pretty obvious jokes. Winn cracked a few heads; nearly lost his job. But old Winn, he's never been grudging in his prejudices. He hates Menzies. He distrusts the South Australian government at least as much as he distrusts the Brits. Take it up with him and he'll quote you his great hero, H. L. Mencken' – Nick imitated Winn's high bark – ' "I tell you it's no more possible to live in the world without picking up its prejudices than it is to go to Hell without perspiring!" '

They turned along North Terrace. The Saturday shopping traffic had slowed to a crawl between the Royal Visit stands. The Holden pick-up was overheating. Near the War Memorial, Nick drove up on the pavement and opened the bonnet.

'Pass my cap, pal!' he called to her.

Georgina picked his stained engineer's cap off the floor and clambered out. Using it as a glove, Nick opened up the radiator with a great hissing which scattered the pavement shoppers. He went to the pool behind the War Memorial and returned with his cap full of water which he poured into the radiator.

'The dead have their uses,' he said.

'Is it yours?' asked Georgina climbing back in.

'This old bomb? No. It belongs to a friend. It's crook, but I hire it from him because he needs the money. Back in Melbourne,' he added drily, 'I'll have you know I drive a Mercedes with automatic transmission. That's the life I'm staying clear of.'

'But what do you *do*?' Georgina was striving to imagine Nick in a suit and tie.

'I run a geo-survey outfit. We work for the oil companies, mostly. Anywhere in Australia they want to prospect for oil, I send people out to produce the geophysical contour maps. If it's an aerial survey, I go out myself in the Tiger Moth.'

105

Georgina was just settling for a mental picture of Nick in a pilot's helmet and goggles when he pulled in beside the South Australian Hotel. They walked under the wide veranda and up through the chandeliered entrance hall to the Terrace Bar. Winn had already gone through to the dining-room. They found him sitting at the table with a napkin round his neck and a schooner of beer in his hand, his mouth full of buttered roll. He gestured at them to sit down.

'You've heard,' he said when he could speak.

'Heard what?'

'Richard Schneider. He's been found dead.'

When this dramatic statement made no impression he waved his roll impatiently. 'Schneider. Doctor Schneider. The man who wrote that piece years ago for the *Journal of Science*, which the British wouldn't let him publish.'

Nick frowned. 'You mean the biochemist who worked for CSIRO?'

'Yes. Head of the CSIRO research division of human and animal nutrition at Adelaide University. Found dead, no further details. I've just been talking to Eddie Roberts, head of university biology. He doesn't know any more than I do, but he's worried.'

'This article . . . ' Nick began.

'Exactly. The article. It was at the time of the British A-tests in the bush in the mid-fifties. I saw a proof copy. Schneider was a world expert on the effects of fallout. He conducted thousands of tests on sheep. He concluded that radioactive fallout over Adelaide would get into the food chain through grazing animals and fish in the streams, and the levels were sufficiently high that they would eliminate the reproductive systems of humans and animals.'

Nick burst out laughing. 'Schools are full,' he said.

'It's no joke, Nick. The Brits chose Schneider because he was the best. He collected animal thyroids, he studied Iodine 131 concentrations . . . and the Brits and the Australian safety committee under Ernest Titterton, they just rejected the whole thing. He couldn't publish. I tried to get to see him, but he wouldn't talk to me. He'd signed the Official Secrets Act.'

Nick called a waiter over. When they had ordered

lunch, Winn embarked on a more scientific explanation, until Nick waved the white flag of his napkin.

'Okay. Understood. But you haven't explained what all this has got to do with today. You tell me that Doctor Schneider is dead. That he was found dead in the biochemistry lab—'

'Still working on food chains—'

'Yes. But what of it? The atomic tests are old history.'

'I don't know, is the answer. But something's wrong, Nick. This town is full of top brass from England, all keeping their heads down. . . . '

'The Queen's coming here, pal. The Queen. Royalty. Not your favourite topic, I'm well aware. But you know that top brass come with the package.'

The journalist shook his head and stared dolefully at the plates of steaming oxtail soup put down in front of them.

Georgina was looking at the soup as well. She said nervously: 'It was Dr Schneider that our biology teacher mentioned last week, I think. A connection with that unknown disease the cattle have been getting. She said this famous Adelaide scientist had been doing research—'

Winn Vellacott and Nick spoke together. 'And?'

'And was looking for the answer. That was all, really. Sorry. I was trying to remember where I'd heard his name.'

The three of them looked down in silence at the soup in front of them. Nick put on a solemn face.

'I saw a film about peanut butter in Melbourne,' he declared. 'An all-American couple had lost their way in New Mexico. After driving for hours across an empty plain, they arrived at a nice suburban bungalow. They'd been getting worried because they'd heard there was an atomic test site in the area, so seeing this made them a lot happier. Nobody answered the bell, but the kitchen door was open so they went in and made themselves peanut butter sandwiches. Then they saw the bungalow was occupied. A man and a woman were sitting watching television. They rushed in to apologise, and realised that the television wasn't switched on; they were dummy people. . . . ' Nick started to laugh.

'Why?' asked Georgina, beginning to giggle herself. 'Don't be mean! What happened?'

'What happened was that the young lady with me let out a loud scream which almost got us thrown out of the cinema, because of course this was the bomb zone, this was ground zero. There was a great explosion – *boom!* – and a heap of timber on the ground, and slowly, slowly the planks begin to move. . . .'

'Yes!'

'And the all-American couple crawl out and of course they're okay because if you eat peanut butter sandwiches it protects you from atomic radiation, *and*— '

'Mm?'

'So does oxtail soup!'

Gurgling with laughter, Georgina tasted the oxtail. It was hot and peppery and appetising. Soon only Winn sat with the soup in front of him: then he, too, began to spoon it up, if not with such a good grace as the others. Patting his mouth with the napkin, he turned back to Georgina.

'So how is my super-sleuth? My double agent in enemy territory?'

Blushing, Georgina explained to Nick how Edward Catchpole had come into their lives. 'It's not enemy territory!' she protested. 'Really, none of us knows him, except Helen plays tennis with him sometimes. And the other one. . . .'

'Collins. Major Collins.'

'Yes. Well, I don't think my father knows him well. He never mentions his name.'

'Ah.'

Nick said: 'Winn, don't come the raw prawn with me. Who are these characters?'

'Collins is head of the British defence liaison team in Canberra. Seconded from Intelligence, according to my sources; he worked in Army Intelligence in London after the war.' He shot a glance at Georgina. 'Not what you might call a natural for ushering Her Majesty through her social engagements. And Catchpole's not the kind of bloke who's ever shaken a champagne-bottle before popping the cork.'

'What's his job?'

'Head of Royal security. Supposedly. But he's too senior to be doing a job like that.' Vellacott banged the table in frustration. 'They're not talking. None of them will talk. I've staked 'em out and all I get is a handshake and baloney about the hot weather. But there's something happening, I know. There's something out there.' He shook his head and took a gulp of beer. 'How about you, Nick? Found your gold reef yet?'

Nick Kemp's pause was fractional. 'I'll come up with something.'

'You always have, mate.' Vellacott winked at Georgina. 'Has Nick told you about the haunted house?'

'What haunted house?'

'Up at Riverland Corner. Friends of mine live there. They'd hear this sort of roaring, fluttering noise on dark nights. I spent a night with them once and heard it; I've never been so shit-scared in my life. Nick was passing through. I got him to come up and take a look. There was a derelict barn nearby, built on sandy river-flats. Nick found footprints and followed them, and where the wind had swept through the barn and swept the sand he found – didn't you? – dozens of human teeth and bits of yellowing skeleton. Wait, I'll tell you. The barn had been built over an old Aboriginal burial-ground. The Abos had held ceremonies there since the dreamtime. This old blackfella was coming along with what they must have used – a bull-roarer, pieces of wood on the end of a string which he'd whirl round his head and it would make this banshee din. He showed it to us, before Nick got him to go away. My mates pulled the barn down: maybe that's why he never felt the need to come back. D'you suppose, Nick? You know more about Abos than I do.'

Nick nodded. Their steaks had arrived, and he was eating. After a moment he said: 'Make a note of that, Georgina. A headline for the *South Australian Gazette*. "Winn Vellacott Sensation! Fabled Local Journo Admits to Not Knowing Everything!" '

'Go jump in the lake, mate. I'm off to take a leak.'

'He's not himself,' said Nick lightly, when the journalist had weaved out between the tables. 'See, he's hardly touched his steak. He's like a blackfella when he's hunting a story, Winn. He hardly eats or drinks until he's tracked it down and delivered the *coup de grâce*. If we let him into our deadly secret about the green stone, it will be all over the *Gazette* tomorrow, friend or no friend.'

'If I'd been his wife, I'd have run off, too,' exclaimed Georgina. She giggled again, for no reason. She was drinking cider, in memory of that lunch with Nick at school all those years ago, and Winn must have ordered the alcoholic kind because it was making her head spin.

'It's not malice, pal. It's commitment. Winn's idealistic. He's on the side of the angels. If you ask him, he'll say: "Listen, mate! South Australia started life as a free province. I want to see it stay that way!" '

Georgina put her finger to her lips. Winn Vellacott stalked back to their table, buttoning his flies. 'Listen, I've got to push off. I'm seeing Martin Amory at three o'clock.'

Georgina gave a start. 'Oh. Are you?'

'What's that?'

'I'm going there for tea this afternoon,' she said. 'Not with Sir Martin. With Robyn, his daughter.'

'Fine. Let's go.'

'Now?'

'Yes. You don't mind getting there early, do you, sweetheart? We'll leave Nick to settle the bill.'

With a wink at Nick, Winn gestured for the bill. 'No worries,' he said. 'This is on expenses. Old man Murdoch will pick up the tab.'

Behind Winn's back, Nick Kemp nodded at her. Georgina saw, and understood. She would play along. She waited for Winn Vellacott to sign the chit, then she went out with him to stand under the portico while he waved his arm at taxis. On the wide balcony above her head she could hear the discreet clamour of a wedding reception, people meeting and greeting. An immense loneliness descended upon her; she belonged nowhere and to no one. All her anchors were up, and she felt that she was dragging them, pulling on them like the strings of the puppet fathers she'd played with long ago.

'Georgina!'

She looked around. It sounded like Dirk Miller's voice. Then she saw Winn, standing by a taxi.

'Georgina!'

Obediently she ran down the steps.

It took them more than forty minutes to reach Glen Osmond. On Princes Highway they sweltered in a traffic jam while a police car and two ambulances weaved through in a clangour of sirens. Winn grew excited. He stuck his head and most of his body out of the cab window, trying to see what the trouble was. At one point he got out and began hurrying down the road on foot; but then the traffic started moving and Georgina had to hold the door open so that he could hurl himself back in.

'Looks like another messy one,' he panted. 'That'll be the ninth in town this month with deaths or serious injuries. I don't know what's happening; Adelaide's gone bush. Drivers doing crazy things – turning into major roads without looking, going the wrong way down the dual carriageway, running down the High School football coach on a pedestrian crossing. . . .'

'It's the heat,' suggested Georgina. She could feel the leather seat sticking uncomfortably to her back through her thin blouse.

'That's what people always say. The heat gets blamed for everything.'

Slowly they crawled past the accident, a policeman diverting them down the middle of the highway. A green Ford Zephyr lay on its back over a fence, its wheels in the air. It appeared to have driven up on the pavement (for no visible reason) with such impetus that it had careered into the air, overturned and impaled itself on the iron railings. Firemen were working around the wreck, from which there came a buzzing, flapping, shrieking noise such as Georgina supposed the Riverland Corner bull-roarer must have made. She averted her eyes, though not before noticing that what she had taken to be a woman's arm hanging through the car window was – horrors – a leg covered in blood.

'Are you okay?' asked Winn Vellacott.

'I think so.'

'It's not far to go. I saw one of our boys there, so there's no point in stopping.' Vellacott sounded disappointed. 'Did you see the Abo woman talking to the police, holding her baby?'

111

'No.'

'I think she may have been walking in the middle of the road and the driver swerved. They do that sometimes, you see, Abos in from the bush. You'll hear silly gossip that it's a deathwish. My guess is, the poor bastards just get confused.'

'Or hostile.'

'Hostile?'

'I was just thinking. . . . ' Actually about the Aborigine and the fire he'd built on the hill above Mountfoot . . . measure for measure in a sort of way. She'd seen it in his face, too – the blankness, the awful spiritlessness, like the Masaccio 'Expulsion from Paradise'. Except that the cause of *his* loss was not the stealing of knowledge but having knowledge stolen from him – that magical knowledge which Aborigines lost when they were expelled from the places of their dreaming, without which all other forms of knowledge, she supposed, must seem ungrounded, like all of one's past detaching itself and floating out of reach.

But Winn Vellacott wouldn't know about that. She looked at him and saw the brown snuff-stains around his nostrils. It evidently needed a lot of extra help, keeping on the side of the angels.

'Is there anything else you can tell me about Catchpole?'

The sudden question flustered her. 'Why? I mean, I don't think there is. He took Helen and me on the rehearsal for the Royal Visit. He seemed okay. A bit stuffy. He didn't say much, except about the security.'

'What sort of security?'

'Oh, for the Royal Progress. Special police, and armed officers in the crowds. Troops, if need be.'

'Troops!' The man from the *South Australian Gazette* scribbled in his notebook. 'That's one I hadn't heard before. Did he mention any names you can remember? Major Collins, for example?'

Georgina shook her head.

'What about the PM, Robert Menzies? No? There's a good old Empire Royalist that Catchpole would get on with. Your father, too.'

He relapsed into silence.

'Why don't you like my father?' Georgina asked abruptly.

'Don't get me wrong. I've got nothing personal against your old man. It's what he represents. Look at it this way, Georgie. For the greater part of our short history we Australians have been convicts and the children of convicts. We throw off those shackles – and what do we do? We put on cultural chains instead, letting the Brits write our history for us. We're a nation of bloody recidivists!'

The taxi dropped them at Mountfoot. Winn Vellacott had his notebook in his hand and what looked like the same stub of yellow pencil he'd brought to Wellington Square. Anxious not to disturb his interview with Sir Martin, Georgina disappeared round the side of the house and went looking for Robyn. Not finding her, she returned to the veranda and settled in the hammock, where she could look down over the wide clearing of lawn towards Adelaide, half-hidden by the eucalyptus trees.

She'd last spent time with Robyn Amory on Australia Day. Robyn had just passed her driving test; she borrowed her father's old Hillman and they drove down the coast to Moana, the place where (so Robyn said) the surfies hung out in search of a good reef-break.

It seemed to Georgina, lying back sleepily in the hammock, that, not finding any surfies to make fun of, she and Robyn had gone on after that to somebody's twenty-first party down in Port Victor . . . but her eyes were closing . . . it had to be the cider . . . and when she thought about the smorgasbord lunch they had eaten on trestle tables in the garden to the sound of 'Devil Woman' (or was it 'Sealed with a Kiss'?) it was not Robyn but Dirk Miller sitting beside her, and the smorgasbord had somehow transformed itself into a tropical salad eaten out of scooped pineapples at a 'Night in Hawaii' organised by Edward Catchpole . . . and she was wearing a muu-muu in hibiscus colours and dancing hulas with Dirk (who looked half the time like James Dean and half the time like Elvis Presley) while Helen Manifold, dressed in a patterned blouse tied with a large pussy bow and a piecrust frill of white organza on her skewered hat, stood watching on the sidelines.

She could not have dozed for very long, because when she woke with a start she could hear raised voices through the open door. One of them was Winn Vellacott's. They had come into the garden-room; she couldn't think why. Unless Sir Martin

113

Amory had walked away from an argument and the journalist had pursued him.

'*You must have had an idea,*' Winn was saying.

'*Why? Why should I? I wasn't the keeper of Schneider's conscience!*'

'*Martin, you were good mates, you told me so. You worked together on those British tests in the fifties.*'

'*Yes, the fifties!*'

'*And you stopped the same time he did. You felt that the truth about radiation hazards wasn't coming out—*'

'*It's common knowledge! I've made no secret of my views!*'

'*But you kept in touch with Schneider! You corresponded. You compared notes—*'

'*Not on everything—*'

'*On fallout! Fallout levels over Adelaide—*'

'*Richard Schneider had his own figures. Other people had different ones. That's all I'm prepared to say, Winn. Go and talk to the Australian Safety Committee. Talk to Ernest Titterton.*'

'*Come on, Martin! Give it to me straight. What was he working on? Why did Schneider kill himself?*'

'*You've got no evidence.*'

'*When you—*'

'*No evidence!*'

'*When you walked out of the A-test programme you said something I made a note of. . . .*'

Georgina could hear the rustle of Vellacott's notebook.

'*You said – here it is, you said that science has a tolerance level in nuclear weaponry, just as the body has a tolerance level in the treatment of cancers. . . .*'

There was a silence in the garden-room. Georgina listened.

'*Martin, I'm sorry, old mate. It wasn't personal.*'

'*I'll tell you this much, Winn. And then you get out of my house. Richard Schneider – yes, he'd restarted soil and air sampling. Also collecting thyroid glands of sheep on the Glenthorne research farm, to check radioactive iodine levels. What his laboratory calculations show, I haven't the faintest idea. Maybe he didn't finish them. That's all. That's it. You know your way out.*'

Steps came towards the veranda door. Georgina froze. There was nowhere to run and hide. She shut her eyes and pretended to be asleep. The footsteps – Sir Martin's, she thought – came out past her and crunched on the gravel, fading away round the side of the house.

She opened her eyes, and slid out of the hammock. Her legs felt shaky. What radioactive iodine levels were she had no idea, nor what the Australian Safety Committee were supposed to be making safe. Dirk might know. She would ask him. But that mention of cancer – and Winn Vellacott's hasty apology – and the tone of Sir Martin's voice when he replied . . .

Georgina hurried down on to the lawn. Fresh smells of eucalyptus and juniper came to her on the breeze. She turned to look back at Mountfoot. At an upper window again she saw it – an old woman, pale and wrinkled, the skin drawn as tight as a death's-head, who twitched the curtain and was gone.

She drew a deep breath. Out in the sun emptiness it was scarcely possible to believe in a sky that wasn't blue, in air that wasn't as clear and pure as the living things it nourished. But her heart was knocking in her chest like earth on a coffin, and when she saw Robyn wheeling her bike up the drive she ran to meet her, in a terror of being alone.

G eorgina kept track of Helen Callender's rôles in the theatre simply in order to know which productions to avoid seeing. Once, last year, when a group of sixth-formers from Malvern had been taken to London to see *The Apple Cart*, Georgina did not discover until she got there and read the programme that Helen had taken over as Orinthia, the female lead. As they all piled down to the stalls, Georgina hung back and fled up a corridor which took her to the street. From a coffee-shop opposite she watched and waited till the play was over. The next day she was up before the headmistress, who accepted her stifled explanation with such a gentle unbending of her usual severity that Georgina left her study with tears in her eyes.

This time, though, there was no escape. Helen's play was running for a full week. On the first night, a Wednesday, she put on a black dress (what Helen had once in her hearing called 'George's crematorium dress') and went in the car with her father. They had to park some way away, on Frome Road, and walk in under the lights of an outside broadcast crew from Adelaide's television news station. A reporter pushed a microphone in her face.

'Excuse me, young lady, are you Georgina?'

'I beg your pardon?'

'Are you Helen Callender's daughter Georgina?'

'No. I'm sorry. She doesn't have a daughter.'

By this stratagem she was safely away up the steps and into the crowded lobby. Ornamental bronzes leered down at them from the lime-green walls. Douglas was cornered by newspapermen, and assumed a practised smile. She noticed the silver in his hair.

She felt a hand on her arm. She refused to look round. A familiar voice in her ear said: 'This had better be good, Georgie. I've missed a real good stock-car race at the Bonython Stadium to come here tonight.'

'Dirk!'

116

He gave her a very casual kiss on the forehead. 'I thought your dad was supposed to be the famous one?'

'It runs in the family.'

'So what are *you* famous for?'

She considered this. 'For being unlike anyone else you know!' she declared.

He laughed. 'I'll say.'

Her father was calling her. But she had the tickets. Dirk had taken her arm.

'Sally says it's your birthday on Friday,' he said.

'Yes.'

'You busy?'

She considered again. 'I don't know.'

'How about if I take you out dancing? The Penny Rockers are on at the Greek Hall, Friday night. Okay?'

Dancing at the Greek Hall. The idea filled her with horror. She shook her head.

'Okay?' persisted Dirk.

'I can't. Sorry.' Shakily: 'I'll probably have to stay in for a birthday dinner. You know, I'm really sorry.'

He stared at her. 'You kidding?'

'My father's calling,' she said. 'Look, some other time?'

Dirk shrugged. 'I'll give you a bell, maybe,' he said. And stalked off.

Douglas came up and took her arm. They went in. The auditorium was filling up. Georgina could see the large pink head of Edward Catchpole in the third row. Their own seats were further back. Douglas greeted a man she hadn't seen before, dressed in a dark suit, with silver close-cropped hair and an intelligent face. As she waited to be introduced, the lights went down and the man hurried forward to join Edward Catchpole near the front.

As one of the set texts for the Certificate, Georgina had read *Measure for Measure* and found it hateful. Angelo's lust and Claudio's bravery and fear she could understand. The Duke of Vienna's petty and complicated machinations seemed to her as stagy as pantomime. As for Isabella, she was surely the most contrary creature in the whole of Shakespeare – ice-cold, self-obsessed, lacking in any glimmer of humanity, so that at the end she could scream imprecations at her brother Claudio and welcome his death, because he had weakened enough to beg her to save his life by sleeping with Angelo. Reading the part, Georgina had read her stepmother into it – her coldness, her self-interest, her sharp wit – and she fully expected her to play Isabella to perfection on stage.

And so she did. But not as Georgina could have anticipated, or anyone else, except perhaps for a man in the third row. Helen's Isabella was no frigid old maid but a young woman struggling to control an almost insupportable sexual desire. Her white novice's robes had blood-red hems and cuffs, and from her very first words, hoping for strict restraints upon the nuns of St Clare, she came before the Adelaide audience as a divided soul. Her chaste novice was the more tormented by guilt as her lust for Angelo grew, a lust fuelled by their thrusts and parries of argument over Claudio's life. Her breast heaving, her face flushed, her lips parted, Helen's Isabella devoured Angelo with her eyes even as she spurned his advances:

> '. . . were I under the terms of death,
> Th'impression of keen whips I'ld wear as rubies,
> And strip myself to death as to a bed
> That longing have been sick for, ere I'ld yield
> My body up to shame.'

Here was the feverish guilt which explained Isabella's self-tormenting rage at her brother Claudio; here the desire for Angelo which justified her calling upon the Duke to forgive him! Georgina sat enthralled, unable to look at her father beside her. No wonder Shakespeare gave Isabella nothing to say at the final curtain! How could she bear to be paired off with the witless Duke when it was Angelo she coveted with all her heart! And as the play ended it was not the Duke's pompous dispensations which held every eye in the Union Hall, but Isabella's unexpected motion of yearning and despair towards the disgraced Angelo, forced to wed Mariana the go-between.

Not until it was over did Georgina notice that several people had apparently walked out. Although the restrained applause grew much louder when Isabella came forward in her white-and-red to take a bow, a number of parents who had brought their children were muttering in affronted voices.

'Sex and filth all the way through. Fancy letting children—'

'A disgrace!'

'Sex on the brain, Shakespeare had.'

'Did you see how she looked at him? A nun and flaunting herself!'

'It should *never* have been a set play. I shall complain to the Examinations Board. . . . '

And a loud male voice: 'What a sheila to stuff in a nunnery!'

Douglas and Georgina slipped through a side-door and went backstage. Douglas was oddly quiet. He had passed no comment on the production. His jaw was tight; a dull redness had settled on his cheekbones. Georgina, following him, quickened to the excitement in the air, the embraces, the flurry of congratulations and messages. If it was like this in Adelaide, what must it be like in the West End?

Alone of the cast, Helen had her own dressing-room. Edward Catchpole had got there before them. Bearing in his arms a large bunch of yellow hothouse roses in crackly paper, he hovered behind the chair in which Helen Callender was sitting in a scarlet *peignoir*, her face mask-white with make-up remover. Around the edges of the mirror she had stuck good-luck telegrams signed by people Georgina had never heard of.

She turned up the mask of her face to them and smiled. 'Was I good?' she asked.

'Fabulous! You were fabulous!' Georgina bubbled.

Douglas did not reply. Helen repeated her question.

'Wasn't I good?'

'You,' said Douglas heavily, 'were a revelation.'

'Thank you, my darlings. George, will you make your father supper tonight? I've got a bloody first-night party with the cast, it could go on for ever. You'll find escalopes in the fridge.'

Georgina nodded. Edward Catchpole was still standing there with his sunburst of flowers, dwarfing the room. She said politely: 'You must have enjoyed it, too, Mr Catchpole.'

'*Enjoy* is not the word I would employ, Georgina. It was magnificent. Caviare to the general.'

'Ah!' Helen laughed; the tinkle of ice in an empty glass. 'Dear Edward, thank you. If you wait a moment, I'll find some water to put them in.'

Douglas took a step back, as if the sweetness of everything was setting his teeth on edge. Helen's wimple lay abandoned on the floor. He bent to pick it up, then checked himself.

'Well, I think there are too many generals in here,' he declared abruptly. 'Georgina, are you coming?'

Away from the overheated dressing-rooms there was a chill in the air. Outside, Georgina looked around for Dirk. The thrill of Helen's performance was beginning to wear off, to be followed by a feeling of her own inadequacy. She looked down at her small, annoyingly pudgy hands, milk-white under the street-light. Helen was so expressive, the way she motioned with her hands, her long fingers. If you were beautiful and expressive, what did it matter being such a cow? Men were still attracted to you, loved you, forgave you. As they walked back to the car – Douglas moodily striding ahead – she saw Dirk standing with a group of students by the Mawson Laboratories. Putting her hands in the pockets of her skirts, she bent her head and hurried on in her father's footsteps.

Georgina was asleep in Wellington Square by the time her stepmother walked that same route, in the opposite direction. A tall figure kept pace with her in the darkness.

'It must be under the dressing-table,' Helen repeated.

'Was there anything valuable in it?' asked Edward Catchpole. 'Addresses? Billets-doux? Anything from me?'

'All you damn well think about, you men of secrets.' Helen was slurring her words a little. 'Discovery. Betrayal. Compromise. All in the scope of one, of one *handbag*. Who cares?' She gave a hoot of delighted laughter. 'Did you watch Mariana doing her dance at the moated grange tonight? She insisted on it, you know. This town is full of Isadora Duncans attempting self-expression without having anything to express.'

'She cornered me, your Mariana, when I came to take you to dinner. Announced she was Italian. I think her Mediterranean culture extends all the way to making lampstands out of Chianti bottles.'

Shaking with suppressed mirth, they reached the Union Hall. It was in darkness. Helen stopped by a side-door. Putting her finger to her lips, she drew a key out of her pocket and turned the lock. Catchpole vetted the shadows; there was nobody about. Silently they flitted into the theatre and made their way backstage.

Her dressing-room was unlocked. Helen pushed open the door and switched on the light. Her bag was invisible under a towel beneath the dressing-table; she went immediately to it, almost as if she had hidden it there. Catchpole closed the door and shot the bolt. He strode over to the cupboard and pulled back the curtain. Isabella's vestments hung there demurely.

'Put it on,' he demanded.

'Put what on?'

He yanked the nun's habit off the hanger, his hands bruising the white linen with sweat. 'Put it on!'

'Don't be silly. Someone might come.'

Edward Catchpole took two quick steps towards her. Helen flinched. Bending his head, he whispered fiercely: 'There's no one here. Now, put it on!'

She reached up her arms around his neck to kiss him. He pulled them down. He began plucking at her dress, as if plucking feathers off a bird. If she'd been his porcelain, he'd be breaking it.

She took a step back. His hands followed her.

'*Be that you are. That is, a woman.*'

'Edward, stop. Stop!'

She undid her blue dress and pulled it over her head. She kicked off her shoes. Edward Catchpole was running the red-and-white robe through his hands. Something he had said about his Japanese plates and bowls . . . he had contrasted their cold prettiness with the violent heat of their kiln-firing, melting the felspar glaze. She took off her petticoat and stockings, beginning to giggle now. Edward had become quite still.

'*If you are one . . . show it now, By putting on the destined livery.*'

'Edward! Stop it!'

She snatched Isabella's habit from him and covered her nakedness. Edward Catchpole picked up the wimple. He placed it over her head and shoulders, smoothing its folds over her breasts until her nipples stood hard to the touch of his fingers.

'I'm drunk,' she said. 'You must be, too. Two drunks, darling.'

'Look at yourself,' he commanded.

Helen turned round. In the dressing-room mirror, framed in the soft glow of the bulbs, she saw Isabella, naked beneath the

121

cotton robe of the Poor Clares. Her face reddened. She threw back her head, as if the triumph of a few hours ago was borne in on her afresh. Hands pressed into her shoulders and pushed her roughly forward.

'Look closer at yourself,' said Edward Catchpole.

Bending over the chair she stared at Isabella. Her mouth opened; her tongue came out between her little teeth and licked her lips. Isabella unfrocked.

'He was panting for me,' she whispered.

With one hand Catchpole was pressing her down. With the other he pulled up her habit, high above her hips. He parted her legs with the toe of his polished shoe.

'Read your telegrams,' he said.

'Read— ?'

'Going around the mirror. Starting at the top. Read them out to me.'

'No, what— ?'

'Read them, damn you!'

Tears started to Helen's eyes. Her hands scattered pots of cream, nail files, make-up pads on the dressing-table as he moved her back and forth against him.

'*To the greatest actress in the world. . . . Good luck as if you need it! . . . To a great beauty and a greater star. . . .*'

'More!'

'*From your devoted fans up here. . . . Best wishes to the most beautiful woman on the English-speaking stage. . . . Good luck, darling and God bless. . . .* Oh!'

'Go on! Go on!'

'*Good luck, you will be fabulous, you always are. . . .* Oh! *. . . Best wishes for a night to remember. . . .* Oh God, yes, yes. . . . *To the best and loveliest. . . .* Go on! Don't stop! *. . .* Oh! Oh!'

Helen let out a long-drawn sigh of self-satisfaction. Her head sank forward; hair covered her face. Edward Catchpole lowered her and let her go. Blindly she felt for tissues on the table. She handed some to him. Catchpole buttoned his trousers. He had let out not so much as a groan of pleasure, but his face and scalp glowed darkly pink and beads of sweat glistened on his nose. He removed his glasses and wiped the mist off them.

'What did you see?' he demanded.

'Mm?'

'When you looked in the mirror.'

'What did I see? I saw a great actress. And a great lover.'

Edward Catchpole chuckled. He seemed to be about to make a retort. Instead he put his glasses back on and picked up Helen's bag. Handing it to her, he said: 'You'd better check and see there isn't anything missing.'

The time according to the clocks was 7.30 in the evening. Throughout South Australia families were quarrelling about which of them should get up and switch over the television from 'Andy Hardy' to 'Rawhide'; while somewhere above them in the sky a communications satellite was slowly, silently disintegrating as it circled the planet Earth.

Astronomers at Jodrell Bank now reckon it could fall right over Australia, so if you're going out tonight take your umbrella, said the chummy voice on Georgina Manifold's radio. *Now, here's one I'm dedicating to that satellite up there, so stick out your antennas, whoops, antennae, for Brenda Lee's latest single soaring in the charts:*

> *All alone am I,*
> *Since you said goodbye,*
> *All alone with just the beat of my heart. . . .*

Georgina curled up on her bed, turned down the page of D. H. Lawrence's *Kangaroo* and shut the book. Her head on the pillow, she surveyed the other presents she had been given: a Voigtlander camera from her father, an ostentatious box of make-up from Helen, a batik from Robyn Amory and the new *Aloha Elvis* LP from Sally Miller. On this her seventeenth birthday she felt as if she was coming out of the mists of childhood into what was turning into a thicker fog.

Helen was at the theatre. Her father presumably was working downstairs. He had offered to take her out to dinner, but he was really much too busy, she could see that. She'd turned him down, as she'd turned Dirk down, as perhaps she would turn down all the men in her life.

> *No use in holding other hands*
> *For I'd be holding only emptiness*

Every second hit these days was a dirge about loneliness. Helen Shapiro, Craig Douglas, Acker Bilk, Elvis crooning 'Are You Lonesome Tonight?' Georgina visualised an entire world of Little Miss Lonelys sitting by their transistor radios being serenaded by disembodied voices – and at this comfortless thought she sat up and threw the book aside. She, Georgina, was not like that. Listen, she could be out on the town with Dirk Miller right at this moment, if she'd wanted to be like Sally, or Robyn even, and tag along as a kind of dumb tailpiece to anything Dirk wanted to do or say. Either way, she sacrificed herself. It wasn't the dancing she hated so much as being made silly and ordinary and taken-for-granted. . . . But where did that leave you? It left her here, alone, high and dry in her bedroom on her seventeenth birthday, listening to the radio, while stupid uncomplicated uncursed people like Dirk's sister went out, flirting and enjoying themselves.

> *People all around*
> *But I don't hear a sound,*
> *Just the lonely beating of my heaaa—*

She cut off Brenda Lee in mid-dirge and went to sit and look at herself in the glass. Probably she was self-destructive by nature; fated to live by herself for the rest of her days. One of the lonely people. On the shelf. While Robyn and Sally went out and had fun, got married, had a family. . . .

The silence was unbearable. Georgina turned the radio back on. *Learn the tremendous possibilities of your own mind,* a deep slow voice was saying. *Explore that mysterious world within you. The free book 'The Mastery of Life' explains how you can master the everyday problems of life and find happiness. Write to the Rosicrucian Order—*

Georgina ran downstairs and out into the garden. The moon had risen. Dusk was thickening the air. It pushed against her, crackling with dry heat; she felt she was walking through paper. Somewhere up there a satellite was tumbling through the pale blue heavens, its signals failing, its systems closing down, its limbs silently dismembering – a suicide in space. Her father had said to her that nobody you love dies completely: but was there a single person in the world for whom she, Georgina, would go on existing if she was to die tonight?

She pushed through invisible, crackling paper, to the side of the swimming-pool. Gazing into its calm waters, she seemed to see a face rising up at her. She knew at once who it was by the braided brown hair, the broad forehead, the wide mouth so like hers. Bella. It was Bella, her mother, come to share her birthday. Gravely she sat down at the pool's edge. She wanted to put her toes in the warm, dense water. She unlaced her shoes and took them off. Then she took her socks off and laid them out in each shoe, tidily.

Nobody you love dies completely. But her father had refused to talk about Bella, he didn't love her, he hadn't so much as spoken her name. She whispered it aloud to the peaceful face that came and went under the water.

'Bella.'

She, Georgina, was now the only one left in the world who loved her mother and kept her alive in her heart so that she could exist here in front of her, her arms stretched out, her smiling face fading and illumining in the darkened water. She wanted to tell Bella that it was all right, her daughter was here, her daughter who loved her. Steadily she lowered her feet, then her legs into the water. At once she knew that it was her mother's element. She was in touch, closer than she had ever been; waiting for her daughter patiently, as she had waited every day by the high school wall.

Distantly from the patio came a voice which tried to break the link. She shut it out.

'Georgina! Georgina! Can you hear me? There's someone here to see you!'

She waited for him to go away. It was now too dark for him to see her, if she sat very still.

'Georgina! Are you out there?'

She did not, could not move. Her feet and ankles had already vanished back into her mother's element, its water blacker even than the surrounding darkness.

Then, out of nowhere, something sprang at her.

With a shock she looked down. In her lap sat Mr Robbins's green tree-frog. Its eyes bulged at her complacently; its emerald flanks gently palpitated. With a gasp, Georgina put out a finger and stroked its back. She murmured aloud: 'I'm sorry, frog. Someone's calling. I've got to go.'

She cupped her hands and put the tree-frog down on the edge of the grass. Picking up her shoes, she walked back to the house. Douglas stood on the patio. He put his arms round her and gave her an unexpected kiss.

'I was worried. I didn't know where you'd got to,' he said stiffly, as if needing to justify the sudden intimacy. 'He's in the hall.'

'Who?'

'I don't know. He says he's a friend of yours.'

Her legs dripping water, Georgina went through to the hall. Dirk Miller stood there. His face fell, comically.

'Your legs are wet,' he told her.

She grinned at him. 'I know.'

'Well. Anyway. You'll have to get a move on, birthday girl. We're going out.'

She opened her mouth to say no. She said: 'Can you give me ten minutes?'

'Seven. And, Georgie,' he shouted after her, 'bring some shoes for dancing in! Okay?'

She drove out with him into the electric night. Helen's make-up on her face made her feel like a masked reveller promenading to a Venetian ball. Her gondola would rub itself along the phosphorescent wooden piers and stop. She would be helped out in a halo of fireflies, a rustle of silk, to meet the Venetian noblemen standing with turned instep on the piazza. Their dark eyes would anxiously quiz her and she, inscrutable in her mask, would wrinkle her nose at their odours of cachou and wig-powder, while her ear would catch the strains of flute and mandolin.

'You look better with your hair cut shorter,' said Dirk.

'Thanks.'

'In fact you look pretty dinky altogether. It would have been a pity to leave you holed up at home tonight.'

'Oh. Well. Are we going anywhere in particular?'

'Downtown.'

She looked at Dirk. He was brooding at the road ahead, his long hands gripping the steering-wheel of the souped-up silver Beetle. The lights went green; he accelerated with a screech of changing gears. She was trying not to think about the swimming-pool. She stared at her hands to steady herself.

'Do you think I ought to paint my fingernails?' she asked.

'If they'll let you. Mum won't let Sally.'

'Helen does. She's always painting herself. It's like the Forth Bridge.'

'Your stepmother? She was bonaroo in *Measure for Measure*. Real dynamite.'

'You think so?'

'Dynamite.'

'Acting is her life.'

'I'll say. Listen, do you drink lager?'

'Not really.'

'Wine?'

'Sometimes.'

'I thought so.' With a triumphant flourish, Dirk pulled the Beetle into the kerb. He disappeared. Georgina contemplated a Coca-Cola sign which wrote itself in red neon and flashed on and off. She thought of a word – something beautiful, not Coca-Cola, perhaps *millefeuille* or *peaseweep* – filled with a thousand fireflies illuminating its transparent tubes of glass.

Dirk returned. He was carrying four bottles in a paper bag which he thrust in her lap. He took a bottle-opener out of the glove-compartment and held out his hand.

'Pass me over a couple of bottles, would you?'

'What are they?'

He uncapped one and handed it to her. She put it to her lips. It was bubbly and very sweet, with a not unpleasant lemony flavour.

'Barossa Pearl,' announced Dirk. 'Take it slowly; it's almost a hundred per cent pure alcohol.'

'I don't mind if it is.' She took another gulp. 'Why are we sitting here.'

'Don't you know? Hey, this is Adelaide, remember? No drinking within two hundred yards of a dance hall! No purchase of alcoholic liquor after six p.m.! I had to get a mate of mine to buy this lot so I could collect it later. But I was kidding you about Barossa Pearl. It's weak stuff. It won't hurt you.'

Dirk reached into the pocket of a corduroy jacket in the back seat and brought out a hip-flask, from which he took a swig.

'What's that?' asked Georgina.

'Brandy.'

'Can I have some?'

He looked at her and grinned. 'My, my. This is going to be a wild night.'

128

She had a sip of brandy, and felt it glowing inside her, like the fireflies. Everything was electric: the lights, the cars. . . . 'Why did you come for me?' she asked.

'I'll tell you later.' He drained the hip-flask. 'Let's go.'

She got out of the car. Dirk gave her his arm, like a beau, and walked her up the street, past a used-car lot and a Greek Orthodox church. At the end they turned into a squarish white building with glass doors like a cinema. Boys in black stovepipe pants and girls in full skirts and pointy shoes stood waiting in the foyer for their partners. Dirk bought tickets, and they went through into a swirl of cigarette smoke and a pounding of electric guitars.

The Penny Rockers, as she supposed they were, thrummed on the stage, shouting down microphones:

> *You don't need me to show the way, love,*
> *Why do I always have to say, love,*
> *Come on, come on, come on, come on. . . . '*

'There's Angie!' cried Dirk, pointing at a dancer in a yellow blouse. 'Hi! Angie!'

But Angie, twisting up and down and around like a corkscrew, was concentrating too hard to notice. Like all the girls here she had puffed hair and was wearing five or six paper-nylon petticoats which rattled like maracas as they jiggled.

'Let's dance,' shouted Dirk. He squeezed her arm. Georgina looked at him blankly. Her brain was reeling from the brandy and the spiked lemon drink and the sour-sweetness of scent and sweat. She stumbled through hen-parties of girls on chairs, and groups of boys with Brylcreemed hair whose names floated towards her and were drowned by the beat. To her relief, as they reached the dance-floor, the music changed, the Penny Rockers left the stage, and an Elvis Presley lookalike got up and began crooning something she recognised from her *Aloha Elvis* LP.

Gratefully she fell on Dirk's neck and let herself be propelled round the floor. Over his shoulder she looked at Angie and some of the others. They all wore thick white powder and heavy mascara round their eyes which combined with their abstracted gaze to give them, under the dance-hall lights, the pallid deathly look of creatures who passed their lives on the deep ocean floor.

'Is Sally here?' she shouted.

'My sis? Strewth, no. Don't go by appearances, Georgie. Sally talks up a storm, but emotionally she's still in the world of hula-hoops.'

His arms tightened around her. Georgina felt sick. Any moment now the Presley imitator would finish spreading the treacle of 'I Can't Help Falling in Love with You' and the Penny Rockers would come back.

'Can we go now?' she asked.

'What, leave?'

'Please!'

'Why?'

'I'm starving. I haven't had anything to eat.'

'But we've only just got here!'

'Please.'

He pulled her off the dance-floor with a scowl. 'You're a hard one to please,' he said. 'If it wasn't your birthday. . . .'

'I'm sorry.'

'Come on. I'll buy you a pizza.'

It wasn't late but most of Adelaide had shut down for the night. Dirk took her three blocks north to Hindley Street, where a night-life of sorts was kept going by Greek and Italian immigrants. At a place where a juke-box was playing the new Ray Charles, he stopped and took her in. Georgina ordered a Pizza Neapolitan. Dirk had an espresso.

'I'm sorry for spoiling your evening,' she said again. 'I'm not much use, am I?'

'Hey, listen. We didn't have to stay at the Greek Hall. And you were okay. Vince said that you look smashing.'

'Who's Vince?'

'You met him. The one with the leather jacket and black string tie. You're a mystery, you see. You're different from the other chicks. And you don't meet many new faces in Nowhere City.'

'Are you going to leave, when you've got your degree?'

'Maybe. Depends if I do post-grad work. I want to go to Berkeley in California. Have you been to California?'

She shook her head.

'Berkeley's got a good toxicology department. That's poisons.'

'I know.'

'Oh. Right. You do biology. Well, toxins are going to be the subject of the future. Poisons are all around us: in the atmosphere, in the ground. In us, even. And we're creating new ones all the time. Did you know you can't catch fish anywhere in the Spencer Gulf round Port Pirie because of the industrial pollution? A guy I know got warts from just swimming up there.'

'What about iodine?' she asked, thinking about Schneider and the sheep.

'Iodine's an extremely poisonous halogen element with radio-active atoms. Especially Iodine-131. It's beginning to be used in medicine. If you swallow a particle of I-131, you can trace it all the way through the body. I mean it, Georgie. Poisons are a growth area.'

'Have you heard of something called the Australian Safety Committee, run by someone Titterton?'

'No. What's that?'

'I don't know. I thought you might. So you'll try for Berkeley?'

'Unless I flunk out. And I might go anyway. The surf's good in California.' He grinned at her. 'There's more to life than sitting on a lab-stool sucking a pipette.'

'Yes, I know.'

'Do you? You weren't going to go out tonight. It's your birthday, and you were going to stay in like a house-plant. Is that what you did on your sixteenth birthday, too?'

'Yes. It wasn't my fault.' She drank a glass of water. 'I was stood up.'

'Were you? Who by?'

'It was half-term. I was going up to stay in Scotland with the brother of a schoolfriend of mine, Wendy Veevors. His name is Andrew. I really . . . I liked him a lot. Except that he was mad about rugger and I wasn't, and I wouldn't always trail along and watch him play, I think that was the reason, looking back now. He sent a telegram via his parents saying he wasn't going to be there, he had a vital weekend rugger game. I knew it wasn't true because Wendy had told me, and I was so angry, I thought it was just so *immature*. I went on a long walk in the snow and promised myself I'd never get involved with anyone my sort of age again.'

Dirk took her hand across the table. 'You've got involved with me.'

'I know.'

'Does it feel wrong?'

'No.'

'So do you always break your promises?'

They laughed. Dirk called for the bill and paid it. He asked her: 'What would you like to do now?' and without waiting for a reply: 'Let's go down to the beach. It's beautiful, down south of here. No one about at this time of night. We can swim, lie on the beach.'

'Oh? Without bathing-costumes or towels?'

'I've got a couple of fresh towels in the car. That's all we need.'

She resisted, as they walked back to the car.

'I'd love to, but not yet. Not tonight.'

'Come on, Georgie. It'll be fun.'

'No, really. Thanks for tonight. I've had a lovely time.'

'So why end it now?'

'Because I want to go home now.'

He shoved his hands in his pockets. 'Do you like me that little?'

'Oh, Dirk. I do like you. Of course I do.'

'Then, why? Are you scared of me? Scared I'll do something to you?'

'Oh, come on. That's silly.'

'It's you who's being silly. I suggest a drive to the beach and you make it sound as if I'm propositioning you.'

Frostily he drove her home. Georgina sat with the empty bottles of Barossa Pearl on her lap, smelling the citric acid. In Wellington Square he stopped the car.

'I really did enjoy tonight,' she said. 'Thank you for giving me a nice birthday after all.'

'I'm glad you enjoyed it.'

'Dirk—'

'That's okay, Georgie. I've been thinking, what you said about your friend Andrew. I think you expect too much out of people. You should relax and enjoy yourself more, let yourself go, you know?'

'Good night.'

'You're better with short hair!' he shouted after her. Turning, she saw the Beetle accelerate loudly into the night.

The sitting-room was in darkness. Her father must have gone to bed. Helen never got back much before midnight.

Georgina went upstairs, treading softly. It was her mother who had made her cautious, she decided. She had made her aware of how women were treated, and how men's vanity could override every rational impulse in themselves, even the impulse to respond to love. It wasn't just the young and silly ones, as her father had been young when he abandoned Bella for Helen. It was all men: it was Nick Kemp, it was Douglas now, the two of them trying to recapture their youth. Her mother had discovered all this the hard way. But what was the answer? Was it merely and long-sufferingly to make the best of it?

Georgina went to the window by her dressing-table and stared down, holding her breath. She felt disorientated, in limbo like the satellite. What had happened at the pool . . . an illusion, perhaps it was best she thought of it like that. But she was thankful that she would never need to feel *dis*illusioned, because clouds had blanketed the moon; the garden was black and invisible, as empty of faces as the night sky.

'Why won't Edward Catchpole come?' asked Douglas. Sitting on the bed, he watched Helen, firm-backed in her slip at the dressing-table, brushing the straight satin of her hair. The brush hesitated for a fraction.

'It's not a question of *won't*. He *can't* come, I've told you, because of pressure of work. He sent his apologies. And, anyway, we've got this other man coming, your old boss or whatever—'

'Freddie Collins—'

'So that makes up. I don't know why you keep on about it. The whole dinner's for you and your chums. I don't even know them, apart from Nick, of course. And Madge Plummer.'

'You met Barry Michaels last night. His being over from England is the whole reason we're giving this dinner.'

'I know he's got capped teeth, because he smiled at me. I know he's got three gold rings on his right hand, because I shook it. I know he's a film executive from your British Lion, because it's the first thing he told me. That doesn't add up to *knowing* the man. Or perhaps it does. By the way, have we got enough drink? I don't know their drinking habits.'

'I stocked up at lunchtime. Beer—'

'Let's not suggest beer.'

'Plenty of wine. What are we eating?'

'Veal. If the cook stays sober. We start with Port Lincoln oysters with ham and Worcester sauce, and finish with fruit. Did you remember the garden torches?'

'The mosquito flares, yes. I got Robbins to help me put them up.'

'Robbins! He's a menace, that man. I'm convinced he's trying to poison poor darling Ottoman; just because I lined the fence with dog repellent! I found her frothing at the mouth this morning.' Helen made a moue for the lip-gloss she was trying on. She stared at herself in the mirror, then patted her lips with a tissue. 'Thank God Robbins isn't coming, too,' she added, 'or we'd have a full house of lively and cultivated men. I told you he invited us to a barbecue last week?'

'No.'

'He popped his head up over the fence, in the way he does, and said: "Terrine and I would love it if you could all come across for a barbie on Tuesday week." A *barbie*! I said: "I'm terribly sorry, we'd love to come, but we're vegetarians!" ' Merry laughter from the dressing-table. 'I think Mr Robbins got the message.'

'You've met Freddie Collins, haven't you? He's a friend— '

'Darling— '

'A friend of Catchpole, I think.'

'Darling, have you seen my Elizabeth Arden? Oh God!'

Helen got up and hurried to the door. Douglas heard shouts from Georgina's room. Helen bore back a small glass bottle with a stopper.

'I give the Child make-up for her birthday and she shows her gratitude by nabbing my Blue Grass,' she complained. 'A girl her age shouldn't need scent anyway.'

'She *is* seventeen.'

'You wouldn't think it, darling. She's so ungraceful, so *sloppy*. The Myer Emporium is running a series of ninety-minute charm schools to teach young ladies deportment and dress sense. I think I might buy her a season ticket.'

'Go easy on her. She's never going to look like you.' Douglas got up and put his arms around her. 'How's your head?'

'Please don't, darling. It'll come back if you start getting in my way. Will you go down and tell Mrs G to start laying the table? What did I do with that. . . ?' Helen's fingers darted among the bottles, boxes and little pots on her dressing-table as Douglas withdrew from her and went to the door.

'Thank God there are no infants coming!' Helen called after him. 'They'd be breaking the glasses and eating the flea-powder. One Child is quite enough.'

The dinner-guests divided neatly between the whisky and the gin. Georgina dispensed the drinks. Major Collins she immediately recognised as the man with silver hair she had seen on the first night of *Measure for Measure*. She tried to remember what Winn Vellacott had said about him. Despite his well-cut worsted suit and shiny black shoes he looked less intelligent up close. His jawline was strong and belligerent – so much so that the rest of his face retreated from it, sloping back to a small narrow cranium as it approached the seat of the brain.

Who he was, and what he was doing in Adelaide were not discussed. Georgina watched him. Unlike Barry Michaels, whose eyes behind his square black glasses never stayed in one place but veered unhappily round the room, Collins examined everyone in turn, as if looking for gestures and mannerisms, and what they might reveal.

It was *Measure for Measure*, of course, they all talked about first (apart from Barry Michaels, who had just flown in from Honolulu, but redeemed himself by appearing eager to be told the name of Helen's agent). Freddie Collins, it turned out, had sent her a first-night good-luck telegram, a fact which Helen appeared to find unaccountably droll. Madge Plummer, an Adelaide lawyer, arrived looking like the Duchess of Windsor in a black-and-silver trouser suit and pearl choker. She accepted a gin-and-tonic from Georgina with a piercing scream.

'*Darling!* You must be Helen's daughter!'

'More of an *objet trouvé*,' intervened Helen with a quick smile.

Helen held court. Dressed in a Gauguin-pink cocktail-dress with a cinched waist and a floppy black satin bow in front, her lipstick the colour of strawberry fool, she told amusing stories about the cast and the audiences. Douglas stared into his whisky. Only Nick Kemp hadn't yet made an appearance.

'Madge, I was telling Douglas about the poor girl who plays Mariana,' said Helen, graciously bringing the Duchess into the conversation. 'Whenever she can't remember her lines, she curls strands of hair round her finger and sucks it until the prompt arrives!'

'Has she ever acted before?'

'I believe she played the barmaid in their last production of *Hamlet*.'

'Forgive me, but there's surely no barmaid in *Hamlet*?' returned Collins, wrinkling his narrow brow.

'There is in the interval.' Allowing a moment for their laughter to subside, Helen looked up at the starfish clock on the wall. 'Ah, well, only another two performances. Shall we go and eat?'

'Captain Kemp isn't here, yet,' Georgina objected.

They all looked round, but the mention of Nick's name failed to produce him in the doorway. Helen returned to the kitchen; the others marked conversational time. Douglas told his story about the professor of literature writing outback Westerns. Madge Plummer wanted to know of Barry Michaels whether the film of Gallipoli would be in 3-D so that she could watch it through red-and-green stereoscopic spectacles.

'Douglas here has got to finish the script first!' replied Michaels, patting him on the back. 'We're aiming at the international market with this one. It's a biggie. That's why we went to the top of the tree for our script-writer, eh? We estimate that American audiences will fall for the Australian angle. They are two great countries with a lot in common nowadays. Except – ha! – Australia got convicts the way Americans got pilgrim fathers.'

In the pause, Madge raised her glass. 'Either way it's good for divorce lawyers,' she remarked.

The doorbell rang. Mrs G ushered Nick into the drawing-room. His hair was wet; he was out of breath. He gave Georgina a hug and a kiss, and shook hands with the others as Douglas introduced him.

'There's a reason I'm late apart from the rain,' he said. 'I called in on a mate of yours, Duggle. Winn Vellacott.'

'He's no friend of mine,' retorted Douglas. 'He came to do an interview for his rag about the Gallipoli film – Barry, you should hear this – and described it in print as another British raid on Australian history. Accused *me* of cultural landlordism: I should have known better than to talk to a local reporter.'

'Winn's all right. Or he was,' said Nick. 'Someone ransacked his flat this afternoon. Drawers pulled out. Books pulled off the shelves. Mattress slit. Whoever it was took a couple of silver cups and a clock to make it look like a common burglary, but Winn says it's political. They took all his notebooks and his tape-recorder.'

'Gosh, you mean all that stuff— '

'Yes,' said Nick, cutting Georgina short. 'He's pretty upset. But I know Winn. He'll sink his teeth in deeper and hang tight.'

Collins asked casually: 'All what stuff, Georgina?'

'What?'

'All the stuff, you said, that this man's been working on.'

'Oh, yes.' Georgina glanced desperately at Nick. 'Wasn't he doing something on Mr Catchpole and the security side of the Royal Visit?'

Nick raised his eyebrows. 'Could be.'

'Hardly a subject to waste notebooks and a tape-recorder on,' observed Collins.

A chilly silence fell, for the few seconds which passed before Helen reappeared and summoned them all to eat.

She sat in the middle of the table, between Barry Michaels and Major Collins. Madge opposite her, had Nick and Douglas on either side. Georgina was placed at the far end between Nick and the film producer. Nick was unusually quiet. The others, keeping well away from uninteresting subjects like Australia, talked about Home.

There was a drugs scandal, there was a spy scandal, there was a sex scandal. Barry Michaels was pressed greedily for details. About the first two he knew no more than they did. The sex scandal, involving a government minister and a prostitute, was stronger stuff. Barry Michaels could see a film in it. He retailed the story scene by scene, ending dramatically with the disgrace of the minister and the suicide of a go-between. Major Collins nodded solemnly.

'I knew him,' he said. 'The minister, I mean. Not a bad chap, but, you know, he was never properly vetted. In our business everyone is checked out the moment they set foot in the door. That way we pick out the rotten fruit. But a minister, in my experience, can come in at the top of the tree with a security clearance that isn't worth the paper it's written on.'

'What is your business, sir?' asked Georgina, getting her own back.

'Well, my dear. . . . ' Freddie Collins paused, smiling.

'The Major and I go back a long way, Georgina,' Douglas interrupted. 'He was my boss for a couple of years after the war in an outfit which used to check out deserters and all those strange displaced people with stories to tell who collect up at the end of a long war.'

Georgina flushed. She put down her knife and fork.

'You mean military intelligence?' she said. 'Isn't that what Mr Catchpole is in?'

Collins's smile faded. Helen stood up and began piling the plates and discarded oyster-shells. Nick began paying attention. His eyes alight, he repeated the question.

'Well, is it?'

'Edward Catchpole is here for the Royal Tour,' defended Collins. 'We all are, in a way. How well do you know him?'

'My wife plays tennis with him,' said Douglas, staring at her. 'Don't you, Helen?'

'Yes, I do,' answered Helen. She called for the plates to be collected and sat down. 'He's very good for my game,' she added, smiling at Madge Plummer.

'Well, then, you should know that Edward is an adviser like the rest of us,' Major Collins said. 'He's a bit of a boffin, I suppose you could say. I met him first years ago, when I was working with Harris in Bomber Command. The last three or four years he's been with the British Joint Services Commission in Washington. All quite above board, I assure you. Although, Kemp, I'd be obliged if you didn't pass any of this on to your journalist friend.'

'Off the record, you mean,' said Nick. He nodded, wryly. 'Dresden, eh? Those were the days!'

'What's the political temperature like back home?' Collins had turned away to Barry Michaels. 'Labour Party's in a bit of a mess again, isn't it? There's no real leadership any more, that's the problem.'

'It's all a mess.' Draining his glass, Douglas banged it down on the table. 'England's a mess. That's why I came away. Attlee started the rot. All those pieties about austerity and the New Age, it was like living in a Welsh chapel. Then Suez blew the candles out. Then Macmillan arrived and waved incense around. And here we are with political scandals, a record number out of work, no power or influence in the world—'

'That's it,' interjected Collins.

'We came back, didn't we,' went on Douglas, darting a look at him, 'from a "war to end war", expecting the socialism of comrades-in-arms, to find the whole country turned into a kind of pasture for apathetic milch-cows chewing the state cud! Corruption and apathy, from top to bottom. Thank God my old man didn't live to see it. He stayed in his practice in Ravenglass, dispensing pills and cough mixtures, and drinking himself to death. He'd had the same confidence trick pulled on him, when he came back from the Great War to a "land fit for heroes". Some heroes they turned out to be!'

Nobody spoke for a moment. There was a busy passing of mashed potatoes and carrots to put beside the sautéed veal on their plates.

'Please start,' said Helen. 'I don't know why you have to be so fierce,' she added sharply, as if Douglas had directed his venom at her. 'Anyway, your father didn't drink himself to death. He died of throat cancer. George, will you eat your dinner? If you're worried about your diet— '

'I'm not— '

'Veal won't make you put on weight. Madge, some more of anything?'

'No, thank you, darling.' Madge picked her bag up and got out a tin of cheroots. 'Would anyone mind dreadfully if I smoke?'

Under the influence of the wine, conversation fragmented. Douglas talked to Freddie Collins about Gallipoli and versions of patriotism. Madge had leaned right across the table to get a light from Helen; but Helen was being monopolised by Barry Michaels, who wanted to know the glamorous details of her Russian émigré past: her ancestral home on the Polish border, her escape to the West as an eighteen-year-old in 1945 in the car of a Soviet general attached to the Allied Control Commission in Berlin. As she talked, Michaels gazed into her eyes and puffed on a cigar.

'You're kidding!' he remarked from time to time.

Nick Kemp waited until Helen was out of the room organising the coffee before he leaned over to Georgina and whispered to her: 'Do you like being called George?'

'No, I don't.'

'Then, why does she call you it?'

'She pretends it's out of affection. I know that really she thinks Georgina is too pretty a name for me; she thinks I don't deserve it. Anyway, she mostly refers to me as "The Child". I don't mind.'

'Child!' Nick looked amused. 'You seem pretty grown-up to me. Douglas said you'd gone dancing at the Greek Hall.'

Georgina blushed. 'It was awful!' she exclaimed. 'God, if that's anything to do with growing-up. . . !'

'Well, I've been to Adelaide dance-halls in my time. Believe me, they're the height of sophistication compared with some. I've been to the annual race-meeting dance at the kind of town where jockeys are weighed on a pair of bathroom scales which have sunk so deep into the bull-dust that you can't take a reading. There's a one-finger lady pianist, a trombone and a drummer. It's ties-only, and nothing to drink. The pub across the street is the only place to get booze, and that's strictly no-ties. A bouncer stands outside with a pair of scissors, and cuts the tie off anyone going in . . . it's God's truth! If you went prospecting up Tarcoola way, you stayed chaste or you stayed sober.'

Freddie Collins cut across Georgina's reply. 'Did I hear you say you're a prospector, Kemp?'

'I have prospected, yes.'

'Out in the bush?'

'Out in the bush.'

'Do you run across many blackfellas in the bush?'

'Only if they want to run across me.'

'Oh. I thought the outback was crawling with 'em?'

'It used to be,' answered Nick agreeably. 'But we killed a lot of them off, you know. We shot a lot early on. Then we started poisoning them, mostly with alcohol. It was friendlier, and it didn't use up expensive ammunition. That's why Abos aren't included in the national census, unlike cows and pigs. The federal government would have to come up with reasons why their population was dwindling so fast.'

'That is an unusual view, Kemp.' Collins looked with amusement at the others, who had stopped talking to listen. 'Most people would say that the Aboriginal doesn't need any incentive to go on the bottle. He just likes getting drunk. Two beers and he's ready to fight, they tell me.'

'So he does. But we're the ones smuggling him the liquor. The only way to cure the Abos of alcoholism is to get them back on to the land of their ancestors. Then they won't be unhappy; they won't need the booze so much.'

141

'Aha! A radical!' The Major looked as if he had hooked a fish. 'I'm all in favour of giving blacks equal wages, Kemp. If they want to drink their money away, that's up to them. But once you let them start claiming land because it belongs to the spirits of their ancestors, there'd be no stopping them. All this talk of Aboriginal *dreaming* . . . I reckon it's their way of bamboozling people into granting them squatter's rights.'

Madge Plummer nodded. 'Legally it's a hornets' nest,' she agreed.

'You think that giving Abos back large tracts of bush country is legally out of the question?' enquired Nick.

'I would think so.'

'What do the Abos say to that?'

'What Abos?'

'The ones you've talked to.'

Madge Plummer sat back. 'I don't have Aboriginal clients, because I'm not involved in Aboriginal legislation.'

'Has anybody here had a discussion with an Aborigine?' asked Nick.

Into the silence came Helen and Mrs G carrying a tray of coffee-cups.

'My husband will no doubt soon be speaking in Aboriginal,' Helen said as she poured the coffee. 'Nick wants to take him off on Wednesday on an expedition into the desert. If you ask me, I'll be lucky to see them alive again.'

Collins nodded gravely. 'The outback can be a dangerous place, Mrs Manifold.'

'What's the point?' asked Barry Michaels, slurring his words. 'There's nothing out there, is there? Bloody miles of nothing, from what I hear. How do you describe the outback if there's nothing to describe?'

'Heat and dust,' offered the Major.

'Sand, sand and more sand.'

'No colours. No trees— '

'Miles and miles of dry scrub.'

'Stones, empty petrol-drums, abandoned cars— '

Their flippant suggestions were cut short by Nick Kemp. He had wetted his finger, and was slowly moving it round the rim of his wine-glass. The sound he produced, pure, quivering, moaning, unearthly, filled the air and gradually reduced them all to silence.

'Listen,' he said. 'Michaels is right, there's nothing that words can describe. This is what the outback looks like. It's the closest I can get.'

The moaning grew louder and louder.

The walls of the house in Wellington Square began to shake. They heard a sudden crash. Helen gave a shriek. Nick got up and strode to the patio doors. The howling grew louder as he opened them and went out into the dark.

'It's the wind,' exclaimed Douglas.

'Yes, yes, the wind,' other voices chimed in. The Major laid his hand comfortingly over Helen's clenched one.

'Nothing to worry about, my dear,' he said.

They waited. Nick returned, blinking painfully.

'It's the shaft on your patio awning, Duggle,' he said. 'I've tied the awning down so it won't flap. But I shouldn't go out for a bit. The wind's from the north and it's like walking into the teeth of a sandstorm.'

He disappeared to the cloakroom. The others sat on over their coffee, talking about the Royal Visit and listening to the winds batter the walls and roof.

'It's what the Queen calls "inclement weather",' said Douglas.

'What the Queen's speechwriters call "inclement weather",' corrected Freddie Collins.

'Left to herself, the Queen would probably say "Christ, it's pissing with inclement weather again!"' said Barry Michaels and laughed uproariously.

'In any case the sun will be shining by the time the Queen arrives,' remarked Madge Plummer, touching her pearls. 'The sun always shines on Royal visits.'

It was half an hour before the wind let up sufficiently for Freddie Collins to look at his watch and decide to make a move. Madge Plummer also got up to leave, after kissing Helen fulsomely on both cheeks. The British Lion executive swallowed his brandy and sat smoking his third cigar. Nick, who was staying in Adelaide, offered to drive him back to the South Australian Hotel.

'I'll give you some free advice,' Barry Michaels replied, staggering to his feet. 'You're in the wrong country for prospecting. Fool's gold is all you'll find out here.'

Nick laughed. 'I thought that was Hollywood,' he said.

They all went outside. The gale had blown the clouds out of the sky. In the moonlight they saw the desert all around them. The grass in the front garden was white, the bushes were white, the road and the square and the roofs of all the houses were white with blown sand. Sand crunched under their feet. It brushed off the gate and the car roofs on to their hands; it got under their jackets and shirts and dresses.

Helen shivered. Something alien had invaded. The illusion of England had evaporated. The guests got quickly into their cars and departed, skirting the branches and 'For Sale' signs which the storm had blown into the street. Only Nick lingered. He bent down and scooped up a pinch of sand where it had collected against the kerb. He made Georgina hold her hand out, and dribbled the sand on to her palm.

'It's hot!' she exclaimed in surprise. Nick grinned.

'It's the real thing,' he said.

When they'd all left, Douglas went up to bed, taking his lecture-notes with him. He listened to Helen moving about downstairs. He tried to remember the last time they had gone to bed at the same time. Putting down the notes, he called out to her.

'What have you been doing?' he demanded, when finally she appeared, peeling off polythene gloves.

'It's Ottoman, poor darling. I'll have to take him to the vet. He's been sick all over the carpet.'

'I expect it's all the stuff you put down in saucers.'

'It's nothing to do with that. Ottoman never touches it. That man Robbins is poisoning him, I'm sure of it!'

She came over to the bed, lifted the sheet and tickled his feet. He made a grab for her. Instead of running away, she let herself be picked up like a child, coming all cuddlesome into his arms as she used to do. Putting out her small pointed tongue, she licked his ear. Douglas felt such a shock of frustrated sexual longing stream through him that he almost dropped her.

144

'My poppet, my baby doll,' he murmured. The long drought had broken: he laid her on the bed and smothered her breasts and throat and face with kisses. And then she broke away.

'Darling—'

'Don't speak!' he implored. He turned her mouth to his to stop her breaking the rules of their old game. 'I love you, oh, so much. . . .'

'Then, will you do something for me?'

'Anything, my baby.'

'Don't go on Nick's expedition. Not tomorrow. Go some other time.'

He lay back stunned. 'What's this?'

'We've been invited to the official reception on Thursday to meet the Queen. It's on board *Britannia*.'

'My poppet, you go. I can't. I can't cancel. It's all fixed up.'

'I can't go by myself.' She kissed him. 'Please, darling. If you love me.'

A hardness had come into her voice. He looked into her eyes. His throat went very dry. He demanded: 'Who got you this invitation?'

'Does it matter? It's in recognition of you more than of me.'

'Catchpole! It was Edward Catchpole, wasn't it!' He shook her. 'Catchpole! Catchpole! All I ever hear about – Catchpole! Have you slept with him? Well, have you? Do you sleep with him?'

She tore away from him. She went to her dressing-table, picked up the hairbrush to brush her hair.

'You and your stupid jealousies!' she burst out. She flung down the brush and started taking off her dress with trembling fingers. 'All you ever do is sit at your desk all day and brood about the real life you're missing out on!'

'Oh, do I? You're the one who lives in a fantasy world; you're the one who tells lies! It's not me who lies about Catchpole! I don't fantasise about my past – all that make-believe about your Russian émigré parents when your father was actually a debt-collector in Leeds!'

'Oh, right, darling, of course you don't. You *live* the lie instead, the lie of loving me. All those poems' – she mimicked his voice – '*When first you think you hear Love's old sweet song beware The unfamiliar ear. . . .* They aren't written to me! Oh, no, they're written to Bella!'

'You can't say that!'

'They are. Do you think I don't know? I see you looking down at me in bed and you're looking at a stranger! I don't exist for you any longer. You make love to Bella. You write your poems to Bella. They're your way of keeping secrets. Of living the lie of our love for each other!'

She burst into tears. As Douglas threw back the sheet and got out of bed, she ran from him into the bathroom. He beat on the door.

'Helen!'

When she came out she was still crying. She stumbled to the bed and buried her head in the pillow.

'And you call me a whore!' she sobbed.

'I did not!' Roughly he turned her over. Her nightdress, unbuttoned, fell to her sides. 'You say I don't love you. You never give me the chance to show it any more.'

He lay on top of her, pinioning her, feeling between her legs. She kicked at him, shouting: 'Is that what you mean by love? Anybody can do that!'

'Like you and Catchpole, you mean!'

'You bastard!'

She was crying again. Douglas was inside her, bearing down on her, cursing her with every breath. She scratched and kicked.

'I hate you!' she cried.

'Whore! You whore!' Great rasping breaths broke from him like sobs. He came out of her, still holding her flat with his arm across her shoulders; and he pumped himself to an orgasm across her belly. Then with a groan he threw himself back on the bed and stared up at the ceiling.

Helen said nothing. When she returned from the bathroom she took a sheet and wrapped herself in it, and went downstairs.

Eventually, Douglas closed his eyes. Sleep must have come, because all at once he was revisiting a place he had been in his dreams many times before, so that not only was the scene familiar to him, but also what was about to happen.

He was a boy of twelve again, on holiday in the Lake District. He was walking towards some old mine-workings that lay on the other side of the river above a belt of trees. Ever since he first came to the valley he had wanted to explore up there; now that he was all by himself he tip-toed across the stepping-stones, went straight to the spot where he could duck under the barbed-wire fence, and walked up through the wood.

Birds were singing. It was high summer; he walked through splashes of light, and came out on a disused road. It led to rusted mine-machinery in the undergrowth around a blocked-off tunnel. A path led to the crown of the hill. He pushed his way upwards through ferns and brambles.

And stopped. And marvelled. Invisible to anyone beneath, the modest hill had been gouged out into an enormous crater. From where he stood on the lip, sheer chalk cliffs fell fifty feet or more into an astonishing lake of round green water, silent and still.

He trembled in his sleep. Each time it was a sight he had never seen before, never imagined finding; and yet he knew it so well it was as if he had returned to his very beginnings. Across from him a broken white road curved down into the crater, to where a rusted corrugated-iron tower reared out of the green water. To throw a stone down and break the skin of the crater-lake would be sacrilege. The silence was absolute, the stillness unbroken. No wind. No birdsong. It was all his. It existed for him. He took possession of it, and at once felt a great peace steal over him, into which he settled, dreamlessly.

Some time that night, though, he woke up and found Bella in bed with her back to him. Over her pyjamas she was wearing her long green pullover (as she often did in winter when they were first married and couldn't afford a properly heated flat) and for extra warmth she had moulded herself into the contours of his sleeping form. Gripped by the old irritation – how he hated to be suffocated and held back so young in his career! – he pushed her roughly away—

And as Helen, who must have got back unnoticed into bed, protested in her sleep, he stared down at her, feeling prickles of cold sweat starting on his skin.

It was Douglas Manifold's idea to give the Colonel Light Memorial Lecture in the Union Hall, surrounded by the props of a painted Vienna.

'The last time my wife Helen Callender played in *Julius Caesar*,' he told his audience of two hundred, 'the director at the Old Vic saw Caesar's Rome as a sandpit surrounded by broken rusty scaffolding, its denizens dressed like beggars. Here, at the Union Hall, Duke Vincentio's Vienna consists of painted flats behind which its inhabitants cower, or plot, or spring out to chase whores and bawds. But Shakespeare of course never went to Rome or Vienna. He wrote both plays about England. And my contention is that these screens behind us tell us as much about England now as about England then.

'*Measure for Measure*, I must insist, is a play about secrecy. All the corruption and injustice in the play stems from the oppressive secrecy of a government which puts itself at such a distance from its citizenry that Vincentio has to quit Vienna before he can discover what's going on. And yet so trapped is the Duke in his own habit of camouflage that he adopts idiotic disguises and unnecessary stratagems to prove what's been staring him in the face all along: that the civil servants of a secret state will get away with murder, because nobody else will know in time to stop them.'

'*Is he all right?*' whispered Robyn Amory to Georgina. They had come in the sixth-form school party.

'*Why?*'

Robyn puzzled. '*I don't know. It's just—* '

'*He didn't sleep last night. I think Helen came back late. That's why she's not here.*'

At least, she didn't think Helen had come. Nick was here, sitting in an aisle seat, and all the usual people (no Dirk, unless he was standing at the back). But Robyn was right. Her father's eyes were red-rimmed. His voice had a flat, harsh,

148

exhausted note. And this evening he was going into the outback. She began to worry for him.

'As many of you will know,' Douglas was saying, 'I am in Adelaide to write a film about Gallipoli. Some of you may well have relatives who fought and died there. A few of you may even be veterans of the Dardanelles campaign. You will know better than most how official secrecy can be a double-edged weapon – first obstructing the lines of communication in battle, and then covering up the full enormity of the mistakes that were made. Decisions in England have always been taken behind the kind of screens you can see on this stage – whether shielding the discussions of the Duke and the Provost from public view, or rearranged to form the high walls of Angelo's garden. None of us can easily expose them. "For", as the Duke's deputy Angelo says, "my authority bears a credent bulk, That no particular scandal once can touch But it confounds the breather."

'You will all remember the particular scandal Angelo has in mind. Given by the Duke plenipotentiary power over Vienna, he has used that power to blackmail and deflower, or so he thinks, an innocent virgin; to break his word; to instil a reign of terror. But is Angelo so unusual in this?

'Men don't change, believe me. As Isabella declares of them: "Man, proud man, Dressed in a little brief authority, Most ignorant of what he's most assured – His glassy essence – like an angry ape Plays such fantastic tricks before high heaven As makes the angels weep."

'A civil servant, Edward Catchpole. . . . ' Douglas paused, and recollected himself. 'Catchpole, yes, told my wife recently a little-known story which illustrates what can be done today behind the screen of official secrecy. It's about Britain's last Prime Minister, Anthony Eden . . . how it was that Eden gave orders to his Secret Service – directly after the fiasco of Suez – gave orders to arrange the assassination of Colonel Nasser with an exploding safety razor. In this case, the head of MI5 can be said to have played the part of Escalus in *Measure for Measure*. He refused to pass Eden's instructions on to our spies in Cairo.'

Douglas stopped to drink water. There was a whispering and muttering in the hall. Georgina, not daring to turn round, could hear a scraping of chairs. Some of the audience must be walking out. She stared at her father, willing him on. Douglas

149

put the glass down on the rostrum with a shaking hand.

'It seems to me that the most contemporary lesson we learn from this very contemporary play is that we have no excuse not to face the truth about ourselves and about what is happening around us. When there is something rotten in the state we don't cure it, as the Duke tries to, by abdicating responsibility. The Duke Vincentio may kid himself that he has won the hand of Isabella and doled out measure for measure. But in the production which has just finished here it is plain from the look that my wife lavishes on Angelo that the rottenness remains—'

'*Is that your friend Captain Kemp over there?*' Robyn Amory was nudging Georgina's arm.

'*Yes.*' She glanced round. As she did so, she saw Winn Vellacott. He was sidling down the gangway. When he reached Nick he bent down and whispered something in his ear. Nick at once got up and followed him through a side-exit. Georgina looked back at her father, her heart beating.

'There is a riddle here to which we each must find our own answers,' Douglas was concluding, his voice unsteady. ' "What news abroad i' the world?" asks Escalus of the Duke. And Vincentio replies: "There is scarce truth enough alive to make societies secure, but security enough to make fellowships accursed. Much upon this riddle runs the wisdom of the world." I leave you to ponder Vincentio's riddle. Thank you for listening to me.'

The applause was polite, doubtful. Someone shouted out a question, but Douglas wasn't taking any questions; he had already left the rostrum and was striding backstage. Georgina didn't want any questions, either; she could see Sally Miller making faces at her. She jumped up and ran on to the stage and into the wings, looking for her father.

'Daddy!' she called out, pushing bits of scenery and racks of costumes out of her way. 'Daddy!'

No answer came. Instinctively she went down the corridor and up the stairs into Helen's old dressing-room.

The room still smelt of her stepmother's presence. A bottle of her scent stood unstoppered on the sink. Her father was standing in front of the dressing-table, a red-stained tissue in his hand. First-night good-luck telegrams lay scattered on the chair. On the mirror was a message in lip-stick, half rubbed out. Only the word LOVE remained.

'Daddy, you were very good,' said Georgina, putting her arm through his. 'Aren't you coming home now?'

Douglas didn't move. 'I don't think I really knew what was happening,' he said slowly. 'That's the thing, isn't it? You never really know until it's too late.'

'I thought you were very good,' repeated Georgina. She bit her lip. Douglas turned round. He kissed her and gave her a hug.

'You're pretty good to tell me so,' he said. 'Give me five minutes. I'll meet you out by the stage door. Then we won't have to see all those people who bought their tickets thinking I was going to talk about Shakespeare.'

'Okay.'

As she went out, Douglas was rubbing the last word off the dressing-room mirror.

TWO

At six o'clock that evening the Transcontinental Express left Adelaide on its marathon journey across the outback to Perth on the west coast. It was seventy-two hours before the full moon. At the last minute a non-connecting carriage had been attached at the back of the train and several dozen Aborigines shepherded into it.

'The city and corporation of Adelaide will have offered them a free ticket to go and shoot the breeze with their kinfolk,' observed Nick, pulling down the window. 'They're cleaning a lot of Abos out of the Big Smoke for the Queen's visit. By the way, Duggle, I hope you've brought the right clobber with you. It's going to be hot as a fire in a peppermill where we're headed.'

'I got what you told me to, Captain. And if I die of heat exhaustion out there just throw my body in the cook-pot.'

Douglas spoke more lightly than he felt. He had prepared for this trip in a ferment of anger and self-pity, scarcely thinking what he was about. Now that he was committed, he was taken aback by the scale of Nick's preparations. A whole bunk in their sleeper compartment was piled with geological equipment: chunky leather-cased boxes with dials and buttons, yards of coiled cable, batteries, electrodes, and a kind of cattle-prod which Nick apparently would stick in the earth to detect variations in its magnetic field. He had also brought a gun, and boxes of food.

Over dinner in the restaurant-car, Nick described the plan. At a little town just past Tarcoola, where the Trans-continental stopped to pick up water, they would collect Nelson. They would take him on the train a couple of hours further to a maintenance halt called Fisher, where the Land-rover, sent up a week ago on the tea-and-sugar, would be waiting.

'Tea-and-sugar?'

'It's the goods train which runs every week or so between Kalgoorlie and Adelaide with provisions for the maintenance workers along the track. I loaded the Land-rover on to a

155

flat-car; there's a trolley-man called Bill at Fisher who'll be looking after it for me. It's a company vehicle, so he'd better. As it is, I couldn't leave my prospecting gear in and hope to find it waiting for us.'

Nick flicked open a can of beer. Douglas looked out of the window. Although the sun had gone down, he could already sense a difference, an emptiness, in the darkening landscape through which they swayed and rattled.

'Do you really think we're going to find anything?' he asked.

Nick nodded. 'I've spent my life travelling hopefully. It's time I arrived. Number one – we know there's uranium out there, and that's the richest mineral to prospect for, richer than gold or black opals. Number two – we've got a guide who says he can take us to it. Number three – there's a socking great area of South Australia, where the Nullarbor Desert runs into the sand-hills, which we know almost nothing about geologically. There hasn't been one proper aero-magnetic survey. Even the tectonics are a mystery. We know quite a bit about the Musgrave and Everard Ranges at the northern rim of the Officer Basin. But where the Officer Basin meets the Gawler Crater . . . well, without getting technical, at the boundary of any rigid plates in the earth's crust you can get some surprises thrown up.'

'Like uranium?'

'Possibly. We shan't know for certain until we take some samples. The classic prospector's technique is to go up a riverbed and take test measurements. We can't do that. Where we're going there's almost no surface water. From such geophysical maps as there are we know that most of the area consists, like many deserts, of marine sedimentary deposits. But there could be some older volcanic outcroppings which the nineteen fifty surveys completely missed.'

Douglas nodded, amused. This was the Nick he remembered from the past – resourceful, serious, knowledgeable, the situation at his fingertips. He had felt his daughter's disappointment when Nick first breezed in; he wondered what she would make of him now when there was everything to play for. The geology tuition over, he said: 'You and Georgina seem to be getting along okay.'

156

'Of course. She's one in a million.

'If I had a kid, I'd like it to turn out like her.'

'What was she saying back on the platform about Winn Vellacott?'

'Georgina's got sharp eyes. She saw Winn pull me out of your lecture yesterday. He's been following up the death of Richard Schneider, a nutrition expert who's been doing research into whatever it is that's poisoning cattle. He'd just got a copy of the Coroner's report which said the guy hadn't died of a heart attack in his lab at all. He'd gassed himself in his car with a hose from the exhaust.'

'Vellacott marched in just to tell you that?'

'That and some newspaper cuttings he wanted to show me. When Winn's on the trail of something, it makes him single-minded. Particularly after his apartment's been turned over by the police. Schneider apparently had cancer, though, which seems a perfectly good explanation to me for doing away with yourself. I shouldn't want to stick around if I had terminal cancer. But Winn's convinced there's more to it.'

Night had fallen. There was too much light in the restaurant-carriage to see the stars. They went back to their sleeper and turned in. Nick's voice came out of the darkness.

'Just like old times, eh, Duggle?'

'Ay, ay, sir.'

And it was true that, as Douglas laid his head on the pillow in the rushing night, he felt the beast on his back begin to retract its claws. He had said nothing over dinner about Helen. Nick was the last person on earth to tell about it. All those nights in Nick's Marylebone flat after he left his wife, pouring out his guilt about Bella, and his love for Helen, with Nick saying little but making it plain he, Douglas, had gone too far to turn back. What could Nick tell him now? That he'd got his just deserts?

This morning he had accused himself of being a coward again, by running away. He had come within an ace of abandoning the expedition and going to confront Catchpole face to face, supposing it was ever possible to confront such a shadowy, slippery bastard. But what would that have solved with Helen? It was best to get right away from Adelaide, right away from the talks, the film-script, the self-recriminations. Out here with Nick was his chance to become whole again.

Douglas woke around seven and pulled back the curtain. Looking out of the train window, he felt like a voyager who falls asleep in port and wakes up in the middle of the ocean. The ground stretched away to the horizon flat and featureless, a pinkish colour in the early-morning sun. Gum-trees there were, and very occasional fenced tracks of what might have been pasture – except that there was no stock, the fences were collapsing, and any attempt at boring for low-saline groundwater had evidently failed.

'You ain't seen nothing yet,' remarked Nick. He was standing fully dressed by the other bunk, checking some equipment.

'Nothing's what I'm looking at. Are we nearly there?'

'It's the next stop. We're past Tarcoola. Feel like some breakfast? It'll be the last proper meal you get for three days.'

Over leathery bacon and eggs, Nick talked about Nelson.

'You'll see, he's not like other Abos to look at. A bit lighter-skinned, and his hair's a reddish colour. He claims his paternal grandfather was a white man, and he's got plenty of airs about him, as well as the Nelson blind eye. I met him when I stopped off in Ooldea on the way back from Kalgoorlie, to try to find a mate of mine who was making a film about the railway. He'd got hold of Nelson – this was the time the Abos had been cleared out of Ooldea by the Government – and Nelson was talking about how he'd taken his pregnant wife Lil up to have his child born at the site associated with his dreaming, and they'd been turned back by patrol officers. He saw me and came over. He said we shared the same hair colour and must be of the same tribe, cheeky beggar. But he was entertaining. And bright. He'd obviously picked up a good education at the Ooldea Mission – you know the kind of place, where they wait to distribute the food until the end of Christian service. He talked about how his ancestors had been forced westwards by the gold-mining around Tarcoola— '

'How old is he?'

'Damned if I know. Twenty-three? Twenty-four? But he looks much older now. He's changed, gone native.

158

It's the Yalata reservation, it's got no spiritual meaning for the Pitjantjatjara, they lose touch with themselves. They drink heavily and become delinquent. This last time I saw Nelson, when he came up with the green-stone, all the spirit had gone out of him. He's thrown away his mission clothes, everything except a pair of baggy pants. He doesn't look me in the eye any more. Just stares into space most of the time; lies on his back and stares up at the stars, or else smokes his pipe. He told me he'd come a long way to find me. Whatever he means by that – it wasn't easy to get him talking. Still, he seems to know where the uranium comes from, that's all that matters to us. Let's just hope the beggar's here where he said he'd be.'

The Transcontinental began jolting and slowing. Douglas had an image of Nick's 'little town' resembling an American frontier town; he looked for the main street of shops and houses leading away from the station. Instead he stepped down on to the bare red earth, on which a few galvanised-iron shacks surrounded a tank of stagnant water.

Small black children ran alongside the train holding up dingo pelts. A couple of Aborigines from the rear carriage had made to get off, and were being pushed back inside by the guard. Douglas stood looking around for the remains of a mission like the one at Ooldea. All he could see was an iron shed, above the door of which had been nailed a wooden board with the words inscribed in peeling paint: 'The Earth Is The Lords And The Fullness Thereof.'

'Let's go quickly,' said Nick. 'Time's short.'

He led the way past the iron shacks and two rows of railway cottages, round the back of the makeshift chapel to a dusty area fenced off by the tall thorn-bushes. Here, in a midden of broken glass, bully-beef cans and shelters made from asbestos sheets and fruit-boxes, sprawled the Aboriginal camp. Piccaninnies with flies in the corners of their long-lashed eyes played in the burned-out wrecks of old cars. Their mothers squatted on the ground, pendulous-breasted, brushing the black tangled hair off their faces. A couple of young Aborigines were tinkering with the engine of a Holden pick-up; they stopped and stared at the two white men with a gaze which displayed neither resentment nor curiosity.

A large camper-van, wheel-less, rested on its axles in

the dust. An awning of brown hessian stretched from its roof to a couple of sticks in the ground. Under this shade sat Nelson Kulpinya. He was wearing a ragged pair of green cotton trousers and a red Paisley-pattern scarf as a headband. As they approached, he got to his feet, scowling.

'You didn't say nothing 'bout another white bloke,' he said gruffly to Nick. 'This bin between you and me.'

'This is Mr Manifold, my driver,' replied Nick. He winked at Douglas. 'Meet my friend Nelson.'

Douglas proffered a handshake. The Aborigine took it suspiciously. He had fine hands, surprisingly smooth, with long fingers. In appearance Nelson was indeed lighter than the other Aborigines. Although he shared their heavy brow-ridges and deep-set eyes, his nostrils were narrower, more European, and his lips less full. His bushy hair was the same reddish colour as Nick Kemp's, although whether it was natural or ochred Douglas had no way of telling.

Nelson held out his hand to Nick, palm upwards. 'You bin got my stone,' he declared.

'Yes. It's on the train,' said Nick easily. 'So is your wages. We'd better get on board or it will leave without us, eh?'

Nelson stared at him. He turned on his heel without a word and went inside his camper. The two men waited. Nick looked at his watch.

'What do you think?' Douglas asked after a minute. 'Is he coming?'

'He'll come!'

They waited another minute. The Transcontinental blew a long whistle. The door of the camper opened and Nelson re-emerged. So far as Douglas could see, he had done little except put on a blue shirt, plimsolls, and a bushman's hat. In his hand he carried not a spear and spear-thrower but a pipe and a large tin of tobacco. He ducked under the awning as he passed and picked up a swag tied at each end with string.

'Let's go,' said Nick.

They made it to the train just as it began to move, and clambered on board with the help of a steward, whose face twitched disagreeably.

'Has he got a ticket for this coach?' he asked, indicating Nelson with his head.

Nick nodded, catching his breath. 'It's in my compartment.'

'I hope so, otherwise he'll have to get out at Watson, next stop.'

In the compartment Nick shoved his prospecting gear to one side so that Nelson could sit down. For the first time Douglas was able to get a good look at the Aborigine's right eye. It was milky with cataracts: a crippling disability if Nelson had had to hunt for his own food.

The other eye, brown and baleful, was studying him. In embarrassment Douglas stuttered: 'You were at the Mission, weren't you? The Mission in Ooldea?'

Nelson's gaze didn't flicker. 'Mission bin finish long time,' he said in his gruff voice. 'Ooldil Gabbi all gone. Plenty sand up to here.' He raised his hand up to his chin.

'He means the outbuildings,' interrupted Nick. 'The sand-dunes have buried them, too. Ooldea soak used to be the only unfailing source of water for hundreds of miles around, which is why the tribes used to gather here. But the railway engineers in the thirties drew off the water and perforated the blue clay bed underneath, so that was that. There's a legend about Ooldea Water, Nelson will tell you. About Karrbiji the marsupial creating it out of the water in his skin bag, and Ngabbula the lizard chasing him. Isn't there an emblem-stone buried there, Nelson, which the medicine-man knew about?'

'The *nungan* use meteor-stones,' said Nelson, deliberately avoiding the question, as if emblem-stones were too sacred for idle conversation. Nevertheless he repeated the legend of the Water, miming Ngabbula's chase, the great clubbing which Giniga the cat gave him, and Karrbiji's friend the emu heeling the sand to reveal to the first men where the soak was. As he spoke, Douglas was amused to notice how Nelson's pidgin was gradually expanding into the clear missionary English he'd been taught as a boy. Somehow it made him seem younger, though Douglas still had no way of telling his age.

'Where's my stone?' Nelson demanded when he'd finished Karrbiji's story.

Nick fished it out. Nelson took it from him. He weighed

161

it in his hand a moment, then leaned over and put it in the pocket of Nick's shirt.

'Many many green stones,' he remarked.

Nick nodded. 'You will take us to the place?'

Instead of replying, Nelson took out his pipe and filled it with tobacco. Then he unrolled his swag. Among its contents – sugar, a bag of flour, tea, a tin billy, a few pieces of ochre and some coins on a string – was a gleaming silver cigarette-lighter. With a flourish, Nelson lit his pipe.

'There is money for you,' said Nick.

'How much?'

'Plenty of dollars. Enough to go to the Big Smoke.'

Nelson considered this. He shook his head. 'Adelaide no good.' He puffed his pipe. 'I don't want your money. I'll take you there by-and-by. But first we go to my place, Yadina.'

'Where's that?' asked Nick.

'On the way.'

'What's at Yadina?'

'Water. I have to test it. See if it's good.' He launched into an explanation which Douglas couldn't fully understand, of how a patrol officer a long time ago had put wood across the sites of 'men's business' north of the railway-line to stop the 'business' and keep the *tjilpi* away. These sites had to be unblocked. Yadina was one of them.

'What's "men's business"?' asked Douglas when Nelson had finished.

'Aboriginal ritual,' replied Nick shortly. 'The *tjilpi* are tribal elders and medicine-men. It sounds like typical interference by the state government. You come across it all the time in the bush.'

The steward came by. Nick held up Nelson's ticket. The steward nodded, wrinkling his nose at the blue tobacco smoke.

'About thirty-five minutes to Fisher,' he said. 'They know to stop for you. There's no one else.'

Douglas understood why when they got there and unloaded the packs and geological equipment. A blazing sun in a blue-white sky shone down on ten rusted oil-drums and a few dozen railway sleepers piled in squares beside the line. A hundred yards across the tracked dirt stood Fisher. It consisted of a small bungalow, two galvo shacks, a dunny and a trolley-shed. Beyond, in every direction, the flat, sandy, stony, Nullarbor Desert stretched to the bottom of the sky.

The Transcontinental quietly, apologetically slid away from them. Douglas glanced round to see the ghostly faces of passengers to Perth and Kalgoorlie craning out at two white men in bush-hats standing in the centre of nowhere – and then they were gone. Where the coaches had been, the emptiness smouldered to the pale horizon.

'Is this it?' he muttered.

Nick slapped him on the back. 'There are two environments in the outback,' he remarked. 'One is called Something. The other is called Nothing. This is neither: this is Civilisation. Here's Bill Rigg. Let's go and have a dekko at our luxury transport.'

A dog was barking. A man with wide shoulders and a narrow head shadowed by a broad-brimmed hat had emerged from the bungalow. One hand in his pocket, the other carrying a six-pack of beer, he strolled across to them.

'G'day,' he remarked. 'Drink?'

He handed out beers to the two white men. Nick glanced at Nelson, who shook his head.

'This is my mate Douglas,' Nick said. 'How's the old truck, Bill? Did you get it off all right?'

'No trouble. It's in the trolley-shed.'

Bill Rigg led the way. Under the shed's iron roof it was hotter than outside. The beer, cold out of the bungalow refrigerator, was already like lukewarm tea. The Land-rover looked as if it had seen better times. The canvas by the driver's window had a rent in it. The roo-bar was bent; so was one of the two struts that went in a V-shape from the front of the bonnet to the top corners of the windscreen.

Nick examined the Land-rover carefully, patting it like a farmer at an auction.

'I checked the petrol and the oil-level,' said Bill. 'Topped up the water in your radiator, though. Out here it evaporates as fast as a prossie's smile after she's bagged your money.'

'Thanks.'

'Your tyres could do with a squirt. I got a pressure reading of twelve pounds.'

'Yes. That's what they should be. Where we're going, the softer the better.'

'And where's that?' Bill Rigg tipped his head back to drain the beer, but kept his eyes on Nick.

'Surveying.' Nick was fiddling with the carburettor.

'Surveying, eh? I thought you might be prospecting. Though I guess you're not so daft as to think there's anything in the Nullarbor. Eh, sport?'

Nick slammed the bonnet shut. 'Thanks for everything, Bill. How much do I owe you?'

'Come and have another beer. We'll settle up in the house.'

'Keep it on ice until we get back. Three days.' Nick took a twenty-dollar bill out of his pocket and stuffed it in the railwayman's pocket. 'It's past ten, and we've got a lot of ground to cover. We'll have to scoot off, pal. Just give us a hand with the stuff, will you?'

They secured the luggage and equipment between the racks of spare tyres in the back of the Land-rover. Nelson fiddled with the two-way radio. The shed was suddenly filled with the yodelling voice of Rolf Harris singing *Sun arise early in the mor-ning*, to the accompaniment of Aboriginal didgeridoos. Nelson's face split into a wide grin for the first time since Ooldea. He clasped his hands round his knees and fell back on the ground hooting with laughter.

'Powerful white fella medicine,' he said, and convulsed again.

When the loading was completed Nick drove the short distance to the water-tank. The others followed on foot, and helped him fill the canvas water-bags and string them along the side of the Land-rover where evaporation would keep the water cool. Nick tested the transmitter. Then he checked his compass against the compass built into the Land-rover's dashboard. Suddenly, there was nothing left to do.

Nick looked at them, his face glowing, his eyes dancing.

'What are we waiting for?'

Shouldering his swag, Nelson clambered into the back. Douglas climbed in beside Nick and slammed the door. As

Nick put the Land-rover into gear and drove out of the siding, Douglas looked back to where Bill Rigg stood watching them, his arms folded. The fearful loneliness of such a companionless existence made him think of his own recent life and flooded him with self-pity.

'Could you survive, living by yourself in a place like this?' he asked.

'Bill chose it.'

'It's a living death. A dog, a radio, and the tea-and-sugar once a fortnight.'

'It's no worse than some of the outback cattle stations and weather stations. You find people like Bill everywhere in the outback. That's what Australia's for: people running away, people keeping their distance. There's nowhere better, if you're a loner. The more you retreat from the edges of the place, the more you can explore into yourself.'

Douglas Manifold looked at him. There was much he didn't know about Nick, but it didn't matter. Old friends didn't hold your ignorance of the past against you, in the way that women, wives, always held against you what you didn't know about them. He said: 'You were tapping your earphones.'

'I was what?'

'Just now, using the transmitter. Tapping on the earphones. Don't you remember those ruined farmhouse buildings outside Sully-sur-Loire? We were so far ahead of the bloody unit that they had started shelling us, thinking we were the German front line. You'd just got the transmitter to work and then the goddam earphones started playing up. . . . '

'I don't know how the hell *you* remember. You were under the table!'

'So were you!'

They laughed. The Land-rover jolted over the flat Nullarbor sand, throwing up a clatter of stones against the chassis. Apart from salt-bushes and a few clumps of mulga in the distance, the whole visible planet was empty, flat, colourless, while they, plumb in the middle of it, were so quick with life.

After an hour, Nick headed for the shade of a solitary mulga and stopped, to let the engine cool and to top up the water. As the hours jolted by, this ritual was the only break in the monotony of their journey. Nothing in the landscape

165

changed. Only the sight of an occasional bounding rabbit, and once in the far distance (Nick pointed it out) a solitary kangaroo. Sand, stones, bushes, rabbits, lizards, all partook of the same hard steely colour, as though the only way to survive in this emptiness under the burning sun was for everything to take on the indestructible consistency of mineral. To Douglas it was exhilarating because of its absoluteness, a quality rare in nature and nonexistent in the man-made world, which he defined to himself as an infinity of perfection. He had felt some of the same exhilaration in the middle of the ocean crossing to America – but waves were always changing and playing, like fire. In this barren desert nothing changed or ever had changed. Nick glanced at him, reading his thoughts.

'It's the one place we haven't stolen from the gods,' he said.

Eventually Nick turned the vehicle towards a clump of tall mulgas on the horizon. There were blue-bushes here, and some other low smoky-grey bushes with fleshy dark-green beet-shaped leaves, cupped for drawing up the night condensation.

Nelson got out of the back. He rubbed and pummelled his legs with loud groans, while the other two unrolled the canvas awning from the side of the Land-rover and propped it up with the bonnet struts. Lunch was bully-beef sandwiches. Nelson joined them for it. When they'd finished, Nick got out a map and spread it on the ground.

'Here's Fisher. And here' – indicating a black cross – 'is where Nelson reckons we should hit the sand-dunes. We follow a straight line two hundred and fifteen degrees north-east to this point. Then Nelson takes over.'

Douglas looked at the map. Half of it was a vacant yellow, the rest a vacant orange, the two colours meeting where the Nullarbor joined the sand-dunes of the Great Victoria Desert. Other than that, it was a geographical blank, except for two islands of blue towards the top.

'Are those lakes?' he asked.

'Yes. That's Lake Maurice. The other one's Lake Dey-Dey. We skirt well to the south of them.'

'Why not use them for picking up water?'

Nelson politely covered his grin with his hand. Nick shook his head.

'No chance, old pal. They're salt-pans. Deadest of all. If we were coming their way a million years ago I'd have taken your advice.'

'Much obliged. So tell me, where are we aiming for?'

A brown forefinger hovered between them and came down on a patch of orange, over to the east from the cross. Douglas looked up at the man who was going to guide them through this trackless country. He met a milky cataracted eye which seemed to be staring past him into the far distances of time and space. On the map the Aborigine's finger had left a dark smudge, obscuring their destination.

They set off again, Douglas behind the wheel. There were more stones scattered on the ground now, like the gibber of the northern deserts, and he drove slowly. The sun was a blister in the blue-white sky; it burned through the roof, it scorched the air they were travelling through. Douglas had put his elbow on the open window. A few minutes later he realised his mistake and withdrew it, to find the skin already a painful red. At once he followed Nick's example and rolled down his sleeves.

It was his first intimation that they were being punished for having the temerity to exist at all in this dead land. Not dead; worse than dead. In this place life had been extinguished at source, before Death could get a hold and scatter the landscape with bleached bones. This, surely, was a blueprint for Armageddon.

'A thousand Hiroshimas and everywhere could look like this,' he said.

'Mars already does.'

Douglas paused to consider this. 'You think— '

'Why not? Why should we be the only ones? The reason we can't find other intelligent beings in the universe must be because they always succeed in unlocking the logic of nuclear energy and blowing themselves apart. They'd reach that stage of technical proficiency before they got the know-how to communicate with other planets like ours. Maybe there are people at Palomar or somewhere sending out signals right now: but by the time anyone hears them we'll be long gone.' Nick paused. ' "The light shines in the darkness and the darkness comprehendeth it not." '

They drove on, sweating. In the back Nelson stirred and grunted. Gradually a pencil-thin elevation on the horizon grew taller and more distinct. It was the ridge of the first sand-hills, where yellow met orange on the map. Nick, who had been consulting the compass, called a halt. Nelson emerged and stood on top of the cab, squinting. Without a word he pointed to a place where the ridge dipped, almost straight ahead. Nick grinned in triumph. He had plotted them to their first target.

The depression, as they approached it, turned into a long sand-spur rising gently towards the height of the dunes on either side. To Douglas's surprise the sand was firm underneath his wheels. As he gained height, though, it became finer-grained and softer, and the dunes kept on rising higher on either side. As soon as they were in the lee of a dune, Nick ordered a halt.

'We'll turn in early so we can be on our way before dawn,' he announced. 'It's best to travel in the cool of the morning and evening, and take longer rests in the day. Else we'll get crook and so will the old truck.'

They pitched camp. This amounted to setting up the awning from the Land-rover and collecting mulga branches for fire. While the billy was heating their stew, Douglas came back from the Land-rover with their sleeping-bags. Nick was fiddling with the radio. The clipped voice of a newscaster brought a sudden rustle of starched shirts to their bivouac:

'Her Majesty the Queen and His Royal Highness the Duke of Edinburgh arrived in South Australia today to an outpouring of loyalty and devotion from the people of Adelaide. After the Royal plane touched down dead on schedule at five-thirty, Queen Elizabeth, wearing an iridescent green dress, was greeted by the Premier of South Australia, Sir Thomas Playford, and Mr Glover the Lord Mayor of Adelaide. The Royal couple then got into an open car and smilingly acknowledged the ovation of cheering crowds as they were driven down Young Street, Port Road and Commercial Road on the way to Port Adelaide where the Royal Yacht 'Britannia' awaited them. Tonight the Royal couple will enjoy a quiet al fresco dinner aboard 'Britannia', resting in preparation for tomorrow's Royal Progress to Adelaide Town Hall. Excited Adelaiders commented that the Queen looked as youthful and lovely as she did on her last visit nine years ago. Comments such as* 'magnificent', 'amazing', 'gorgeous' and other superlatives were among the tributes which will be repeated many times before the Royal Visit ends on Thursday night.

'Two prehistoric tritons have been restored to normal life, after having been frozen solid for five thousand years, Moscow Radio reported today. . . .'

Nick switched off the radio. Douglas grinned at him.

'When do we start prospecting?' he asked.

'Oh, I'll do a sweep or two tomorrow, in the dunes. There was no point in the Nullarbor. It's all marine lime-stone down there; relatively recent sedimentary formations. You need older, harder rocks for what we're looking for. Cambrian limestones for oil reserves. Cretaceous strata for opals. Gold and uranium in granite conglomerates. I don't expect much from these dunes, but you never know what sand can cover – faults, pressure systems, anything can be going on under here. There could be gold-yielding calcite, like there is at Nichols Nob.'

'No maps?'

'No maps. Or only very basic ones of the tectonics. No magnetic-intensity maps of this southern rim of the Great Victoria Desert that might have told us what the underlying rocks might be, or where the outcroppings are.'

'What happens if your instruments register something good?'

Nick laughed. 'We take an astro fix on the latitude and longitude, get drunk, and go home to stake our claim! Pass me a beer, will you, Duggle?'

'If you fellas get rich, then what?'

Nelson had thrown down his swag and come to squat by the camp-fire. Douglas and Nick looked at each other.

'There'll be spondoolicks enough for all of us,' replied Nick after a pause. 'That's not what I'm here for, primarily.'

'Nor I,' said Douglas. 'I hadn't given a thought to it.'

Nelson gave a broad grin. He prodded the fire with a stick of mulga; sparks flew upwards. Holding his plate in cupped hands like a begging-bowl, he kneeled and proffered it so that Nick could hand out his helping of stew.

When they'd finished supper, Douglas walked up the dune and looked down over the Nullarbor plain. The light was begin-ning to fade. The plain stretched away as flat and bare as a billiard-table, with the clumps of distant mulga sticking up no higher than nap on the grey baize. All around the horizon a pallor of white began to rise towards the darkening blue. It was a stained-glass blue, the last colour to lose its light in English church windows at the end of the day. The stars were out; as the brightness died they congregated until the sky was scattered with cities of lit windows.

Nick and the Aborigine were a hundred yards away on the other side of the dune. Douglas was alone, under a stupendous bowl of sky so unobstructed in any direction he had the giddy feeling that it was about to descend below the horizon, below his feet, spinning on the axis of his little mound of sand. Its vastness chastened his soul; he experienced a momentary pang of longing for the green littleness of England, confined, limited, domesticated, in which the human genius could rise above its mundane surroundings and conquer the universe. Without confinement, energy could never explode into creation.

His brain whirling, Douglas removed himself back over the hill. Nick and Nelson were talking in low voices by the puny light of the camp-fire. Without interrupting them he unrolled his sleeping-bag, took off his boots and glasses, and went to sleep.

Within minutes of closing his eyes, it seemed, a brown hand was shaking Douglas awake. He sat up, and found himself shivering. The night must have been cold: the outside of his sleeping-bag was shiny with condensation. Nick brought him over a mug of tea. He clasped it in both hands and felt the warmth returning.

'What time is it?' he asked.

'Getting on for six. It'll be light soon. Nelson's cooking up some porridge. We ought to be on our way by first light.'

The sunrise revealed a different planet from the day before. Gone was the colourless flat emptiness of the Nullarbor. The sand-hills were red, bright red, the colour of haematite. Their sides were covered in thick clumps of flaky-white spinifex, and the gullies between them were dotted with grey mulga and occasional desert oaks.

The high sand-ridges were often no more than fifty yards

apart. Travelling between them, Nick said, reminded him of navigating through the long high swells of hurricane-waters after the hurricane itself had moved on. The ridges all rolled east-north-east, at right angles to the prevailing winds from the Nullarbor which over thousands of years had raised them in parallel waves across the desert. Nelson had deliberately joined the sand-dunes at a place where their route would run parallel to the ridges, but even so there were times when the hills had to be crossed. In the heavy Land-rover it was a difficult time-consuming task enough. Without Nelson to guide them, Douglas could not imagine how it might be done at all.

Nelson had not got back into the Land-rover. Instead, barefoot now, he loped ahead of them along the top of the ridges, scanning for any dips in their height or ramps of sand that would make a crossing easier. Every now and then he set fire to a thicket of spinifex. That way, from the crest of the higher sand-hills, he could look back along the line of smokes and check the course he was taking.

For all that, they averaged barely more than five miles an hour. Bush-bashing through the mulga, they accumulated a mat of undergrowth on the windscreen. It started at the front of the bonnet and gradually rose halfway up, until there was only a thin strip of clear glass remaining between the mulga and the sun-visor and they had to stop to push the stuff off. Much more time-consuming were the flat tyres. As well as the needle-sharp spinifex grass on the ridges, the sand was scattered with three-cornered jacks, millions of triangular sharp-spined burrs which could pierce through sandals and sometimes tyres as well.

The first flat came ten minutes after breakfast, on a back tyre. They all got out. Nick shovelled the sand away while Douglas fished out the iron plate and slid it underneath the jack. The tyre was squashed as flat as a camel's foot; they nudged it off and replaced it with a new one from the rack. Every hour or less the same ritual had to be repeated, except that where there was a slow puncture, often a piece of wood embedded in the rubber, Nick simply pumped the tyre up and went on.

The red sand was especially treacherous in the lee of the dunes. The only way to cross, they discovered, was in one go, without losing momentum, if they were not to get buried up to the axles and have to dig themselves out. At the top of each sand-hill Nick would flick his eyes across to where the Aborigine was beckoning them and at once drive and slide down the route he had chosen, avoiding the spinifex clumps. On the steering-wheel he had taped a tally-counter of the kind used by sheep-hands. At the top of every ridge he clicked it, to check the number of dunes traversed since they had left the Nullarbor.

The hard going was soon made more uncomfortable by the blistering sun. Neither man complained. There was no time to think beyond the next sand-hill crossing, the next swerve round a mulga, the next flat tyre. Around midday they stopped for a lunch of bully-beef and tomato sauce, shared with several thousand of the black flies which swarmed and pestered every time they left the cab. Douglas smeared on zinc cream. He felt like up-ending one of the canvas water-bags over his head, but their water-supplies were too limited for that. Nelson was the only one of them in his element. Apparently untroubled by his hours of loping in the blazing heat he was full of energy and a new friendliness – probably, Douglas guessed, because they were heading towards his Yadina rock-hole, sacred, so Nelson had told them, to the Wanambi water-serpent of the dreamtime who created water-holes for men.

While Nick rigged up the radio transceiver aerial, to call his contact at an airfield outside Port Augusta, Nelson took Douglas by the hand.

'You come 'longa me,' he insisted. 'You clever fella, but you bin know nuthin' 'bout my country.'

Within a few yards' circumference of the Land-rover, the Aborigine proceeded to show Douglas the tracks of a dozen different creatures who had passed that way – lizards barely marking the sand in their rush across it, the bigger, more ponderous tracks of goannas, the tracings of insects and spiders, the prints of the black crow, and the little circular footmarks of rabbits. He showed Douglas how the yellow-white spinifex grew in circular clumps which propagated outwards for defence, the outer branches bending downwards, taking root and starting a new plant. Inside each spinifex ring lived a self-contained community of lizards, insects and small mice, the sharp spines of the plant protecting them from predators except when hunger drove them to scavenge further afield. Everything in this baking wilderness of sand and scrub had evolved its own protective devices – even the mulga grass whose outer stalks, as they dried in the heat of the sun, bent inwards to form a tented shade over the fresh green shoots at their base.

'If we left you and drove away,' said Douglas, 'what would you eat? How would you survive?'

'Blackfella tucker. Kangaroos.'

'How kangaroos? You don't have a hunting-spear.'

Nelson shrugged. He waved vaguely at the ground. 'Lizards. Witchetty grubs. There's plenty tucker if you go see. And water.' He pointed at the roots of one of the silver-grey bushes in the gully. 'Plenty to drink!'

Douglas was unconvinced by this. He was about to ask for a demonstration, when Nick called to them.

'Radio's working! Let's go, if you're ready.'

They set off again on the slow painful journey across the fossilised sea of orange-red sand and undergrowth. Nelson jogged on ahead, setting fires, searching for landmarks, beckoning them up sand-hills which the four-wheel-drive vehicle somehow surmounted, slithering and straining. Occasionally they came to salt-pans – baked flat pitches of reddish ochre which Nelson would test but often avoid. Once a kangaroo watched them pass, a joey in its pouch. But for hours on end there was nothing to see except sand and mulga, and the undergrowth gathering on the windscreen.

Just before dusk fell they came to a wider, flatter gully than usual. Nick stopped.

'I want to do some measurements before we camp,' he said.

Douglas helped him unload some of the boxes they had stowed at Fisher. The cattle-prod turned out to be the sensing head of something called a proton precession magnetometer, a portable instrument like a large radio slung round the neck which gave readings of faults and anomalies in sub-surface magnetic ores. Nick put this aside for the time being and instead began setting up a complicated console attached to electrodes pushed into the ground at distances of several hundred feet apart.

'It's called induced polarisation,' he explained. 'I don't suppose that means anything to you. It's a new technique,

173

nobody's quite sure what it can be made to do. Basically it penetrates the ground deeper than anything else, up to two thousand five hundred feet. By measuring the resistance between the electrodes you can find disseminated magnetic particles in a host rock. Copper, for example, or gold disseminated in quartz veins. It's the same principle which the Allies applied in the later stages of the war to submarine detection – you may already know that, Duggle, from your intelligence days. Would you mind manning the console? I'll tell you what to do.'

For the best part of an hour, until the figures on the dial became indistinguishable from the swarming bush-flies, Douglas called out figures and wrote them down. Nelson meanwhile had been building a fire, using the mulga bush on the windscreen as its base. By the time Nick returned with the cables and electrodes, spears of flame were already twisting and snapping the dry scrub.

'I'll look at the figures tonight,' Nick said. 'My guess is that there isn't much down there except carbonates; maybe some water-bearing strata. We're still on the marine limestone shelf.'

His voice was heavy with disappointment. Douglas asked: 'How can limestone produce Nelson's bit of rock?'

'It can't. But we're still a day's journey away from that, so Nelson says.'

The sky was clear. A cool wind had sprung up. They washed their faces out of a bowl, and threw the dirty water over the Land-rover's acid-soaked battery. Douglas combed his hair. The three of them drank soup and ate tinned baked beans and sausages. Then, because Nelson's fire was too good to waste in sleep, they sat round and told stories, while the sky darkened and stars came out.

Nelson, sucking on his pipe, told them the legend of the mythical Wild Turkey Man who stole fire from mankind and tried to extinguish it in the sea. It was a burning bush, like Abraham's, the only fire in existence, and if two valiant Hawk men had not snatched it back from the thief at the last moment the world would have become a cold and lifeless place.

Nelson himself was a Wonambi man, and he described how the great serpent-god, in his incessant search for water, had writhed this way and that across the desert, throwing up the sand-ridges on either side of his body. It became clear to Douglas, as he listened, that for Aborigines of the central desert all of the barren land around them was somehow consecrated to a dreaming; all of it was sacred in some degree. Nelson, who appeared to regard his missionary education as a whitefella attempt to cheat him of his birthright, behaved like a keeper of the holy flame. He had returned to his old religion; he talked with the passion and protectiveness of a convert for whom every hole dug in the desert earth, every man-made defacement of the landscape, was a violation of his own body and spirit. In the firelight, as he spoke of it, his one good eye hardened and glinted like a knapped flint.

For Nicholas Kemp, alone among white men, he seemed to have an affinity. Douglas had forgotten the reason, and puzzled over it, until Nelson leaned across and ran his hand gently through Nick's red hair.

'You brother longa me,' he declared in his guttural voice. 'You and me go down together.'

'You do me an honour,' returned Nick gravely. 'My ancestor treated you people badly. Now the wound is healed.'

'Which ancestor?' Douglas asked.

'My grandfather.'

'Son of Kemp's Pinnacle?'

'Yes. Albert Kemp. He was a prospector. Like us, I think I told you. After the Victoria gold-rushes in the eighteen sixties, South Australia wanted a gold-rush of its own. Aboriginal legends started going the rounds of the prospectors' pubs about lumps of gold in the hills north of the Burra copper country. Expeditions went out, with Aboriginal guides, but nothing had been found. So my grandfather decided to go and take a look for himself. Up near Leigh Creek he found a lode of gold-bearing quartz, and like a fool he advertised the fact. So by the time he'd staked his claim and started digging he was in the middle of a miniature gold-rush with half of Adelaide forming syndicates to peg every block in sight. Typical of the Kemps, my dad used to say.'

'But how did he treat the Aborigines badly? What's this wound you've been healing?'

'Well, the trouble was that the Leigh Creek miners were rooting up Aboriginal land. They fossicked everywhere; they sank hundreds of shafts in the search for gold. They cut down the vegetation, shot the kangaroos, polluted the streams . . . and it wasn't as if they compensated by employing Aboriginal labour; dammit, they outnumbered the local Aborigines. So the Abos were starving to death. The only way they could fight back was to raid the white settlements when the miners were at work. They'd steal food and drive the miners' horses and cattle off, or spear them. It caused a lot of friction. The miners were often hardened convicts from the East Coast, you have to remember. Not a morally fastidious lot. Anyway, my grandfather kept *his* mineworkers in check, until the massacre happened. That was in 1872, around the time the Alma Mine was established.'

Nick fell silent. He poked the fire with a mulga stick, frowning. Sparks flared and died. Nelson sat as still as a stone, gazing into the flames, his face cavernous in the shifting flare.

He muttered: 'Plenty shoot 'em. Plenty blackfellas killed.'

'The thing was,' Nick went on, 'my grandfather had a club-foot. He must have thought it was the mark of the devil; anyway, that's how he behaved. Despite his standing in society he decided that no woman would have him, which is why he chose to go fossicking in the outback. He didn't even live in Leigh Creek. He built himself a house down by the mine at a place called Waukeringa. He lived there with a black native woman, probably Pitjantjatjara; he called her Maria.'

Douglas stared. 'An Aborigine!'

'It happens more often than you might think, out here. And Aborigines – Nelson will tell you – often see physical deformity as a sign of power rather than of weakness. Anyway, Maria bore my grandfather a son, whom he baptised George on the tenth of February 1870 – I've seen the register in Port Leigh. But then something happened. I wonder if Albert's sister Emily announced she was coming to visit him from Adelaide? Anyway, he turned Maria out of doors, to live in the saddle-shed. She died there soon after. I'd always heard it was a cold, but I found a note from my grandfather after he died saying it was syphilis caught from the miners who came to the saddle-shed and raped her.'

The fire flared. Nelson kicked it.

'Either way the local Pitjantjatjara decided that my

grandfather had humiliated them. He writes in his diary that he heard the sound of bull-roarers every night. They came in through a window, one of those nights, and abducted the baby, George. Just carried him off! Albert saw red. I suppose he loved the child; anyway, he'd gone to the trouble of hiring a nanny from Adelaide to help raise him. So he set out with a party of servants and miners to get the baby back . . . and the thing got out of hand. The miners saw their chance to get revenge for their speared cattle. There was a large camp of Pitjantjatjara a few miles away. They surrounded it and shot down every last Aborigine, men, women and children. About fifty in all.'

'And George?' asked Douglas after a moment.

'No. Albert never found his son. He left Leigh Creek shortly after that. He went back to Adelaide where he married my grandmother, club-foot and all.' Nick turned to look at Nelson. 'What do you think of that – brother?'

Nelson took the pipe out of his mouth. 'I know it,' he said. He leaned forward, and spat into the fire. Slowly, sparing not a glance for his questioner, he put the pipe back between his teeth and sucked at it. The two white men stared at him.

'I don't think my grandfather should take all the blame,' Nick continued. 'It's down in Aboriginal folklore as a massacre but you've got to remember the Europeans killed about twenty thousand Abos during the white settlement of Australia, not including those who died from being driven off good land into the marginal country. . . .'

He paused. Nelson was shaking his head.

'Whitefellas still poisonin' us,' he declared. He waved his hand. 'Poison in the air.'

'Not now, Nelson,' said Nick. 'Not any longer.'

There was an awkward silence. Douglas couldn't leave it there.

'Do we know what happened to the half-breed baby, George?'

'No. The kidnappers probably rubbed him with charcoal and took him out of reach of the white settlements. Or else one of Albert's miners killed him in the raid and was too scared to say so.'

Nelson stood up. 'Nuthin' get finish up yet,' he said.

He bent and picked up his swag and carried it into the darkness beyond the circle of firelight.

Douglas felt the wind chill on his back. For the first time since Adelaide he experienced a moment's longing for the luxuries of civilisation: a hot bath, a soft mattress and a pillow. He unrolled his sleeping-bag and wormed into its warm cocoon. The last thing he saw before his eyes closed was Nick still sitting with his arms on his knees, staring into the fire, still musing on the past, he thought sleepily, as though the future wasn't worth thinking about . . .

In the updraught from the air-conditioning the venetian blinds rattled once, twice. Through them a cage of shadows fell on the crumpled sheet. Helen got out of bed. Naked, she yawned and stretched her arms above her head, palms outward like an ivory figurine. Edward Catchpole, in a silk dressing-gown, sat up on the pillow and reached out for his glasses, the better to study her long slim back, the tight roundedness of her hips.

Without a word she began dressing. Through the shut windows came the faint frantic clanging of a fire-engine. She peered out through a chink in the blinds.

'Fires.' She stood with her back to him. 'Sometimes, you know, I feel as if I need a fire-break in my body, to stop burning up inside.'

Catchpole regarded her. He said: 'You've been very quiet today.'

'Have I?'

'Is everything all right, dear heart?'

'Yes.' She dropped the blind. 'The papers are talking about arsonists.'

'The police won't chase them. Too busy drilling and parading and cleaning their boots for the Royal Progress.'

'Shouldn't you be out there, organising the security? Isn't this your big day?'

'I've done what I came here to do. Most of it.'

He got out of bed and went and fiddled with a drawer in his desk. He came back with a packet of Russian Sobranies, lit one and handed it to her.

'Here. A gift from the Enemy.'

'Thanks. It's what I need.' Helen dragged hard on the cigarette. 'I may as well tell you, Edward. I'm planning to get a divorce.'

'Oh?'

'Don't go all cold on me. It's nothing necessarily to do with you. It's on grounds of cruelty. I've been in touch

179

with my lawyer in London. I might see someone out here, while Douglas is away.'

Very deliberately Catchpole tied the ends of his dressing-gown cord into a bow. He asked: 'How has he been cruel to you? No, don't tell me. I'd better not know that kind of thing. What will you do?'

She turned her head a little towards him. 'Go back to England, I suppose.'

'Will you go back? Straight away?'

'Larry Olivier wants me to join his company at the National.'

'Yes.' He plunged his hands in his pocket, meditating. Then he said quietly: 'Don't go yet, Helen. Stay here till I'm through.'

She flicked her ash, as she always did, into one of his precious bits of oriental porcelain. He flinched.

'How long will that be?' she wanted to know.

The telephone began ringing.

'Two more weeks. Three at the most. I'll know when I'm coming back to London.' He went into the living-room.

'Why should I wait for you?' she cried after him. 'Give me one good reason!'

Thoughtfully she finished dressing. Snatches of Catchpole's conversation filtered through from the next room.

'*Yes. . . . No, right off the scent. . . . Rumours, no more than that. . . . Levels, what levels? His instrumentation was all wrong! . . . I know. . . . No, it hasn't changed anything. If the Yanks won't let us use Nevada we're still free. . . . Yes. . . . Goodbye, and good luck.*'

He came back and started putting his clothes on. Helen stood at the window, looking out through the blind at the barred sunlight. He came over and lifted her hair, letting it ripple through his fingers.

'Wait for me,' he commanded.

'Why? Whatever can keep you in this place?'

He made no reply to this. After a minute she said: 'I'm going to make some coffee. Do you want some?'

Catchpole grunted, putting on his shoes. 'Not for me.'

There was the sound of the fridge opening. 'Where have all your steaks gone?' she called out to him. 'All you've got in here is wrapped Danish bacon and Italian salami!'

Catchpole didn't answer. In his grey suit and polished shoes he came and stood in the kitchen doorway.

'You really need someone to look after you,' said Helen, sighing.

As she brushed past him, he put out a hand to caress her.

'No. Leave me.' She edged around the living-room, running her fingers over his desk, his sofa, his cabinets of oriental porcelain; all the while stealing glances at him. 'Sometimes I wonder if I'm on display here, like one of your Chinese pots,' she complained. 'To be taken out and fondled and put away again.'

'Helen, promise you won't go back without me.'

'They are *your* pots, aren't they? You're not really care-taking anything for anyone? It was just another of your secrets!'

'You know all my secrets. The secrets of my heart.'

'Those might be the least interesting.' She turned the lock on a display-cabinet, and took out an exquisite Kakeimon rose-bowl decorated with birds and trees on the white glaze. 'You're always telling me that knowledge is power. You think you know me, Edward. Don't you?'

'I know only as much as I need to know, and you let me know.'

She examined the rose-bowl carefully, turning it over in her fingers. The tip of her tongue poked out between her teeth. 'What if I dropped— ?'

'No! Don't!'

Too late. She had let the bowl slip, and not on the carpet but on to the splayed foot of the cabinet where it shattered. At once Helen burst into tears. She ran to where Catchpole stood rigid, and clung to him like a penitent child.

'What shall I do?' she sobbed. 'Oh, Edward, tell me what to do!'

Edward Catchpole's hands balled into fists behind her back. Slowly they relaxed, and held her to him.

'Divorce Douglas,' he declared. 'Marry me.'

181

O n the expanse of hot sand, stretching to the horizon, a
foot clumped down clad in a frogman's flipper. Georgina
raised her head from the beach-towel. A figure in a black rubber
wet-suit was looking down at her. Its mask came off to reveal
a freckle-faced boy of about eighteen with curly red hair and a
wide toothy grin.

'G'day!'

Georgina raised herself on one elbow, the beginnings of a
scowl on her face. 'Hallo. Did you want something?'

'Yeah. Just to introduce myself. I'm Bill Read. I saw you
were here by yourself.' His eyes flickered briefly over her red
bathing-suit. He pawed his rubber mask. 'I thought maybe you'd
like to watch me practise.'

'I'm not here by myself.' Georgina shaded her eyes and
scanned the waterline. A flash of green surfboard, riding the
breakers . . . Dirk. She sighed.

'It's the Aqualung Navigation Championship this afternoon,'
said Bill Read. 'I'm one of the top divers. We're practising
right up the beach, look!' He pointed. Sure enough, a shoal
of rubber-suited frogmen were flapping in and out of the water
and clambering up netting on to a sailing boat anchored off-
shore. He added graciously: 'You're the best looker on the
beach!'

'Oh. Thanks. Perhaps my friend and I will come over a bit
later on.'

Not that it was *that* much of a compliment, she reflected,
after Bill had clumped back up the beach taking his toothy
grin with him. The competition was not strong. Dirk's idea had
been that they'd have the Glenelg beach to themselves because
everybody would be up in town waiting to see the Queen go by,
or else getting ready for the big excitement that night when the
Royal Barge was due to sail up the Torrens to the Music Festival. Instead they'd all taken this special holiday to come to the

beach instead: fathers in blue blazers licking ice-creams, mothers reclining pinkly on towels watching their nippers dig puddles in the sand, grandmothers in hair-nets knitting comforters under candy-striped beach-umbrellas – and Georgina, looking pretty good, she thought, in her new swimming-costume, lying on her solitary towel in the middle of this mêlée as she waited for Dirk to stop showing off on his surfboard.

She looked in her school-bag for the sun-tan cream. Dirk came running up the sand in a fine cold spray of sea-water and flung himself down on the towel beside her.

'Who was that?'

'Who?' She searched her bag.

'The goof in flippers.'

'Oh, him. He's the State Aqualung Champion. He wanted me to go and watch him because I'm the most beautiful girl on the beach.'

'Oh, baloney.'

'What!'

Dirk was looking down his nose at her, amused. 'Baloney that he's the State Aqualung Champion.'

'That's not what you meant!'

Dirk took the sun-tan lotion from her. She rolled over on her tummy. He began kneading the cream into her back above the bikini strap, massaging her neck and shoulder muscles so pleasurably that she groaned and had to turn it into a cough.

'Do you like me doing this to you?' he asked.

'It's okay. I was thinking about . . . about that scientist, Doctor Schneider. Do you think it was suicide? Or do you suppose someone murdered him because he knew too much about radiation levels?'

He was running his fingers down her spine.

'Dirk?'

'Yes?'

'What do you think?'

'You know why they called bikinis after the American atomic test on Bikini Atoll?'

'Seriously. What do you think?'

'I don't know. This bloke Winn Vellacott – what makes him so sure? It sounds to me as if your dad's right, it's the journalist trying to create a story to write about.'

'But there *were* atomic tests out here, Winn says. The same time as the Bikini Atoll ones.'

'Yes, but they were in the newspapers. Don't move—'

'It's cold!'

'And you'd need a lot of fallout before it got in the food chain. You'd need a north wind blowing tons of sand from the testing area over Adelaide before anything like that happened. You're just over-dramatising, like a lot of girls your age.'

'And you're so mature, I suppose!'

'I know a thing or two.' Dirk paused. 'I know Flippers was right about how pretty you are.'

Georgina pulled a thread out of the towel, carefully. 'You never used to thing that.'

'You've improved since you came to Australia.'

He capped the bottle of sun-tan cream. She took it from him. The brush of his fingers against hers sent a shock of joy through her.

'Do you know Marble Hill?' she asked, blinking at him in the bright sun.

'The ruin up on Norton Summit?'

'Yes. Where the British governors used to go. It's a fabulous place. I go there sometimes. Why don't you come?'

'It's private.'

'But nobody sees you, the way I go in. We could have a picnic up the tower. You feel on top of the world. Last time I went I saw a forest fire, like the one which burned the house down.'

Dirk's face on the towel was very close to hers. He was wearing his ironic smile. She went on, defensively: 'It's true. There was a stand of silver gums in the gardens, with lawn all around. The trees just caught fire, with a kind of roaring, whistling noise. I thought it must be spontaneous combustion or something. Then I saw the two figures.'

'What two figures?'

'I don't know. I thought they were shadows of the flames at first, because they were running in and out. I couldn't see them properly; I couldn't see what they were doing. It was incredibly stupid, because if the wind had been

184

the other way the fire could have spread down the hills all the way into Adelaide. I just couldn't move. I just stood on top of the tower and watched.'

'What then, Georgie?'

'Someone must have seen the smoke, because the fire-siren went off. I thought I'd better clear out in case they thought it was me. So you see . . . ' she ended vaguely.

'I see it's time for a swim.' Dirk jumped up and held out his hand. 'Come on.'

'But I've only just put my sun-tan on!'

'So what?'

He pulled her up off the bath-towel and made as if to carry her down to the sea. Georgina struggled free and ran from him down the sand. The water was like cold fire licking at her ankles, running up her legs. She plunged into it, her heart dancing.

When she got back to Wellington Square, later that morning, Georgina found her stepmother doing her exercises in the sitting-room, observed by Ottoman stretched out weakly in his basket.

'I thought you might be looking at the Queen,' Georgina said. 'To see if she was doing it as well as you.'

Helen was evidently in a good humour for once, because she didn't rise to this remark. Instead, straightening up, she said: 'George, if you have a second, I think you and I should talk.'

They sat over coffee in the kitchen – Helen in her exercise kimono, Georgina in the shorts and shirt she had pulled over her swimming-costume.

'I know you don't like me very much,' Helen began.

Georgina was silent.

'Darling, I don't blame you. Stepmothers are always wicked. They're the ones blamed for breaking up the marriage, because it's so hard for a child to blame her father. People forget that it's often worse for a child when her parents carry on in a marriage that's gone sour. The wonderful thing for Douglas now is that he's got you.'

'He's got both of us.'

'Yes, darling, but especially you.' Helen's eyes were moist. She put out her long fingers and clasped Georgina's wrist.

185

'You mean so much to him. You know what a secret person he is in some ways. It's as if he stores up his feelings and lets them out in his writing. But I know he loves you very much.'

'Because I remind him of Bella.'

Helen flinched. 'Because you're his daughter, George. Let's not bring your mother into this. I never met her.'

'She met you. I mean, she saw you. You were playing Helen of Troy at the Lyceum. She went to a matinée. When she came to pick me up from school, she'd been crying. I asked her why, and she said that it was because Faust had sold his soul. I didn't understand, then.'

A fly was buzzing in the window-netting. Helen got up.

'I know you want to exclude me,' she said, her voice shaky. 'Even though I've loved Douglas all these years and tried to make him live up to himself. Well, I can't fight the dead, and I don't mean to try. You might just get what you want, little Miss Sanctimonious. And, if you do, it won't be my fault.'

In a shimmer of yellow silk Helen left the kitchen, stage right. Somewhere a piano lid slammed down. Searching vainly for her mistress Ottoman dragged herself into the kitchen and was sick over Georgina's shoe.

Jolting on their way north-east again in the first grey
light before dawn, they scared an emu which crashed
away through the mulga, its body stately and upright above
its pounding undercarriage. The sun came up in another
mercilessly clear sky. Once again Nick and Douglas had to
take the choice between the devil of treacherous sand-hills
and the deep grey-green sea of mulga, mallee and salt-bush
undergrowth. Although fewer spinifex hummocks waylaid them,
the ridges were becoming more jumbled, as if the serpent-god,
waterless, had thrashed around in its agony.

Nelson kept his distance in front of them. He only
stopped when they got bogged down, or had a puncture,
and had to repeat the infinitely tedious ritual of digging out
and jacking up on the iron plate which itself kept sinking
into the sand. As they approached Yadina, Nelson gave every
appearance of reverting once more to pure Aborigine. Naked
now except for a cloth around his loins he was striding out with
an assured deliberation, as if an ancestral path, visible only to
him, lay beneath his feet and led him towards the place of his
dreaming.

Aboriginal beliefs, so far as Douglas had been able
to tell, were closest to those of the Homeric Greeks.
Hesiod had written of the semi-human gods creating living
things before transforming themselves into mountains, valleys
or watercourses, and leaving parables of themselves for men
to learn from. The great Scottish anthropologist Sir Arthur
Keith had come to the opinion that of all the existing races
of mankind the Australian Aboriginal was the only one who
could serve as their common ancestor. It no longer looked like
a ridiculous supposition. Here was a race which over thousands
of years had evolved a completely successful hunting–gathering
economy. It included a system of naming and classifying every
aspect of its environment which was as efficient as anything
modern science had invented. From the tiniest burr to the sun

and stars, everything had its place in the Aboriginal order of things, an order at once mythological and practical. This was the intricate satisfying mechanism which the white man, since the first settlement, had inadvertently or deliberately proceeded to destroy.

He mentioned some of these thoughts to Nick, who had been uncommonly quiet during the morning's drive. Nick had heard of the Arthur Keith theory.

'My theory of evolution is different,' he said. 'Mine is that mankind is progressing from Aboriginal innocence towards a state of perfect understanding of the world around us. The problem is that the closer we get to universal knowledge the more it scares us into wanting to return to a state of Aboriginal innocence. I think the Chinese have got it about right. Everything goes in cycles. We get to the point of conquering nature, and then there's a giant catastrophe and we all go back to being little fishes swimming around in a scummy sea.'

'Is that determinism or fatalism?'

'Fatalism. If you were Nelson, wouldn't you be a fatalist?'

In the shade of a tall mulga tree they stopped to rest the Land-rover. Petrol was pouring through the carburettors; the engine needed to cool before they could top the radiator up with water. They were hungry and wanted to eat lunch, but Nelson would have none of it. Impatient, he explained that the Yadina rock-hole was less than a mile away.

They took a drink, and drove on. Almost at once the ground began to rise and the sand-ridges to flatten. They found themselves on an open plateau of undulating sand, dotted with mulga trees and low scrub. A ghost gum reared its flaking antlers into the cobalt sky. Beyond it the ground fell away into a natural amphitheatre, sloping towards an arena of flat sheet rock.

Leaving the Land-rover on the ridge they scrambled down. Nelson was there before them. He stood on the grey rock, gazing at a plank of wood which lay diagonally across it.

'Whitefellas bin stopping up our water, stopping men's business,' he complained.

Douglas and Nick each took an end of the plank and lifted it away. Underneath was a long irregular fissure where two pieces of sheet rock had cracked apart. In the middle the fissure widened into a dark hole, no bigger than a hat. Nick kneeled and put his arm down, about twelve inches. When he brought it up there was water in his cupped hand.

'No good?' Nelson was hopping from one foot to the other in a paroxysm of anxiety. 'Is it bin poisoned?'

'Why should it be poisoned?' Nick sipped the water in his hand, and spat it out. Then he sipped again. 'It's fresh water,' he announced. 'A bit brackish, but fresh. Good on you, pal.'

Douglas had brought a plastic cup from the car. He filled it from the rock-hole. The water tasted foul to him, but it was enough to savour the miracle of water at all in this arid wilderness. He offered the cup to Nelson, but the Aborigine turned away. He climbed up the ridge to the car, and came back with the chunk of red-ochre from his swag.

While the other two watched, Nelson dipped the red-ochre into the water of the rock-hole. Then he began annointing himself with the red stone, rubbing it over his face and torso and into the ritual scars on his back. As he did so he wheeled around on the sand beside the rock – slowly at first, then faster and faster, stamping his heel on the ground in time to the chant.

He seemed to Douglas to be singing a story in verses, each one starting on a high keening note and ending in a guttural growl. The singing-dance was addressed to the rock, which Nelson called sometimes Wonambi, sometimes by a word like *tjukuri* which Douglas didn't understand.

'The rock is the serpent-god,' explained Nick Kemp in an undertone. 'It's also his grandfather. . . . '

'His *grandfather?*'

'Nothing to do with his real grandfather. I think Nelson told me he died in the nineteen eighteen flu epidemic, like thousands of Aborigines did, and the Pitjantjatjara don't mention their dead. Calling the rock Grandfather is a mark of respect and kinship. It means the rock has a life-force, a *kuranita*. I suppose it's full of the *kuranita* of the serpent Wonambi, which must make it very sacred indeed. I don't blame him for wanting to come here and release it.'

Whether it was his hunger, or something hypnotic about

189

Nelson's wild, solitary, chanting dance, Douglas suddenly had the vivid impression that the long sheet rock was curving out of the lateral. As he stared at it the whole flat rock from its tail to its square head at the foot of a lichened outcrop of black boulders was moving, curving, twisting, writhing in the shimmering heat, as if the serpent had been summoned to life by Nelson's frenzied exhortation.

Douglas blinked and stared, and blinked again. There was a rustling and hissing in his ears. It must have been a gust of wind ... the leaves shaking on the tree that grew out of a crack in the boulder outcrop ... but for that instant he had equal faith that the serpent-rock was speaking. He held his breath. Nelson seemed to be requesting something of Wonambi. Was it guidance? He was pointing at Nick. Then, as if exhausted, he sprawled full-length across the serpent, his palms outstretched, his ochre-red arms flung wide in a suddenly speechless embrace.

Nelson stayed prostrate. The seconds ticked by. Douglas made a move to get up; Nick signalled him to stay still. The Aborigine raised himself into a squatting position. Out of his headband he took a razor-blade. He extended his left arm, palm upwards, and nicked open a vein. Red blood swelled through the red ochre. Drops of blood fell on the serpent-rock. Only then, with a glance at the two white men, did Nelson kneel and drink from the fissure, raising up the cool water in his cupped hands.

Nick got up. 'Let's bring the food down. We can eat under the tree.'

They climbed the slope. Douglas asked: 'What did you make of the blood-letting?'

'You'd better ask him. I think Nelson will tell you something about giving back life to what gave him life. Now that his ritual business is finished I hope to God we don't waste any more time. I want to take a fix on his place-of-green-stones while it's near enough full moon to see it, then get back before our supplies run out.'

In the twisted shade of the corkwood tree Nick and Douglas ate their bully-beef smothered in tomato sauce. Nelson did not share their meal. In the sparse oasis of the rock-hole he had found witchetty grubs, two small mallee hen eggs, and a grey fruit he called *kalgurta* which he ate raw. In silence he finished his meal; in silence he watched as Nick wielded a geological hammer and a small pick to take a specimen from the rocky outcrop where they sat.

'If we find the uranium lode, you'll need Yadina as a pit-stop, won't you?' Douglas asked. 'Moving men and mining equipment across this Godforsaken territory you'll surely need all the water you can get.'

'That's right. But it's permanent sources of water we'll need. It'll mean an intensive survey of the water table and sinking very deep wells if we have to. Always supposing it's a major find.'

They talked for a while about the logistical problems of creating the kind of access through this waterless desert which would suffice to make a uranium mine worth investing in. Nick tried to draw Nelson into the conversation, with illustrations of the benefits he and his people would stand to gain. The Aborigine smiled and nodded or shook his head. Every now and then he leaned over and patted the Wonambi rock or gently smoothed it with his hand, like the face of a loved one returned after a long absence.

They plunged billy-cans into the fissure to top up the radiator, and filled a couple of the canvas water-bags as well. Then Nelson put back the stone cap which, until the officials had come with planks, had been used to plug the rock-hole and stop its water evaporating. He looked up at the sky and sniffed the air. It was late afternoon.

'We stay here,' he said.

Nick shook his head. 'Sorry, mate. The going's good now; we can make another five miles before dark.'

Nelson stuck out his lower lip. He pointed the way they were going. 'Tomorrow,' he said.

'Nelson, look. It's Saturday, right? You told me *two days*: we've done that already. I want to see this place and be back here tomorrow night. Sunday. Otherwise no money, nothing.'

The Aborigine looked at the ground. He shuffled his feet. Nick put his arm round his shoulders and led him aside. As far as Douglas could tell, Nick was offering more money. He was putting up his fingers. Nelson was nodding and shrugging.

191

It occurred to Douglas that he had barely discussed the finance of this expedition with Nick, as if the money would look after itself, as it did in storybook adventures. To be honest, he had abdicated all responsibility; he had escaped to the one place which forced him to concentrate on where he was, not on who he was.

He made himself think about Helen. What would she be doing? He tried to imagine her lying by the pool at home, or on a shopping expedition with Madge Plummer down King William Street, but it was impossible to hold such disingenuous pictures of her in his mind. Other images supervened.

Through his head ran the terrible lines of Catullus, like a litany:

> My mind has been so broken by your guilt, my Lesbia
> and so destroyed itself by faith in you,
> that now it cannot wish you well if you turn to virtue
> nor cease from loving you in all your vice.

It was no good. His sunburned elbow was hurting – that was the reality. That and the black flies which swarmed around the remains of their lunch and eventually drove him back to the Land-rover.

Nick joined him presently, wiping the sweat off his face. 'Labour problems solved.' He raised his eyebrows. 'If I'm Nelson's brother, then fraternity isn't what it used to be.'

They set off across the plateau of undulating sand-hills. Although the gradients were gentler, the Land-rover's wheels still spun on the powdery sand. Twice they had to dig themselves out. On one occasion Douglas, jumping down from the cab, trod on a three-cornered jack which punctured the sole of his boot and sent a shaft of pain up his left leg. Swearing, he limped back and patched himself up with a first-aid kit under the seat.

The heat in the cab was stifling, made worse by the necessity of keeping the windows up in the high undergrowth to avoid brushing a deadly tree-snake on to the seat. In his dehydrated condition he found that the smallest setback irritated him intensely; even Nick's equanimity exasperated him. He began to understand how Ben Gunn, left alone on Treasure Island, could be driven mad by the emptiness.

Nelson was leading them more slowly, more cautiously

now. Occasionally he made them wait while he shinned up a mulga tree to check his bearings. Just as they began to think they were making good time he came back from one of these reconnaissances towards the car. Shouting to them, he pointed ahead of them, where the sky had become suddenly dark.

'Dust blizzard!' shouted Nick. He drove into the lee of a dune, and leaped out to secure the canvas flaps and tape down the windows and vents. Nelson took shelter in the back. As Nick climbed in and shut his door, the storm slammed into them, rocking the heavy vehicle on its springs. In the tornado of red dust visibility was down to a few feet, the sun a crimson button in the furred sky. For ten minutes or more they sat immobile. Then the blizzard moved on, leaving red dust caking the windscreen and cloaking everything in sight in a rust-red monochrome.

After using more of their precious water they drove on into the cool of the early evening, and into a glorious sunset rapidly fading into dusk. They drove on even though Nelson refused to lead them any further on foot and came back and sat in the cab between them, pointing ahead without bothering to check the compass. They crossed sand-ridges, gullies, claypans, until eventually it was too dark to see anything but the silver undergrowth in the Land-rover's headlamps and the trunks of the mulga shining with a ghostly pallor in the moonlight . . . and finally Nick stopped and they made camp.

Nelson helped build the fire. Rather than accept their food he chewed on dampers made from flour which he cooked himself. Nick set up the theodolite, plotted their longitude and latitude and scaled off a bearing. The long drive had exhausted them. After a sketchy supper they piled mallee on the fire to keep the scorpions away, and turned in.

Douglas lay in his sleeping-bag under a mulga tree. Once again the bowl of night was clear and brilliant with stars. It seemed to him that, as they journeyed on through the outback, the firmament pressed more closely upon them every nightfall, almost oppressive in its intimacy, offering a star for every grain of sand from here to their destination.

He was suddenly overwhelmed with an awareness of *mysterium tremendum*. It shivered through his veins like mercury, cauterising his injured spirit. How right the Aborigines were, he told himself,

193

to locate their sacred places in the desert. Was it not in the desert that the Christian God first revealed himself to the Israelites, filling the wide horizons, speaking to Moses in voices out of the silent wilderness?

Gods were closest to man in the desert. Even an unbeliever would surely apprehend the presence of something other out here, something greater than himself. In the desert, man was closest to a primal sense of his own existence; he was taken back to the very beginnings of things. He, Douglas, had come on this expedition with Nick to recapture the spirit of their wartime experiences, before the guilt began. But the outback was taking him much further back in time, back to all the beginnings in his own life which remained unfulfilled. It took him back to the flooded mine-workings, to the sea-cliff at sunset on his confirmation retreat, to the Iron Age circle of stones in the Western Isles – the moments of unloosed joy when his solitude had merged into the omnipresence of Nature.

The way it was. The way it had ceased to be. He closed his eyes. Instantly he was climbing the hillside again in the valley beyond Wastwater. The sun was cool upon his face. The birds were singing. He knew with a joyful dread that the path would bring him out above the old mine-workings and he would look down again into the bright enticement of that secret lake. A breeze had sprung up; the way was more overgrown and difficult: could he still remember it after all these years? At last he came to the disused road, the blocked-off tunnel and the path which wound over the crown of the hill. In gladness he quickened his step. Nothing had changed. He came to the edge of the crater, and looked down into the green, into a pit of green serpents wriggling and squirming, monstrous, hideous, poisonous things rearing up at him with blind mouths agape—

He sat up, staring-eyed, sweating in the chill of the desert night. What had gone wrong? It was the journey, he told himself, the exertion, dehydration, short rations, yes, and Nelson's idiotic Wonambi ritual, all conspiring. . . . He blinked and shook his head. As he did so, a brilliant flash lit up the sky. Dazed, he heard the crack of thunder. A gust of wind rattled the branches of the mulga tree like a knife-fight, bringing down leaves.

Rain!

He glanced across. Nick was still asleep. Nelson was invisible.

He lifted up his face in the moonlight. No rain came. The stars glittered in the clear sky. He waited for rain to fall, but all was dry. Even the air was dry. And the thunder had come and gone. He tried to go back to sleep. Perhaps he succeeded. But his eyes were open, and he knew where he was, when he looked up and saw, in the configuration of the stars, Bella's face looking down at him.

Then Douglas understood. He listened to himself breathe, he listened to the fire, spitting embers into the darkness, and he found the strength to admit what he had half-known all along: at what moment the portcullis had fallen across his life, and why it would never be raised until penance was done.

A hand shook him awake. It was Nick, hardly more than a ghost in the pre-dawn greyness. He sat up. The camp-fire was nearly out. He grabbed his jacket and put it round his shoulders.

'Looks like we're on our own, pal,' Nick told him.

Douglas struggled to his feet. He blinked around. 'Where's Nelson?'

'He's scarpered. I don't know, he may be hunting for our breakfast. But I doubt it. He's taken a full water-bag.'

Douglas blinked again. There was enough light to see that Nick wasn't joking. 'Nelson's disappeared?' he repeated stupidly. Then, as it sank home, on a rising note of hysteria: 'For God's sake, what are we going to do?'

'We're going to have a good breakfast. Look, you start the billy going while I get more firewood.'

Dawn came up over the landscape which suddenly treacherous, death-beckoning. Nick Kemp had got the map out of the car and spread it on the reddening sand.

'No worries,' he said. 'The route's plotted, all of it. Nelson's green mineral deposit can't be ten miles from here.'

'What do you mean? You can't believe it still exists!'

Nick felt his pocket. He threw something down on the map. It was the uranium rock, glinting green and black.

'That's no figment of my imagination. Don't tell me Nelson picked that up off the ground in Ooldea. He's taken us this far. It's up to us to do the rest, Duggle. You and me. Like in the old days.'

He spoke decisively, the captain to the lieutenant. Before last night, Douglas would have mutinied. He would have refused to budge from camp unless they turned back there and then and ran for home. Now he stood up and threw the dregs of his tea on the fire.

'Let's go, then.'

There were measurements to make first. Using the cattle-prod attached by cable to the proton precession magnetometer, Nick took readings of the rock formations underlying the sand-dunes. By the time he returned to the Land-rover, Douglas had filled the radiator, refuelled, and checked the oil level and the tyre pressures. Their supply of fresh tyres had run out long ago. Now every flat had to be repaired with tyre-mending tools and pumped up by hand.

'Limestone,' Nick said curtly. He kept the map open on his knee. 'Let's make for the high sand-ridges. I need a vantage-point.'

They headed in a northerly direction. Almost at once they were back in the high dunes, saw-toothed and steep, worse than anything they'd faced so far. On some hills the land-rover had to make ten or more attempts to get to the summit, before sliding down the far side in a spray of fine red sand. After an hour of this torture, its engine began to stutter. They stopped in the shade of a mulga to let it cool. Douglas cleaned his glasses.

'I'll drive if you're tired,' Nick said.

'I'm okay. I've been asking myself why Nelson ran out on us. Did you hear the thunder last night?'

'No.'

'I wondered. Maybe Nelson thought it was Wonambi, creating water-holes. I heard him say something to you about poisoning the land, about trails of smoke which have been killing off the old men's sacred places. Is that what he thinks *we* are? Poisoners?'

'I don't know.'

'It bears out what your grandfather found: you can't trust the Aborigine. Nelson's probably buggered off after dingo pelts. Isn't that what they trade in? If we find his place-of-green-stones, he'll look pretty damn stupid.'

'Nelson isn't stupid,' said Nick, after a pause. 'That's what I don't understand.'

They set off again, climbing up the sand-hills, falling back and climbing again. The sun, and the heat from the wailing engine, turned the cab into an inferno. Every time they reached a summit, higher ones blocked the view. Both men were conscious of the risks of an engine seizure in this remote unforgiving country. Nick, who had taken the wheel, grew steadily grimmer and more monosyllabic as the hours passed.

At midday, having covered perhaps three miles, they came to three white gum-trees in a dry creek-bed. Nick pumped the brake pedal, swung the wheel and skidded to a halt inches from the nearest tree. He got out. Crouched over the left rear wheel, he called Douglas over. He pointed to an oily coating on the wheel's inside flange.

'Hydraulic brake fluid,' he explained. 'The brakes have gone.'

In the welcome shade they put up the awning and had lunch, while they waited for the engine to cool.

'We've got enough food to see us through a couple more days,' Douglas reported, his voice uneasy.

'Comfortably.'

'I don't know about the water.'

'Plenty.'

'Or the fuel.'

'That's fine.' Nick threw the empty stew-can with a clatter into the back of the Land-rover. 'What you're saying to me, pal, you're saying you've had enough, you want to get out of here.'

'I'm just pointing out— '

'I know. I know what you're pointing out. I'm sorry, Duggle. I'm sorry I brought you into this. I was asking too much of you.'

'Nick, I can last as long as you can— '

'Oh?'

'All I'm saying is that without food or water that won't be very long.'

'We've got food and water! We've got a car, a two-way radio. This isn't some kids' adventure!'

'Don't get on your high horse. I'm simply telling you that we set out on Thursday and it's now Sunday. That's three days, guided by an Aborigine. We've got food left for no more than that. Finding our own way back.'

Nick laughed, without humour. 'There speaks the voice of reason. Forget the uranium, we're running short of porridge oats. Listen, Duggle. If it'll make you feel better, I'll call up

Port Augusta. My mate Gary Todd is standing by in case of trouble.'

'What could he do?'

'Send a chopper.'

Nick was gone a long time. When he came back his face was strained.

'It's got me beat,' he said. 'I thought it must have been that dust-storm, clogged up the transistors.'

'The radio?'

'The bastard's crook. There's a bloody jinx on it. I can't raise anything but static.'

Douglas felt the panic rise and clutch. 'What are you going to do?'

'I'm going to have a go at cleaning up the engine. Then we're going to head due south from here. According to the map we've come a long way round to accommodate Nelson's bloody water-hole. The railway-line is two days, maximum three days, in a straight line south.'

'Over the dunes?'

Nick grimaced. 'Who knows?'

For the next hour Nick worked on the engine. He cleaned the spark plugs, the fuel filter, and the fuel pump, the sweat pouring off him, his hands slippery. Once he gashed his hand and swore. Douglas took refuge from the heat in the back of the truck, and combed the sand out of his hair. He could still smell the presence of the Aborigine, an odour compounded of tobacco and sweat and something darker, sweeter, perhaps a narcotic. The desert had changed; the atmosphere was stiller than ever. After these days in the bush he had become acclimatised to quietness but this was different, a complete absence of sound and movement. It was as if the tides of sand had frozen, the clouds had stopped still. Only the shadows inched eastwards along the dry creek bed, towards a patch of yellow spinifex. He squatted in the truck, imagining the intricate shadows that a human skeleton could make on the sand.

Nick came round the back, wiping his hands on a blood-stained rag. 'It's ready,' he announced. 'I'm praying that we can make it to the railway line without having to clean the carburettor – that's a bastard of a job.'

'I'm praying with you.'

Driving by compass, detouring to avoid the highest sand-ridges, they headed due south. Within half a mile they had another flat tyre. Then twice in quick succession the Land-rover sank to its axles and had to be laboriously dug out of drifts of sand.

Straining his eyes in the cab beside Nick, Douglas began seeing things that weren't there. Mirages persisted and became lakes of water at the foot of the sand-hills; he yelled a warning to Nick as they dipped down into one. Increasingly the landscape mirrored his exhaustion and defeat. The vegetation looked blackened: half-dead and half-alive. Once they passed through an entire battlefield of dead mulgas, their roots and twisted limbs scattered over the thankless sand. It was a few hundred yards further on that he saw Helen, her arms up round her face, warding off a blow. After that he saw her everywhere, black-haired in her long black dress, standing motionless, dead, stretching her arms away from him.

As darkness fell, to his intense relief the ridges began to flatten. The scrub thinned out. They seemed to have reached a plateau, higher, more open, scattered with saltbush and clumps of bluebush in the depressions. Nick insisted that they camp at once, to conserve energy. Douglas began collecting scrub for the fire. Nick hauled out his prospecting equipment.

That night they shared one of the last remaining tins of bully-beef. Each of them drank two Thermos-cups of water. Nick was preoccupied, muttering to himself. Douglas noticed that the precious magnetometer had been discarded carelessly in the sand.

'What readings were you getting?' Douglas asked.

'Eh? Oh, none that made any sense. The machine's gone troppo. It's pointing to surface or subsurface metallic deposits of incredible magnetic intensity a few hundred yards away. I get a higher reading holding the thing in the air than sticking it in the ground. Tomorrow morning I'll test with the electrodes, do it properly. After that, I swear to you, no more testing.'

Douglas smiled weakly. He felt feverish, light-headed with lack of food and water. After a minute he muttered: 'How much longer?'

'I'll get working on our longitude and latitude in a moment. My guess is another couple of days to the railway line.'

'Guess? Guess? Two days is what you guessed this morning!'

'Look, it depends on the terrain. If it stayed flat like this, we could be down to the railway line in half a day. In any case we've got enough fuel and water to take us safely through another forty-eight hours. After that they'll come looking for us. Don't worry, we've got enough empty tins in the back to stick 'em on mulga poles and signal an SOS.' He laughed croakily.

Douglas asked: 'Are you afraid?'

'Worse things have happened to us, pal.'

'We were younger then.'

'No odds. Our bodies can still do almost as much if we prepare them for it. Ageing is a mental process, mostly. We start weighing up the risks, playing for percentages. We think of all the home comforts we stand to lose if we make a mistake . . . the life we've built up around us. I suppose the thing about me is that I've never surrounded myself with things I couldn't bear to lose. Families, friends, houses, love-letters . . . I've had them all, and kept some, and thrown others away.' He stirred the fire. 'That's why I invited you along, Duggle. And why you agreed. You'd got yourself surrounded. You couldn't see out any more. I suspect you couldn't even see yourself.'

'I can see myself now. Don't much like it.'

'Don't you? Why?'

There was a long pause in the stillness. Only the fire waltzed crazily on the empty sand-floor. Douglas said slowly: 'I don't suppose you've forgotten Bella.'

'Of course not.'

'I tried. Oh God, Nick, I reckon I've spent the last eighteen years putting a wall up brick by brick to block her out of my life. And it, you see, it blocked everything else out, too. All the emotions I had then. All the experiences. I couldn't get back to them, because I wouldn't admit how much Bella had been a part of them. I kept her like a secret from myself. It's a kind of moral cowardice, I suppose.'

There were tears in his eyes. Nick stared into the fire. Douglas told him about the time he had woken up in Wellington Square and seen Bella sleeping where Helen slept. He talked about Edward Catchpole. He poured out his feelings of guilt and resentment, as if he was on some psychiatrist's couch and not stranded with dwindling provisions in the Australian out-back hundreds of miles from the nearest cattle homestead.

'I don't know who it is I resent so much,' he finished. 'Helen or Bella. The flesh or the spirit. Christ, I really don't know.'

Nick was silent. After a minute he got to his feet and picked up the scorched limb of a mulga and threw it on the blaze.

'The deepest scars are the hidden ones,' he remarked, inspecting the cut on his hand. 'Mind or body, it's the same thing. Did I ever tell you I've still got a shell-splinter in my skull, suffered in the course of providing your theme for *DogDay*? Hurts like hell in wet weather!' Nick twisted his mouth ironically, watching the dry mulga blaze up into the night. 'It's time I got a fix on our star position,' he added. 'I should turn in if I were you. Sleep will stop the hunger pangs. We'll get through this, Duggle, God willing. Then is the time to feel sorry for ourselves.'

Douglas watched his friend walk across to the Land-rover, in his legs the jaunty swagger still. Was Nick ever capable of feeling sorry for himself? He'd gathered around him nothing he couldn't bear to lose, that was what he'd said. No one who could hurt him, in other words. Nobody who had reached through and touched him to the quick. The warmth, the openness, the good humour, the appetite for experience – they were all real enough. No secrets there. But deep inside there had to be something hard and self-protective: a bomb-casing marked 'Danger. High Explosive. Do Not Touch.'

With a sudden lurch in his stomach it occurred to Douglas that there was a hardness about his companion which hadn't been there in the old days. He stared with a cold eye on life, on death.

Douglas stood up. His legs were shaky. As if to prove his self-sufficiency, he turned away from the camp-fire and set off at a brisk pace towards a low hill which sheltered them from the east. At once he was as utterly alone as he had been that first night gazing back over the Nullarbor Desert towards Fisher. Surrounding him, the eerie quietness which had lasted all day; not the call of a bird, not the scuttle of a lizard disturbed it. The last non-human sound he could remember hearing was last night's clap of dry thunder.

The moon bathed the sand in a startling radiance; it shaped the leaves of the bluebushes into cupped hands begging for the gift of dew. He stood still and gazed around, catching his breath before mounting the hill. *The deepest scars are the hidden ones.* From his treatment of Georgina's mother stemmed all the lies he had uttered, all the truths he had become unable to express – and it had taken Helen's unfaithfulness to make him aware of it. He fell to his knees and covered his face with his hands, imagining himself back into his own dreamtime, before the gate fell, before the poison spread. Then he climbed the hill to the top.

It was in the corner of his eye at first, a flash of light like a falling star. He blinked. It was still there. He took his glasses off and wiped them clean on his shirt, and stared some more. Far across the sand it glowed, a fingernail of steady light. It was like the tip of a cigar in the dark, except that this was green, a bright green, a phosphorescent green. It shimmered and spilled in the distance, a bright meniscus of light, like a radiance of green water perpetually overfilling a lake.

He tried to shout. His voice wouldn't come. Swallowing, he tried again.

'Nick! Nick! Nick!'

He hadn't the strength to go back and get him. Waving his bush-hat, he bawled again: 'Nick!'

'Are you okay?' Nick came up the hill in easy strides. 'What's the trouble, mate?'

Douglas pointed. Nick Kemp took a deep breath, and let out a whoop of joy.

'That bastard Nelson! What are we waiting for?'

They scrambled back down the hill. Nick took a compass reading; Douglas started the Land-rover. Checking the compass with a torch, they drove due east towards Nelson's place-of-green-stones, travelling quite fast, nine or ten miles per hour, over the flattish undulating ground. The headlights wavered over dead trees, collapsed like the skeletons of kneeling elephants. As they got nearer there were no trees at all, just blackened stumps, none of them more than three feet high.

'Stop the truck!' Nick shouted.

Douglas slammed on the brakes. The headlights had picked out shards of a bluish metallic substance glinting on the ground. Nearby were a couple of empty baked-bean tins. Nick collected up several fragments of the strange metallic clinker and stuffed them in his pockets. He chuckled as he got back into the cab.

'It looks as if some Abos have been this way before us!'

They drove on, bumping over what might have been an old Aboriginal track. After holding back so auspiciously, clouds had extinguished the moon. The night was suddenly dangerous. Shapes of men and monsters danced before Douglas's eyes.

'I can't focus any more,' he said.

'No worries. We're here. I can smell it. Let's camp. We'll find our fortune in the morning.'

It was already midnight. Groggy with exhaustion the two men stumbled in search of wood for a new fire. They found nothing. The pinkish-brown sandy topsoil was bare even of scrub, as if vegetation had been wiped off the face of the planet. Nick called Douglas over. In the pool of his torch-light a rabbit had started up and was bounding in small circles. As they watched the rabbit flopped down, exhausted, quivering.

'What of it?' Douglas asked.

'It's blind. Look at its eyes. It can't see the torch.'

In the end they returned to the Land-rover and bedded down in the back. Douglas plummeted into a dreamless sleep. In an instant he was drawn up from it into the painful daylight. Nick was shaking him. His eyes were bright.

'Come on, pal! This is what we came for!'

Unshaven, dirty, red-eyed, they slid out of the Land-rover. Each of them drank a precious cup of water. The stillness was palpable. Even the flies had vanished. Ahead of them rose a low hill with a curious flattened top. All thought of food put aside, the two men walked towards it, across the scalped earth. Douglas, light-headed, moved his feet like a sleepwalker. The morning sun was on his face. He came, as he expected, to a man-made path which wound up the hill to a wide flat summit.

In the middle was a shallow crater, as wide in diameter as a bowling-green. Slowly Douglas walked the last few yards to the edge, and looked down. Secret and beautiful it lay before him as if he had known it all his life – a round shallow lake of brilliant green, as fragile as ice, as smooth as a skating-rink. He gazed.

'Douglas!'

He kneeled and put out his hand. Close to, the green was glazed with hairline cracks. It was rough with tiny bubbles as if it had been melted under intense heat. Quite easily it came

203

away in his fingers, a kind of sand-glass or mica, some of it in layers as thin as a butterfly's wings.

'Douglas!'

He stood up but he couldn't tear his eyes away. The sun burned off the bowl of green unendingly as the bush burned before Moses in the wilderness. God, the desert god, had re-created for him alone this memory, this beauty, this pure and awesome peace. He listened for the voice which would say to him, out of the burning bowl: *Draw not nigh hither: put off thy shoes from thy feet, for the place whereon thou standest is holy ground.*

There came only a sighing wind across the outback, and Nick's voice calling him faintly. He looked over, and saw the bodies.

Somewhere a telephone was ringing. Helen Manifold blinked. Was it morning? Afternoon? Groggy, she pulled on her cotton gown and blundered downstairs. The clocks had gone mad the day before yesterday; they were still all telling the wrong time. And now the phone . . . what had she done with it? She searched blindly, feeling the dryness in her throat.

The vet had been the last call she'd taken. Ottoman, her beloved Ottoman, had died yesterday at five. In her grief and rage – it must have been Robbins next door, that bastard, who had poisoned him – she'd buried the telephone somewhere and taken the whisky to bed. Now the sun was high over Wellington Square and all the clocks were wrong.

She lifted a cushion on the sofa. The squat black monster shrilled up at her.

'Yes?' she cried. 'What time is it?'

'Mrs Manifold?'

'Yes, what— ?'

'This is Gary Todd, Mrs Manifold. I'm calling from the airfield at Port Augusta.'

'Where? I can't hear you.'

'Port Augusta, up north. Your husband went up to Ooldea with Captain Kemp, am I right?'

'Into the desert, yes.'

'Yes.' There was a pause. 'Mrs Manifold, can you hear me?'

'Yes, yes.'

'Nick Kemp was due to check in his position with me, on a prearranged frequency, every day. I haven't heard from him for forty-eight hours. Can you hear me?'

'Forty-eight hours!'

'No real cause for alarm, Mrs Manifold. Nick's a good bush-man. I expect his radio's gone crook. Just to let you know, I'm going to fly a recce to his last radio fix, or as near as

I can get without going off-limits. I'll give you a tootle as soon as I get back. Cheerio!'

'Wait. Off-limits? What do you mean, *off-limits*?'

The line was dead. Helen let the phone drop. Her mouth puckered. It was too bad. Ottoman, precious darling Ottoman, had been the one creature whose love she could rely on any more. And now Douglas was lost somewhere in the desert. She'd known something like this would happen. Wasn't it why she'd asked him to postpone the trip, so he could come with her to dinner on board the Royal Yacht? Why were men so selfish? And so cruel, so cruel to put poison down to kill her baby kitten who'd not had an unkind thought in her fluffy head.

She rang Edward Catchpole at his office in Government House. No answer. Panic seized her. Supposing, the Queen's visit over, he had gone back to Canberra after all? With trembling fingers she dialled the flat.

'Catchpole.'

'Oh, Edward, thank God!'

'What's up?'

'Why do you say it like that?'

'It's seven in the morning!'

'Is it? Oh dear. Douglas has got lost in the desert, darling. A man from an airfield in Port Augusta has just rung me up.'

'What am I supposed to do?'

'I need to see you. I'm all by myself.' She wailed, 'Douglas is missing and darling Ottoman's just died in agony, and I haven't seen you for two days!'

'Helen, something big's come up. . . . '

'Didn't you hear what I said?'

'Helen— '

'I'm coming round. I'll be there in half an hour.'

She wheedled and cajoled, and within an hour was at the door of Catchpole's downtown flat. The air-conditioning purred like Ottoman; she swallowed, and blinked at the china bowls sitting pretty in their glass cases.

Edward Catchpole had dressed in his most sombre suit. He looked worried, though not on her account.

'I can't give you long, dear heart,' he said. 'Some urgent stuff— '

206

'More urgent than me?'

He kissed her, and frowned. 'You haven't come to see me. You've come about Douglas.'

'Oh, the silly man!' She went and sat down on the sofa, biting her lip nonetheless. Edward stood over her. He took out his spectacles and held them up in front of his nose, examining her. She turned her head away.

'You're really upset, aren't you?' he said with curiosity.

'Not terribly. It's just a bore.'

'You're frightened of losing him.'

'Hardly, darling, when I'm talking to Smithson the divorce lawyer, as you know.'

'No, not that way.' Catchpole lowered his bulk beside her, and began touching her through her cotton dress. 'You're frightened of losing his knowledge of you. Do you see? After the time you've been together it's become part of your self-knowledge, all the little intimate secrets you share—'

'Oh! Secrets – secrets! All you ever talk about!' She pushed his fingers away. 'Anyway, he doesn't know all about me. He doesn't know about us.'

'Really?'

She looked at him, her eyes wide. 'Of course not! What do you take me for?'

'A beautiful deceiver. . . . ' His hands were back. 'A naughty girl who doesn't always tell the truth.'

'Why should I?' She put her tongue out at him. 'What have you ever done to deserve the truth?'

'So he does know?'

'Of course not!'

'Does he suspect?'

He was kissing her, tugging at her dress. The phone rang. He pulled away at once and answered it, keeping his back to her, talking in a rapid low voice. She got up and went into the kitchen to make coffee. He came and stood in the doorway, straightening his bow-tie.

'I've got to go,' he said.

'Where's your milk?'

'In the tin. Condensed milk.'

'First no meat, then no milk. Are you getting an allergy, darling?'

He laughed. 'What does Smithson say?'

'He thinks I should go for irretrievable breakdown of the marriage. The grounds could be adultery or unreasonable behaviour.'

'We agreed I wasn't to be brought into this!'

'Don't worry. I told him that. He thinks I should go for unreasonable behaviour – physical violence possibly. I'll work something out.' She shuddered and clasped her sides as if visualising the scene in court with her, in Gauguin pink, in the witness-box.

'Dearest heart . . . I wish I didn't have to go.'

'What about Douglas? What should I do? The man at Port Augusta said he'd fly as near as he could but an area was off-limits. What did he mean?'

She poured the milk. Hearing no answer, she looked at him. All movement had gone from Edward Catchpole's face. His eyes were stone. He stood still, fingering the knot in his tie.

He said: 'How many of them?'

'Two. Him and Nick Kemp and an Aborigine.'

'Helen, where were they going?'

'I think he said Oolday, something like that.'

'Ooldea.'

'Yes. Edward, will you please stop staring at me?'

'This is terribly important. You're sure it was Ooldea?'

'Yes! What about it?'

The civil servant in Catchpole reasserted itself. He fixed a smile on his face. 'That's fine. It means we shouldn't have too much trouble finding your husband. Excuse me a moment. I'll be right back.'

Frowning, Helen poured the tinned milk into the two coffees. Disagreeable specks of white floated to the surface.

'*Now!*'

She had never heard him raise his voice before. She ran into the living-room. Edward Catchpole put the phone down. On the reddened face he turned to her was the same fixed and terrible smile.

'Goodbye, Helen,' he said.

There were three of them. They lay sprawled on the bare burned ground, back the way they had come last night in the dark. Two, face-down, were in military khaki with white tin helmets and white webbing. The third was wearing voluminous overalls which covered his whole body, and white plastic bags over his feet. His face was invisible under a kind of gas-mask or respirator; he goggled through it at the sky like a drowned fish.

Douglas kneeled in the dirt beside the first soldier, panting. There was no smell of death, and Normandy had taught him all he wanted to know about the smell of dead bodies. He turned the figure over and recoiled with a shout.

No skin. No features. The thing was a dummy, made of wood.

The hair rose on the back of his neck. He looked up; he shouted for Nick. Nick had vanished over the next ridge. Douglas went on to the next soldier, and then the figure in the goon suit. All puppets, made of wood. All wearing curious plastic badges on their chests. He glanced up, right into the face of a rabbit grinning at him. It had lost all the skin and fur round its mouth; its teeth were pitifully exposed, a cartoon bunny. It was shivering with hunger. Douglas ran his sleeve across his eyes. Staring round he saw other rabbits, all poisoned, blind, some in convulsive throes of death.

He had to escape from whatever hell this was. He scrambled on, the sun at his back. Nick was calling to him hoarsely. He ran past yellow marker-posts stuck in the ground, past bits of bright yellow tape stuck in the blackened stump of a mulga. There were railway tracks here . . . a jeep with a dummy sitting at the driving-wheel . . . a steel trough still half-filled with water. On the ground lay more fragments of metal of the kind Nick had collected the night before. Cables snaked through the earth. Only life was missing. Here there was no life at all.

He crossed a dirt track. Nick was there. He was staring

209

into a great burial-pit, dug foursquare into the earth. In it Douglas saw whole aircraft standing. He saw caravans, jeeps, wooden sheds and fences, metal towers, poles, shelters, cables, corrugated steel sheeting. He saw a child's bicycle next to a couple of Centurion tanks and a caterpillar tractor, all packed together like toys in a trunk. Half the giant pit was empty. Was there another army of tanks and caravans scattered across the outback, waiting to be bulldozed in? But all around the emptiness stretched away.

They gazed and gazed. Neither man knew what to say. The enormity of these sights, after days of isolation and in their weakened state, was more than words could utter. Nick Kemp let drop something he had held clenched in his fist – it was the uranium stone Nelson had brought back to Ooldea. Fumbling with his shirt buttons he began to take off his clothes.

'We have to get away,' he muttered.

'What are you doing?'

'Back to the Land-rover.'

'But what— ?'

'Don't argue, mate. Strip off. This place is contaminated, can't you see? Our clothes will pick it up. For God's sake hurry!'

Radioactive. Douglas tore off his clothes and threw them into the pit. Mother-naked, at one with the Aborigines except for the shoes on their feet, they raced back towards the truck. Near the dummies Douglas stumbled and fell. He lay gasping on the hard ground. Nick came back and kneeled beside him. He put his arms round Douglas and lifted him to his feet.

'Not much further now,' he said.

'I can't go any further.'

'Yes, you can, Duggle. Lean on me.'

Hobbling, parched, peeled by the burning sun, they staggered across the deadness. Douglas had lost his glasses. All he could see before him was the crater of green stone which had drawn him across half Australia, to this. Trapped in his nightmare he heard a great clatter in the sky, as though the Last Trump had sounded and the skeletons of the dead had all risen from their graves and were fighting to escape. He looked up. Over the ground a helicopter plunged its shadow. Flying sand stung his unprotected flesh.

When they could lift their faces again, they saw the three figures stepping towards them from another planet. Goon-suited, goggle-faced, they marched at a funeral pace, holding in front of them instruments which clicked and went on clicking, faster and faster, as they came and took the two men by the arms, and delivered them out of there.

THREE

E verything *is all right*. That was all they ever said to her. *Everything's all right, Georgina*. Everything's going to be *fine*.

What were they talking about? How could it possibly be all right? On Saturday night she'd had a premonition of this. There'd been a row with Dirk Miller over the usual thing. Instead of letting him drive her home she'd walked away down Rundle Street by herself. The last cinema-goers had gone home from the York, the Rex, the Hoyt's Regent, and the street was almost deserted. Begonias and cinerarias were wilting in the Royal Parade window-boxes. She walked down past Myer's Emporium and stopped to stare at its fashion window, dimly lit from the interior of the store.

The mannequins were naked. Their articulated bodies, Elastoplast-colour, were cocked obscenely across the piled boxes used for displaying blouses and shoes. Their limbs were splayed at grotesque angles which mocked the mask of gentility on their vacant faces. Everything was as still and contorted as a woodcut of the Dance of Death.

There had been an explosion. Or something like that. Her father hadn't said much when Mr Catchpole brought him home. He had walked in, hollow-cheeked, wearing that strange baggy safari-suit they'd given him, and a funny cap. When he took the cap off she saw they'd shaved his skull. He'd smiled, and made some remark about a cheap haircut. Then he'd pleaded tiredness and gone straight to bed. He hadn't kissed her. Catchpole had pulled him by the arm and said it was better not to, not yet.

As soon as Catchpole had gone into another room, with Helen, she'd rushed upstairs to the bedroom, bringing the jug of water her father had requested. He was lying back on the pillow. The tendons stood out on his neck.

'Did you find the place of green stones?' she'd asked him.

'Yes. Oh, yes.'

'Did you bring any back?'

'No.'

'What were they? Were they uranium?'

'No.' He'd swallowed the water greedily, his face pale under the tan. 'Not uranium. Sand. It was sand fused into green silica by the heat of an atomic explosion directly overhead.'

'So there *was* a bomb!'

'Yes, once. The last bomb tests finished years ago.'

'Then—' She'd broken off, confused.

'I'm all right. They shaved my head like this to be on the safe side. There's nothing wrong with me much except dehydration, so they say. The heat. Not enough water. Nick's in the hospital with it. Perhaps you could find out.'

I'm all right. Well, he wasn't. She could see that. Something was very wrong. Men had come yesterday to look through her father's things. They'd spent two hours locked in his study. When they came out they searched through the whole house, lifting up carpets, looking under mattresses, emptying earth out of indoor-plant pots, poking into record-sleeves, not saying a word.

And now, as she came down from her father's bedroom, she heard Helen and Catchpole shouting at each other in the living-room. She crept down the stairs and listened in, although Helen was yelling loud enough for the whole house to hear.

'You can't do this to me!'

'Helen, be reasonable. . . . '

'Reasonable? After what you've just told me?'

'I've been honest with you—'

'Honest – shit! You've never been honest. You lie, and deceive, and leave victims behind without a word of apology, not a word!'

'I've said I'm sorry.'

'Do you ever take responsibility for anything or anyone? Look at Douglas! What am I going to do about him?'

'He'll need looking after. He must go back to England with you.'

'You bastard! What have I ever done to make you hate me so!'

'It's not my fault. I can't be part of this. It's out of my hands.'

'You and your *bloody* secrets. Treating us like *Aborigines*!'

'I can't stay here any longer. Helen— '

Edward Catchpole must have lowered his voice because Georgina couldn't hear any more except for Helen's frantic sobbing. She crouched by the stairs, shaking. After a minute she heard the door open. Catchpole came out, the same unchanging Catchpole, shining pinkly with health and confidence. Through the banisters Georgina watched him put on his hat and stop briefly in front of the hall mirror to adjust the brim. Then he let himself out. In the silence, as Helen drew shuddering breaths in the living-room, she heard Catchpole's driver open and close the door of the Jaguar Mark VIII.

She entered the living-room. Her stepmother was lying back on the chaise-longue, exhausted from sobbing. Georgina rushed at once to sit beside her and put a tender arm around her. Helen took convulsive breaths. She murmured faintly: 'First Ottoman. Now this!'

'Daddy's going to be all right. We'll look after him.'

'Oh!' Tears welled up again and coursed down Helen's cheek. Georgina took out her handkerchief, folding out of view the blotch where she'd wiped up a chemistry exam experiment. Helen seized it and blew her nose. Georgina's tears began falling in sympathy.

'That awful man! I knew he wasn't to be trusted!' she burst out. And then: 'Is Daddy really ill?'

'I don't know. I'm not supposed to say.'

'He told me the testing-ground hadn't been used for years.'

'Not for atomic bombs.' Helen sat up and dabbed her eyes. Looking at the handkerchief she wrinkled her nose and passed it back to her stepdaughter. 'Apparently there have been other kinds of minor explosions up there. I'm not to tell you or anyone, he said . . . he said "a controlled release of Plutonium". Don't ask me. One happened three nights ago. It was quite safe, he said, except that nobody should have been there. Stupid, *stupid* secrets.'

Georgina's heart was pumping. She thought she was going to be sick. She had heard only the phrase about Plutonium and the Four Horsemen of the Apocalypse reared in her vision, their terrible steeds trampling across the Numdah rugs. What had Sir Martin Amory said? *The most dangerous carcinogen . . . a*

Frankenstein's monster living 24,000 years. Numb with shock, she got up and walked over to the window. What if they *hadn't* controlled the release of Plutonium? What if some of it had got away?

Nick would know the answer. Nick knew all the answers. At this moment she needed him more than anyone else in the world, for his wisdom, his strength. She looked at the starfish clock. It was six in the evening. Leaving Helen, she ran out of the house, wheeled her bike from the garage and headed south towards the Royal Adelaide Hospital in Frome Road.

At the desk she asked for Nicholas Kemp, admitted for surveillance yesterday afternoon. The nurse ran her pencil down the list and shook her head.

'What do you say his name was?'

'Kemp. Nicholas Kemp. Captain Nick Kemp.'

'No one's been admitted under that name. Did you say dehydration?'

'Yes.' She swallowed. 'Or else it's for radio-active poisoning.'

The nurse looked up sharply. 'There's a difference, you know.'

'Yes.'

'Anyway, there are no Kemps here. Otherwise I'd have a note of it.' Seeing Georgina's expression she added more gently: 'Why don't you try the Memorial Hospital? You never know. He might have been transferred.'

'Thank you.' Georgina wandered off. She was close to tears. Her father and Catchpole had both said the Royal Adelaide. She had to find Nick. She'd found him once before. In a corridor she saw a grey-haired nursing sister checking medicine bottles in a cabinet. She went up to her timidly.

'Excuse me. Can you direct me to the Isolation Ward?'

Directions were given. Georgina hastened along several more corridors and up three flights of stairs. Pushing open a pair of double doors, she found herself in an anteroom. It smelt of antiseptic and something sweeter, like vomit. A nursing sister in starched white-and-blue appeared, a bunch of keys jangling at her side like a prison warder's.

'What can I do for you, young lady?'

Georgina followed her hunch. 'I've come to see Captain Nicholas Kemp,' she declared.

'Kemp?'

'Yes.'

'Are you a relative?'

'Yes. Yes, he's my father.'

'Captain Kemp told me he doesn't have a next-of-kin.'

Georgina reddened. 'I'm Georgina Manifold. I'm the daughter of his oldest friend. Please. My father was the one who went into the outback with him. It's very important!'

The nurse stared at her. 'Very well,' she said suddenly. 'Not tonight, the doctors are still with him. Come back tomorrow after lunch. Ask for Sister Jessup. I'm not supposed to let anybody see him, but poor man. . . . '

'Tomorrow . . . ' Georgina repeated dully.

'Don't worry,' said Sister Jessup, bustling her out through the double doors. 'Nothing will change overnight. It takes longer than that.'

Georgina rode home through the gathering darkness. *Don't worry, Georgina. Everything's fine.* But she knew now that it wasn't. Whatever was going on was bigger than anyone was willing to admit.

No lights were shining when she got back to Wellington Square. She put the bike away and went into the living-room. Helen had not moved from the chaise-longue. In the gloom she lay as still as a carving in ivory. On the floor beside her, on a plate, was a half-eaten apple and a knife.

Georgina did not attempt to disturb her. She switched on the kitchen lights and the hall light and went upstairs. Her father's bedroom door was open. Douglas lay back on the pillow, breathing regularly. He was fast asleep. Georgina folded the white sheet at his chin and tucked him up like a baby. Before she left him she stole the kiss that Catchpole had forbidden. Then she went to her room, opening the window to let air in.

The morning dawned as dry as the rasp of a cicada. Georgina woke early and went downstairs to make herself coffee and toast.

In the real world it was the last day of term. In the real world she had School Prizegiving. At 10.30 she was due to walk up and be given a commendation for her portfolio of Adelaide ruins. (She would have won except that the teacher wanted photographs which looked towards Australia's future, not its colonial past.) Already she had purchased odds and ends to give as goodbye presents to Sally and Robyn and a couple of others. Sally was going on to what she said was a top secretarial college, and Robyn to university in Melbourne if her results were OK. There would be hugs and tears and promises . . . and Georgina couldn't face it, she simply couldn't. It was the *not knowing*.

She wandered round the kitchen, putting leftover food away, washing and drying the lunch things from yesterday. Then she picked up the telephone and rang the Royal Adelaide Hospital.

'I'd like to speak to Sister Jessup, please.'

'I'm sorry. She's not on duty yet.'

'Then, can I speak . . . can you put me through to the Isolation Ward, please?'

A click. A man's voice on the line.

'Doctor Elder here.'

'Oh. Is that the Isolation Ward?'

'Yes. Who is this?'

'I'm Georgina Manifold. I'd like to speak to Mr Nicholas Kemp, please.'

There was a pause on the other end of the line, and a click as if Georgina was being put through. She heard a British voice in the background. Then Dr Elder was back.

'Are you a journalist?'

'No, I'm— '

'There is nobody in the ward with the name of Kemp, I'm afraid. Goodbye.'

Georgina put the phone down. She stared out of the window at the brown grass, and the garden hose coiled like a noose on the branch of a dry tree. After some while she put through another call, to the *South Australian Gazette*. Then she got dressed, and bicycled downtown to the newspaper offices.

She hadn't seen Winn Vellacott since he pulled Nick out of her father's lecture to give him the news that Schneider had killed himself. When he came down to reception she saw that his face looked thinner. There were pouches of tiredness under his eyes. He shook her hand, rather formally, and took her up to his partitioned cubicle on the editorial floor. A bleary girl was on her knees under the open drawers of a bulging filing-cabinet, gathering up memos and documents which appeared to have spilled out under sheer pressure.

'Coffee?' she mumbled to Georgina by way of greeting.

'Thanks, I've just had some.'

'So's Winn, but he lives on it. I'll make some anyway.' She slouched out, yawning.

'How's my Georgie,' said Winn Vellacott. He sat on his desk, pushing aside a file stained with the brown rings of coffee-mugs, and stuffed his shirt-tail back into his trousers. 'Psychic, that's how. I was just about to ring Wellington Square to find out how Burke and Wills had got on. I've been trying to get hold of Nick, but I can't raise him.'

Georgina's hands were shaking. She pushed them into her sleeves. She said: 'We made a deal once. If I found out anything to tell you about Catchpole, you promised to help me in return.'

'We did. And I will.'

She began describing what had happened in the past twenty-four hours. After a minute Vellacott stopped her and got out a notepad. When she finished, he was still scribbling.

'You see, they're pretending Nick doesn't exist,' she told him, trying to keep the hysteria out of her voice. 'All I want is to see him! There must be something you can do. Please!'

The journalist looked up. All signs of tiredness were gone. His face was flushed, shining. 'When did Sister Jessup say you could go back to see him?'

'After lunch. About two-thirty, I suppose.'

'I'll take you there. Don't worry, you'll see him, I'll get you in. Now, first, have a look at these.' He picked up the file on his desk and took out of it three newspaper cuttings. 'You, dear girl, have just put flesh on these dry bones. I think you've given me the key to the sardine-tin.'

Georgina scanned the cuttings. They were all recent. The earliest, dated 5 December and headlined 'Britain's Bomb', announced the explosion of a low-yield nuclear device underground in the Nevada desert. This, she read, was the last such test before nuclear disarmament talks resumed in Geneva on 12

221

February. The second cutting was a short news item confirming the establishing of a moratorium by the United States, the Soviet Union and Britain on all nuclear weapons tests so long as the Geneva talks were in progress.

The most recent one, dated 20 February, was taken from *The Times* in London. It referred to a clause in the Conservative government's recent Defence White Paper acknowledging the development of 'a new type of British nuclear bomb' which would bridge the gap until Polaris came on stream. It quoted the Minister of Defence emphasising 'the importance which the British government attaches to keeping, building and maintaining for the UK an indestructible power of retaliation against any threat of nuclear attack'.

Georgina lifted her head. 'I don't see— '

'You will. You will. If I'm right, Catchpole and his mates have been caught with their pants down.' Vellacott's voice was soft, but his fingers were trembling as he slipped the cuttings back in the file. 'If I'm right, it will mean the fall of the Menzies government. I mean it. We can get a decent independent *Australian* administration in Canberra.'

'What about Nick and my father? What's it got to do with them?'

'That's what we're going to find out. There's one person who can tell us: Martin Amory. Are you coming?'

Georgina hesitated. She thought of her School Prizegiving and the silence which would descend when her name was called out. She thought of the empty chair as the school choir sang the end-of-term anthem, Mrs C. J. Carleton's 'The Song of Australia':

> There is a land where treasures shine
> Deep in the dark unfathomed mine,
> For worshippers at Mammon's shrine. . . .

'I'm coming,' she said.

They took a cab to Glen Osmond. Georgina thought of telling Winn Vellacott about the Plutonium, but the memory of what Sir Martin had said filled her with such dread that she could not bring herself to speak the word aloud. Looking at the journalist, bent over his notebook with a frown of concentration, she thought of Sindbad loosing the frowning genie from its bottle.

Had she betrayed a trust, telling Winn all she knew? Try as she might, she could not think that there was any trust left to betray.

Sprinklers greened the Mountfoot lawns. A gardener pottered in the sun dead-heading marigolds as if this was just another day. Winn Vellacott rang the bell. Sir Martin Amory opened the door, and immediately tried to shut it again. Vellacott's foot was in the way.

'We need your help,' he said rapidly. 'Douglas Manifold went on to a nuclear test site, north of Ooldea. We believe he's been irradiated.'

'What test site?' Amory glared at them. 'If this is a trick, Winn, forget it. I've locked my book away. You can't read it. I'm not showing it to anyone.' He paused, looking at their faces. 'What's this cock-and-bull stuff about nuclear testing?'

Georgina forced her tongue round the words. She uttered them: '*A controlled release of Plutonium* . . .'. She could not go on . . . the heat . . . her legs began to buckle. She swayed; she felt herself falling.

She came to on the couch in Sir Martin's study. The two men were discussing something.

'You could be right,' she heard Sir Martin say. 'Supposing that they are British tests, the Australian need-to-know could well be limited to Menzies himself and a couple of his ministers and advisers, plus Ernest Titterton and the Safety Committee.'

'In Canberra?'

'Yes.'

'You mean the Brits could be polluting us and not one single person in South Australia would know about it?'

'Conceivably. If these trials involve fissile material, the fewer people who know about them the better – especially with the Geneva talks going on.'

'The bastards!'

'They must have official approval—'

'Exactly. It's not the Brits, it's those bastards in Canberra. Blow up the desert, gentlemen, just so long as it's the South Australian desert. And if there's radioactive fallout, please make sure it falls over Adelaide!'

'You're jumping ahead.' Amory frowned. 'Though if they're

223

releasing Plutonium by coupling explosive to it the consequences could be messy.'

'Martin, I'm going to blow the whistle on this so bloody loud. . . . '

Georgina sat up. Her dizziness had gone, leaving her with nothing worse than a headache. Sir Martin went for a glass of water and an aspirin. When he came back, she asked the first question that came into her mind.

'Is he going to live?'

'Your father? Oh, I think— '

'No. Nick. Is he going to be all right? Why's he in hospital and I can't see him?'

Amory was silent.

'Why him and not my father?'

They physicist shook his head. 'Radiation can affect people in different ways, depending on their age, their body temperature, their blood flow, their genetic background. Until we know where they were on the test-site, what happened, what they were doing, I can't answer that. It could be that Kemp ingested Plutonium and your father didn't. Or that he had a cut which let it into the bloodstream. It only takes a particle the size of a speck of dirt . . . though to be hospitalised you'd need a bigger dose of ionising radiation than that.'

Georgina swallowed. Nick the hero. Nick who was the toughest of anyone, who had survived shrapnel and bullets, to be hospitalised by a handful of dust! Had he saved her father's life a second time?

She asked: 'How long will he have to stay there?'

Sir Martin hesitated again. 'That depends on how big a dose he got.'

'No.' It was Winn who spoke. he sat, crumpled, at Amory's desk. 'Tell her the truth, Martin. What happens to people with severe radiation sickness. The puking, the shitting, the hair falling out, teeth falling out, the bleeding from the gums, the rashes, the cataracts in the eye— '

'That's enough! Enough!' Amory was shouting. Georgina sat and rocked her head in her hands.

Nick her hero.

'Winn is describing Hiroshima victims,' Sir Martin reassured her. 'I'm sure Nick won't be that bad. To start with, perhaps a skin rash. Some hair loss – except that they'll have shaved his head, like Douglas, to minimise the risk of fallout particles clinging to the scalp. Then a feeling of nausea, cramps, headaches . . . it all depends what effect the alpha particles have had on his neuro-muscular and gastro-intestinal systems. That's what Plutonium does, you see. It lodges in the lungs and emits alpha radiation which can affect the kidneys, intestines, bone marrow, that sort of thing. It can kill the cells, stop them dividing. You'll know this from your biology classes with Robyn. It can take days, or months, or years. Or never. I don't know. Nobody knows.'

'They went prospecting!' Georgina wailed. 'They were miles from anywhere! Isn't anywhere safe any more?'

She stood up and went to the window. At the bottom of the green lawn a man in overalls pushed a frail stick-like creature in a wheelchair slowly across Georgina's line of vision. The wheelchair stopped by a flowerbed. The man produced a pair of secateurs. The woman – for so she seemed to be – took them and leaned over and snipped dead leaves from a flowering bush. Then the pair moved on slowly, and disappeared behind a bank of shrubs. Georgina thought back to the face at the window, and Winn quoting from his notebook. *The body has a tolerance level in the treatment of cancers.*

'I think it's time I took you home,' she heard Winn Vellacott say.

They summoned a taxi and returned to Wellington Square. Winn was silent, brooding. Georgina asked him about the woman in the wheelchair.

'She's Martin's wife,' said Vellacott abruptly. 'It's a terrible sadness.' He added, 'Her grandfather founded the University of Adelaide. Long before Canberra was even bloody thought of.'

Georgina stared out of the cab window. In the gutters, and swept to the edge of pavements, were small mounds of sand, brought by the big storm on the night of their dinner and still clinging on. Sand, it occurred to her, never went away. It just waited patiently for its time to come. It made inroads when the crops failed and the topsoil blew away. One day it would cover Adelaide. One day, sand and ice would cover everything.

She had her key. On the doorstep she said, 'Thanks, Winn, I'll see you at the Hospital,' and shut the door before he could get his foot in it. Helen, in dark glasses, was on the telephone. Seeing Georgina she slammed it down.

'Where have you been?' she cried. 'The school rang. I tried the Millers. I've just rung the police! Does anybody care what's going on?'

'How is Daddy?'

'Your father's asleep, I think. He didn't have a bad night. Better than you, by the look of you. I've made some soup, come on.'

They ate a scratch lunch at the kitchen table. Helen said, 'I've reported that rat next door to the Animal Defenders Association.'

'But you don't *know* that Mr Robbins poisoned Ottoman!'

'I know it – here.' Helen tapped her heart. 'Now, George, listen to me. Your father and I have decided to go back to England.'

'Oh.'

'As you know, darling, Larry Olivier wants me back, and I think it would be best for Douglas, too, so that he can be properly looked after if . . . if the need arises. We talked about it this morning. There's nothing to keep him here. You might have to go back to Malvern for a term or two if you want to do University Entrance. . . . Are you listening?'

'Yes.' Georgina sat there, staring at the view of Old Adelaide on the tablemat. She heard her stepmother's voice in the distance; she was still talking about her father. She stood up, pushing her chair back with a shriek on the polished floor.

'I've got to go now, please,' she said.

'Go? Go where?'

'To the hospital. To see Nick.'

She was out of the house before Helen could stop her. She cycled like the wind. At the Royal Adelaide she sprinted past Reception and down the sterile corridors to the Isolation Ward. She needed to see Nick before Winn Vellacott could turn up licking his pencil. She had to talk to him alone, talk and listen. Then everything might start being all right again.

She plunged through the double doors. The anteroom was empty. Ahead were more doors with forbidding signs on them. She rushed on through. It was a ward with six beds. Five were

226

empty. The sixth had screens up. Trembling, she put her head round.

'You're too late.'

It was Sister Jessup, bending over the rumpled bed. Her keys rattled as she stripped the sheets.

'He's gone. He must have dressed and crept out while my back was turned. Don't worry, he'll come to his senses.'

'Georgina?'

She turned. She took a step back. Edward Catchpole stood there. Behind him was a Military Policeman. A gun was in the holster at his waist. Catchpole advanced and threw back the screens violently so that they toppled to the floor with a crash.

'Where is Kemp?'

Sister Jessup repeated her explanation. 'I'm not a policeman,' she added defensively.

Catchpole made no attempt to conceal his fury. He spoke in a low voice to the MP, who went out at the double. 'How far can he get?' he demanded.

'Anywhere. It depends how strong he's feeling. That material he put in his pockets . . . he'll have giddy spells, attacks of nausea. Without medication he'll be feeling very sick within twenty-four hours.'

'That long?'

'If you don't believe me, ask Doctor Elder.'

Brushing her out of the way, Catchpole bent down to examine the contents of Nick Kemp's locker. It was empty. As he straightened up, the MP came clattering into the Isolation Ward.

'Looks like Kemp's done a bunk, sir. There's a bloke downstairs yammering that his ute's been nabbed from the hospital carpark.'

'Ute?'

'A Holden FJ pick-up, sir.'

Catchpole turned cold blue eyes on Georgina.

'Georgina, this is very important,' he said in a kindly voice. 'Nick, your friend, he doesn't know how ill he is. If we can get to him, we can save his life. If not, it may be too late. I want you to think very hard. If you were him, where would you be heading now?'

Georgina glanced around desperately. They were all looking at her. What would Nick expect her to say? He wanted to be free; he had always wanted to be free. But free to live, surely? Not to die. Not to die.

She took a deep breath, '*Bellerophon*,' she said. 'It's his house-boat. He keeps it on the Murray, out at Mannum Bend.'

'Is that right?'

Catchpole's gaze was making her uncomfortable. In the silence, she dropped her eyes. Then he decided.

'That's where we're going. Georgina, you can come— '

'Oh, no. No, please.'

'Yes. You will come and show us the way. Let's go.'

The MP took her arm. There was nothing she could do. She allowed herself to be dragged out of the Isolation Ward, along the corridor and down a circular fire-escape which she thought they must have used to smuggle Nick into the hospital. Catchpole's royal-blue Jaguar was waiting at the bottom. He got in front. She was placed in the back, beside the armed policeman.

As they drove off, past the main entrance, she noticed Winn Vellacott get out of a taxi.

'Winn!' She pounded on the window with her fists. The MP pulled her away. She lay back in a daze on the rich leather seat, watching Catchpole take a transceiver from inside his jacket and speak into it, exactly as he had done all those light-years ago on the rehearsal for the Royal Progress. The Jaguar sped through the Adelaide suburbs and up into the hills.

The third garage they called at recognised the description Catchpole gave. They wasted no more time but drove on as fast as the roads would allow. The weather was changing. The sky had clouded over; it was humid and sticky, even though they had the windows open. Sitting behind Catchpole encased in his black suit, Georgina saw a brown stain of hair-dye trickle down his pink neck into his collar.

'A controlled release of Plutonium,' she said.

The neck twisted round. 'What did you say?'

'Plutonium. That's what he's dying of, isn't it?'

Catchpole chuckled. 'You young people put two and two together and make six,' he remarked without humour. 'Mr Kemp— '

'*Captain* Kemp.'

228

'Captain Kemp, if we can get him back to hospital, will be ill for a few weeks, that's all. By the time you're all back in England, he'll feel as good as new.'

So going back to England had been Catchpole's idea! Her ears burned with rage. She said: 'If there's nothing wrong, why all the stupid secrecy, pretending Nick wasn't there?'

'Because, Georgina, thousands of people like you have formed the wrong idea about nuclear power. Instead of seeing it as a force for good, the one thing capable of keeping world peace, it makes them anxious, superstitious. What we've been doing in these tests is actually trying to make our nuclear defence equipment even safer.'

'How?'

'I can't tell you that, my dear.' Catchpole chuckled. 'We wouldn't want the Russians to know, would we? That's another reason we must keep it hush-hush!'

Georgina pondered this. They were coming down into the wide Murray valley. 'It can't be safe,' she said. 'Otherwise Nick wouldn't be in hospital.'

'Ah. Kemp and your father, I'm afraid, were in the prohibited zone. They should have seen warning signs and turned back. Now, Georgina, this is where we require your assistance. Which way do we turn along the river for Mannum Bend?'

Georgina gave directions. There had been something wrong about Catchpole's answer, but she'd come back to that later. All she could foresee now, with a thickening misery, was the look on Nick's face when he realised that she'd led them to him. It was no good trying to convince herself that it was for Nick's own survival, or that Catchpole had plenty of other ways of finding out about *Bellerophon*. She cowered down in the seat, and almost missed the turn-off down the dirt-track towards the mooring-places.

At the boat-builders' yard they stopped. Catchpole beckoned over a large man with rolls of fat spilling over the top of his khaki shorts. The man pointed.

'I'd guess ten minutes ago. Not longer. A Holden PJ, that's right.'

They bumped on down, past the clump of stringybarks. The MP beside her was nervously buttoning and unbuttoning the stud on his holster. Georgina could see the line of sweat on his upper lip.

'It's the one at the end,' she said.

Catchpole's driver accelerated then skidded to a halt. Catchpole and the MP jumped out, yelling. Georgina peered out between the front seats.

And saw Nick.

It was a second before she recognised him – the whiteness of his shaven scalp, and a great red rash across it like a scar. A pipe between his teeth, he had untied *Bellerophon* from its mooring and was pulling up the gangway. The pontoon-boat's engines were already clanking underneath the yellow superstructure.

She put her hand over her mouth. The two men were running, shouting. Nick waved his pipe at them. She heard him shout out: 'I'm going prospecting!' Then he went inside, behind the wheel. With a churning of muddy waters *Bellerophon* ploughed out from the shore.

The MP cracked off a shot into the air. Red-and-gold galahs rose into the blue, screeching. Catchpole waded out from the bank. He grabbed out for *Bellerophon*'s guard-rail, lost his balance and fell. An arm reached out from the wheelhouse door and burped the klaxon, once, twice.

Georgina burst out laughing. This was the man she loved. Nick the invincible. Nick the invulnerable. She hugged herself. Nick would sail down the Murray and out to sea, out and away like Hiawatha into the setting sun. She got out of the car and ran to the riverbank. Edward Catchpole was being helped out of the river, his suit muddied and dripping, his hair plastered to his great pink skull. He took off his glasses and wiped them. Drops ran down his cheeks – river-water or tears of rage.

The three of them stood side by side on the bank of the Murray. The sky had cleared; the late-afternoon sun gilded the water and sent up a thin stream from Catchpole's sodden clothes. The klaxon sounded again. *Bellerophon*'s engines fell silent. It began to turn in a slow circle.

As they watched, Nick Kemp came out of the cabin. In his hand he held an axe. He walked to the side of the boat and swung the axe down at the pontoon. He swung again. They heard the cracking and splintering as he ran from one side to the other with the axe in his hand, smashing the pontoons at the waterline.

Georgina understood, a moment before the others did. She

dropped to her knees on the shore. She heard Catchpole scream out, *Get me a motorboat!* but it was too late, of course it was too late. *Bellerophon* dug itself slowly into the inexhaustible gold of the river. First to the level of the deck, then the guard-rail, then the brightly painted cabin, until the waters of the Murray joined above its roof.

She felt the screams coming from her, but they belonged to someone else. All her dreams, all her hopes, were focused on that stretch of river where Captain Kemp had scuttled his last command. What did she expect? To see an arm clothed in white samite lift a sword out of the water? To see Nick rise from the depths and strike out to where the trumpets were sounding for him on the other side? Bobbing to the surface came only *Bellerophon*'s boat-hook. The current carried it away downstream.

Edward Catchpole helped her to her feet. She had been kneeling on something soft; she looked down and saw a cap on the ground, Nick's engineer's cap. With a moan she bent and picked it up and hugged it to her breast. Holding it tight, she allowed herself to be taken back to the car.

They stopped in Mannum to report the hazard to river traffic. It was the policeman who phoned the news through to Helen in Wellington Square.

'He had no right,' whispered Georgina when they set off. 'He had no right,' she whispered again.

'He had every right,' Catchpole disagreed. 'We're all free to make our choices.'

'Free to be poisoned, you mean!'

'Let's not exaggerate. Kemp would have been all right, probably. What we've just witnessed, I'm afraid, is an example of the fear and superstition I was talking about. Don't forget, we're engaged on a programme which is intended to save lives. We have the Bomb to protect us. Really, instead of all this nuclear disarmament rubbish you young people should be made to realise that mankind is in far more danger from mass contraception. The human species is equipped with a margin of reproductive capacity which is sufficient to offset losses caused in war. Contraceptives destroy that margin. It's birth control you should be campaigning against, young lady. Not nuclear fission.'

Georgina had stopped listening. She was thinking of Nick – of the hugs he gave her, his jokes, his stories, his boundless energy. It was impossible, it made no sense, that so much vitality had just been snuffed out as casually as a lighter-flame before her eyes. She rocked backwards and forwards, holding the cap to her cheek, in a misery of loneliness.

He had no right.

They arrived in Wellington Square. Catchpole opened her door and held out his hand.

'I'll take you in,' he said.

'I don't want you to.'

'Come on. Please.'

Helen answered the door. She was dressed in a black jacket with puffed shoulders and a black silk belt round the waist. She looked at Georgina's face, then at Catchpole's. 'You'd better come in,' she said to him. 'There's someone who wants to speak to you.'

'I'm afraid I really can't wait.'

'It won't take long.' She took his arm and pulled him inside. As he stood there, Winn Vellacott appeared in the living-room doorway. The two men stared at each other. Catchpole turned to leave. It was too late for that. Helen had locked and bolted the front door.

'Open the door, please, Helen,' he said in a loud voice.

'No.'

'Let me out at once!'

'Don't you realise?' Georgina cried. 'Nick's killed himself! He went out on his boat and sank it! Nick's dead!'

She flung his cap down on to the floor and burst into tears. Nobody spoke. Catchpole's eyes darted at Georgina, then at Winn.

'You've got it wrong,' he said. 'It was nothing to do with me.'

'Oh, no?' It was the journalist who answered. 'First Richard Schneider. Now Nick Kemp. Two very convenient suicides, Mr Catchpole, from Canberra's point of view, not to mention your own! How many more are going to die before your nuclear trials are completed?'

'I have nothing to say to you.'

The civil servant brushed past him into the living-room. Vellacott followed. 'Is it true that Menzies is about to allow the

United States to defend its new telecommunications station in Australia with nuclear missiles?'

'There is a policeman sitting in my car,' replied Catchpole. 'All I have to do is signal him and you're in trouble, Mr Vellacott.'

Winn stood, arms folded, between him and the window. Catchpole glared at him. 'I have nothing to say,' he repeated.

'In that case, you'd better bend your ear to the story the *Gazette* will be carrying on its front page tomorrow.'

'There is no story.'

'Oh, no?' Vellacott flipped open his notebook, and began reading aloud. ' "Exclusive. Evidence is mounting that South Australian territory is once again being used for nuclear weapons trials. According to reports, the British government with the approval of the Premier and senior Australian officials in Canberra has reopened the atomic test-site north of the Transcontinental railway line, in order to test firing devices used with nuclear weaponry." '

Catchpole turned on his heel and strode into the dining-room. He tested the patio doors. They were locked. Winn Vellacott followed him through, still reading.

' "Questioned about the trials, a senior British civil servant in Adelaide, Mr Edward Catchpole, did not deny that quantities of Plutonium and other fissile material had been involved in the firing experiments; although it is not yet known how many casualties there may have been from radiation exposure as a result." '

'You can't print that!' Catchpole was on the run, now, into the kitchen. Helen was there before him, her back to the outside door, the key in her hand. Catchpole retreated to the kitchen window; he opened it and made to squeeze through, but it was too narrow for his shoulders. Snarling, he returned to the living-room, the journalist still snapping at his heels.

'Mr Catchpole previously served in the British embassy in Washington, where he was delegated to the British Joint Services Commission to discuss the international moratorium on weapons-testing which is now in force. The Australian Labour Party, which has called a special conference in Canberra on the eighteenth of March to debate foreign affairs and defence matters, will undoubtedly now wish to include these new British trials in their discussions— " '

Edward Catchpole tried to seize the notebook from him. The two men wrestled for it. Catchpole fell back against the mantelpiece, knocking one of the green vases. It toppled to the floor and smashed.

'Stop it!' shouted Helen. She pressed her fists to her forehead. Her lover stood in the fragments. 'Don't worry,' she hissed at him. 'It's not Japanese.'

Catchpole had cut his lip. He applied a silk handkerchief to it with a shaking hand. 'I'm not going to talk to you now about writs and injunctions,' he said to Winn Vellacott, who was on the carpet retrieving torn pages of his notebook. 'I'm going to appeal to you, man to man. We're both patriots. The damage you could do with such a piece of speculation and falsehood as that is incalculable. We're already lagging behind the Russians— '

'There's a moratorium!'

'Lagging behind, I say; and you and I know that the only way to negotiate is from strength. Canberra knows that giving us this assistance links Australia to the defence umbrella of the free world. . . . '

'Horse shit!'

'Menzies has gone out on a limb— '

'It's about to be chopped off.'

The civil servant was breathing hard. He made a flapping gesture with his hand. Georgina followed it, to see the MP standing outside the window. He rapped with his knuckles on the glass.

'I appeal to you!' repeated Catchpole. He made for the front door. Vellacott barred his way.

'Give me one good reason.' The journalist was taunting him. 'What about these falsehoods? What falsehoods?'

'Very well. It is true that there was a release of Plutonium. We were testing to see what would happen if something went wrong. If you couple high explosive to an assembly containing Plutonium and uranium, there are bound to be jets of molten metal. One of these plumes went out further than anticipated. But I will tell you now on the record, there have been no casualties from radiation exposure. None.'

'Nick Kemp, for one.'

'No.'

'Oh, yes.' Vellacott stood in the doorway. The front-door bell rang, and rang again. 'I haven't been wasting my time, Mr Catchpole. I've been talking to a nursing sister in his Isolation Ward. You think you can get away with it, but you can't gag everybody. Nick had talked to the doctor about the radio-isotopes in his urine. He knew he was dying.'

'No!'

'The cancers were already growing. He knew there was no hope. He *knew*.'

The MP was back at the living-room window. He had taken off his jacket and was wrapping it around his fist. Helen began to laugh.

'What was it you once said to me?' she asked Edward Catchpole. '*Do the damage but don't leave marks*. A pity you can't take your own advice. Isn't it? Isn't it?'

The MP's arm smashed through the window. At that moment Douglas appeared, at Winn Vellacott's elbow. He was in his dressing-gown. The bald dome of his head shone in the light of the chandelier.

'What's all the fuss about?' he asked.

With a cry Georgina rushed from the room. Behind her she heard raised voices. She wandered into the kitchen, then into the dining-room, aimlessly. She unbolted the patio doors and went into the garden. Clouds left a window for the rising moon. Something moved in the grass. She kneeled. The green tree-frog jumped into her lap. Its flanks quivered as she stroked and stroked it.

After a few minutes she recovered her senses. Gently she put the treefrog back down on the grass and stood up. She had come to a decision, and it gave her the strength to go back inside. The shouting had stopped. Her father was alone in the living-room. He was on his knees by the hearth, picking up bright shards of green glass. On his head was Nick Kemp's old blue engineer's cap. Without looking round, he held up one of the pieces of glass to the light.

'That's all I went for,' he said.

'Oh, no. Oh, no, it wasn't!' Georgina ran to him and hugged him. 'You went because you had to!' she cried. 'I understand that!'

Douglas embraced his daughter. He hugged her tight. They kneeled on the carpet for a long time, not hearing the confused noises, the crunching on the gravel. At last, Douglas stood up.

'You know what? I think Nick made his mind up when the boffins came for us,' he said. 'I think he made his mind up that it wasn't his country after all, Australia. Not any more. He'd come home, to the last place on earth he could feel at home, he could feel close to his gods. And the gods had gone, and in the vacuum this . . . this *evil* thing.'

'Yes.'

'And he wasn't an Aborigine, you see. He was as compromised as the rest of us. Nelson – God knows – Nelson made that clear enough.'

Georgina drew juddering breaths. 'You told me, only people who were never loved go straight into the dark. God so loves the world – doesn't He? He won't send us all into the dark? Tell me He won't do that! You said— '

'I said that nobody one loves dies completely. Nick will always be a part of you. Of both of us.' He raised her face and gave her a kiss. 'That's what you've got to remember, whether it's Nick or me.'

'You?'

Helen came in. Her face was flushed. 'That beastly man!' she exclaimed.

'Which one? Napoleon or Snowball?'

'I don't know what you mean, darling. I'm talking about Catchpole. He wants us out of the country. We'd better start thinking about flights.' She sighed. 'Frankly, I sometimes wonder if I'm going to get out of Australia alive.'

Georgina faced her. 'I'm not leaving,' she declared.

'Don't be silly, Child. You can't stay here by yourself.'

'Yes, I can. I'm going to nurse. I decided just a moment ago. I'm going to apply for the May intake to the Preliminary Training School, and go and nurse at the Royal Adelaide. I'm going to work in the Isolation Ward.'

'Because of Nick?'

'He won't be the last. He's the beginning.'

Helen looked at Douglas and shrugged. 'She's your daughter.'

'Yes, she is.' Douglas put his arm round Georgina. 'I can't leave now, poppet. Nothing to do with Catchpole. I came out here to write *Gallipoli* and I'm damn well going to finish it here.'

'I see.' Helen grasped the lapels of her jacket, pulling them tightly around her. 'And just who's going to look after you? The Child, I suppose.'

'Yes,' said Georgina.

Douglas nodded. Helen stared at them both. Holding herself tightly, she walked towards the window. Glass lay in bright daggers where the MP had punched his way in. She turned, stamping it into the carpet.

'It's because of me, isn't it? You're doing this to get back at me!'

Douglas shook his head. 'You go to London first, that's all. I'll follow.'

'No, it's because of me.' With a groan Helen sank to her knees and trailed her arms on the floor, her neck bowed forward like a ballerina. Douglas stood over her. She raised her hands to him. He took them, but did not pull her up. A tear welled up and ran down the oval of her cheek.

'Come back with me!' she implored.

Douglas squeezed her hands. 'They need you in London. The theatre needs you, poppet. More than I do, I think. I've been too selfish for too long. Go home now. When you're settled back in, then I'll come.' He squeezed her hands and let them drop. 'Now I'm tired. I'm going back to bed. Let me sleep a while.'

He left them there. The two women stared at each other, not sure any longer who was the older or the wiser: Helen in her black jacket, Georgina in her blue dress still muddied from the riverbank. The portrait painter from Douglas's Oxford days would still have made the most of Helen's languorous pose, her tragic eyes, the hair fallen across her perfect face. But he would not have been able to deny Georgina her position in the centre of the room.

A part from the odd headache, and a bit of trouble con-
centrating, Douglas Manifold feels fine. The heat doesn't
bother him. He has moved his typewriter out on to the patio
where he works in slacks and an old white cotton shirt under
a giant sunshade. He can hear Georgina in the kitchen, helping
Mrs G with the lunch things. It isn't a bad life.

Helen has gone back to London. There is nothing he could
give her, right now, that she doesn't pay her agent for. Leaning
over the fence, on her last day in Australia, Mr Robbins begged
an autograph for his daughter. Helen wrote in it: *Terrine, with
best wishes for a quick getaway.* Now that Helen's gone, beyond
reach of jealousy, Douglas can start acknowledging the difference
between love and desire.

He's behind with *Gallipoli*. Barry Michaels has sent him an
anxious postcard. Too bad – the script has needed revising. He's
placed too much emphasis on the bravery and comradeship of
men in war: not enough on the inscrutable forces which send
them into battle. Witnessing the resolute Britishness of his
characters, an audience would have come out of the film with
a warm feeling about men triumphing over the worst that Fate
can throw at them; even if they die, there's a moral victory
in the way they face death with equanimity.

Well, that's no good, blaming Fate. It just gives those
inscrutable forces an alibi. It gives them permission to go on
plotting their power-games, and to go on lying and covering
up when the games go wrong. This is what's happened in the
past few days, after all. Edward Catchpole and his friends in
Canberra got Winn Vellacott's story stopped on the grounds of
national security. Nothing surprising about that. But there are
ways of handling these things, as he told Winn when the man
came round to see him after resigning from the *South Australian
Gazette.* Look at *DogDay.* Look at *All Quiet on the Western Front.*
They can censor the journalist but they can't stop the poet,
the playwright, the novelist, from telling the truth.

Douglas takes a sip of the rather unpleasant liquid which the doctors have prescribed and Georgina is making him take. Revising, he has reached the point in the screenplay where the Australians, dying in their hundreds in the assault on Sari Bair, grumble that the British are using them as cannon-fodder. Unfair and untrue of course, so the historians say. But there are times when a writer finds the past catching up with his story. *Plus ça change, plus c'est la même chose.*

Something lands on his jaw. He swats at it. The mosquitoes have been getting worse; really, it's becoming an epidemic. Tipping back the brim of his engineer's cap, Douglas picks up the typescript and goes inside, into the cool of curtains and venetian blinds. In the living-room, he puts Richard Strauss's *Tod und Verklärung* on the gramophone. It has become a favourite of his – the bitter, percussive Death-struggle giving way to the sustained C-major chords of the transfiguration theme, reconciling all that's gone before like a long ocean wave sweeping up the cross-currents and rolling on.

The Gallipoli script lies on the chair, waiting to be transformed into lines of extras running through olive trees, the *whump* of shells, splints and bandages over shattered limbs. Never again will he write about war, not the kind he used to know. Already it's as out-of-date as triremes and arquebuses. A form of warfare has arrived for which the poet cannot find metaphors. Invisible, insidious, it lacks the human dimension. It has no room for heroes, only for victims. It has no moral connotations. The struggle between Light and Darkness is over in an instant, in a literally blinding flash; and, whichever side claims victory, Darkness wins. Darkness comes into its kingdom –

> and, lo, there was a great earthquake; and the sun
> became black as sackcloth of hair, and the moon
> became as blood; And the stars of heaven fell unto
> the earth, even as a fig tree casteth her untimely
> figs, when she is shaken by a mighty wind

– although all he, the poet-prospector, heard that night in the sand-dunes was a clap of dry thunder, and the thin wind out of nowhere which rattled the leaves on the mulga tree like broken swords.

He will write instead about life, love, friendship, history,

239

children and God (the God who loves man enough to let him exterminate himself). He will write furiously and widely, spread his net over rock-pools but also over the deep ocean. He will write about music, because music dispenses with treacherous words, dispenses with secrecy; music is the last inviolable intellectual freedom.

Out of the window he sees that he is looking at his daughter, in a flowered blouse, wiping her hands on her trousers and whistling for her faithful tree-frog. Strauss's Transfiguration theme is heralded by a flourish of horns and trombones. Douglas kneels by the chair. On the dedication page of the Gallipoli typescript he writes in a firm hand: 'To Georgina, In Hope.' Then, a little giddy, he goes to the window and presses his forehead against the glass.